A Bard's Folktale: Dustland Requiem

Aramis Barron

To R. M., who taught me the importance of pursuing a dream even after waking.

Table of Contents

Introduction

Heeey! Well look who it is! Didja miss your friendly neighborhood narrator, the fantastic Mr. Geroge Evans? I bet ya missed me, didn't you? Of course you did. S'okay, there's no need to be shy. I'll admit it: I missed you too.

I bet you're all amped to know what's happening with some of our favorite people, huh? I'm not gonna keep you waiting, 'cause, after all, you know me—I'm a crowd pleaser. Also, I recently took up a side gig as a purveyor of spoilers, so you don't wanna know all the goodness I shared before (or remember it just fine) feel free to skip ahead. Otherwise, I'ma cover everything we went over before, so here goes.

Last we left off, our trio of high school grads and their resident college drop-out, Glenn, took a little road trip across country, ending up in a mess of trouble down in El Paso. The sweethearts Kody Lehane and Alma Grey found their love nest left a mess by their bestie of best friends, Cris-Don't-Call-Me-Charisma Roberts.

See Kody and Alma were in one of *those* relationships...yeah, ya' know what I mean, and during one of their down times, little miss Crissy found herself with something of a fancy for the bad poet, Mr. Lehane. Being more than a bit of a romantic himself, Kody did what most teenage boys would do, and created some sort of funky love triangle with angles too crazy to imagine. Long and short, he broke his sweetie's heart, and so his lovebird, Alma, flew away.

Mr. Glenn Redcliffe, infatuated with the lady Grey, took her flight pretty hard. Being the slightly psychotic philosopher he was, he did some less-than-stellar things to himself and was left OD'ed in a mess of his own blood by none other than Cris and Kody. They fled the scene to avoid getting arrested, even though they hadn't done a thing (to poor Glenn, anyway).

Seeing as they had no means to make it right, Cris and Kody figured they may as well finish what Glenn had secretly started: finding Alma's surprisingly not-dead brother. Guess they figured there was an off chance they'd find Alma and could head home. Anywho, just a bit too late, they got there to find Glenn's associate instead, who offered Kody an opportunity to catch up to the lady Alma by taking on a mission down Mexico way. And so he went, leaving little Miss Cris behind, 'cause really— hormones and reason just don't mix.

So all by her lonesome, Cris waited in Nevada for her sister to pick her out up. When the elder Roberts daughter finally arrived, she came with a familiar little feline: Glenn's cat, Mr. Allister Theodore Bixby III, Esq., who had been with him right up until his incident in El Paso. With nothing else left, Cris headed home and time kept moving along.

Personally, much as he's screwed things up, I owe it to my boy to show him some love after leaving him out of last season's finale, so let's add about a couple months to the clock and get started where he left off.

1. El Sur Salvaje

"The problem with doin' things the way you're taught is that you accept things the way they are. Makes it all kinds of hard to see the things that need to change."

– The Memory Book of Siggy Martinez

A Few Months Since Graduation: Outer Region of Los Tios, Mexico.

A youth with stormy hair and wild eyes sat waiting on the back porch of the bar on the outskirts of the desolate desert town, not too far south of the U.S.–Mexico border. He was young in years but old at heart, the boy named Sigurd Martinez. He gazed out across the barren landscape, scuffing his leather boots against the desert's dirty floor. He waited for his brother to pick him up, finally allowed to go out on his first mission as part of the newly established trio. After all, he was the one who had done the legwork to put this operation together.

Only a few days past his fifteenth birthday, his maturity and mannerisms far outshined those of his unrefined older brother, Adelais. Siggy recounted all the factors and variables he might need to consider—all of the things he might need to know, although he himself was unfamiliar with such elaborate terms as "factors" and "variables." A hard, quick life was all most of the townsfolk ever knew. But he was determined: he'd be the one to set the record straight.

"He—y, Siggy! Are ya' nervous?"

3

A brazen, sometimes ugly, sometimes lovely dark-eyed girl knelt playfully behind him, leaning over him. A pastel blue sundress hung off her lean, hardened frame, deflecting the heat. Her sunburnt hair draped over Siggy, blocking all but her face from view.

"Lorena, hey. Me, nervous?" he chuckled, "Maybe just a little."

"It's all right little brother, everything's gonna be jes' fine. Adelais won't let anything happen ta' ya'. But here's a little somethin' for luck. Jes' in case."

She tied a blue kerchief around his neck as she took a seat next to him, sliding a comforting hand over his shoulder. Her feet dangled merrily in the sand beside his own. He let out a small breath, clenching his fist. Like she said, everything was going to be just fine. He cracked a smile, turning to her.

"I ain't your brother, ya' know."

She stopped and cocked an eyebrow at him, to which he couldn't help but laugh. She pulled him close and kissed his forehead.

"Close enough."

He watched her as she stood and swayed back inside, each step whimsical yet graceful. The heat of her touch left him warmer than he liked, thoughts lingering to the flourishing hips of his adoptive, slightly older sister. She disappeared behind the thin sheet veiling the back doorway.

"Gonna build a better life fer all of us."

Siggy scratched his head, his repose cut short by the sound of a rundown pickup truck barreling along the gritty path behind the bar. He rose slowly, anxiousness unwilling to relinquish its grasp on his limbs as beads of sweat trickled down his back. The truck's driver slammed on the brakes, bringing the vehicle to a halt before him. His brother's voice broke whatever spell anxiety held over Siggy.

"Sig, the hell you doin' standin' around? Get in!"

Siggy jumped into the back of the truck, holding on to the ledge as his brother floored the pedal. The red pickup hauled off as quickly as it had come. Siggy sat close to the rear window, dust flying up all around. A tan but relatively pale hand slid the glass partition separating him from the truck as a shaggy blond head poked out of the cabin to check on him.

"What's going on, buddy?"

Siggy looked the man over, not overly fond of the new guy. Although, as usual, he couldn't help but examine the man's face. Something about those green eyes always stood out. Siggy shook his head.

"Hey, quit talkin' to me like a kid. I'm only a few years younger than you."

"Yeah, yeah. Just make sure you pay attention and don't get yourself hurt."

The smug grin the passenger wore hinted more kindness than his naïve frame implied—a stark contrast from the calloused driver sitting next to him. A sudden jolt lifted Siggy from the steely bed of the truck as they hit the gravelly, semi-paved road.

"Watch it, Ade! I'm sittin' back here ya' know!"

"Shut it, little brother! If you got an issue with my drivin', walk."

Siggy sighed, still clenching his fists. At least his brother was close by. Long as they had been together, Adelais had always been the law. Long as he was around, everything was all right.

"So, are you nervous?" the passenger called back to him.

"Ya' serious? Just 'cause this is my first time going all vigilante with ya' two don't mean I'm a punk. I deal with these guys same as everyone else."

"Yeah, well I get the feeling that *dealing with them* is probably a little different than what you're about to get used to."

"If a city boy like you can manage to learn it in a few months, I think I'll be okay."

"My name isn't City Boy, it's Kody. Try to remember?"

Siggy rolled his eyes and turned back around, cacti and shrubbery getting smaller with the distance. Wind whipped his ragged hair about. He closed his eyes, sliding his hand along the holster on his hip. Guns were made for killing, and as far as he knew, he wasn't a killer.

Monster butterflies began fluttering around in his gut as the truck slowed down. He waited for the loud thud of the truck door slamming before he tried to move.

"All right, Sig. Out. Let's go."

Adelais peered over the side of the truck, his massive, sinewy stature obstructing all else from view. He scratched at one of the assorted scars blanketing his body as he waited.

Siggy sat in the bed of the truck for a moment longer, eyes locked with his brother's. He tried to summon the strength to move, but it didn't arrive soon enough. Adelais walked off. A hand reached out and clutched his own, helping Siggy out the back of the truck.

"It's okay to be scared, man, this is scary stuff. Believe me; I'm not exactly volunteering to get shot up either. But we can't just sit around and do nothin', right?"

Kody helped Siggy stand and brushed him off. Back on his feet, Siggy found nothing but a small shack a few yards off in the distance. Being the only structure in the area, it stood out, but not as much as Kody with a bad tan in his urban cowboy attire. The city boy had packed some lean muscle onto his otherwise unremarkable body since he'd shown up, but he still wasn't much to look at.

"I ain't scared. I'm just…adjusting," Siggy said.

"Hey, do what you do. Just hoping we can handle this guy. What do you know about him?"

"His name's Alejandro Romero. He's done about every nasty a bastard can do, an' he's worth good money."

Kody scratched his head. "Romero…Romero…as in the Romero family you were talking about before?"

"That's the one. No one messes with them on account a' they're crazy and dangerous. We'll prolly get our asses handed to us." Siggy chuckled, trying to calm his unsteady hands.

"Maybe. Although if we're talking dangerous and crazy, I'd bet on your brother any day," Kody smirked. "All right, Ade's on point and I'm backup. Since this is your first time, gonna start you off easy—"

"Hey! Don't go treating me like a kid! I can hold my own!"

Kody turned back, cocking a grin in Siggy's direction. "I'm not sayin' you can't. That's why I'm asking you to watch the truck. Make sure no one but us gets out. Can you handle that?"

"Yeah, city boy, I got it."

Siggy watched as Kody ran off toward the rear of the shack, disappearing around the far side. Suffering from no over-indulgence of recklessness, Siggy remained near the truck, standing vigilant. With the burden of the holster weighing down on his hip, Siggy cautiously drew the gun, gliding his fingers along the cold, metallic surface of the old-fashioned six-shooter, just like one of his abandoned childhood toys. Hefting its weight from one hand to the other, he got the feeling playing with this wouldn't be as much fun. He slid the weapon back into the holster.

The more time passed, the more his fear gradually gave way to an apprehensive boredom. He blew air into his face as he glanced around, looking for anything worth looking at. Thoughts crossed his mind of what he'd do when he got back to the bar. So far, this job was the exact opposite of what he had expected. He figured it'd be something more like—

Several shots fired off. Instinct dropped him to the ground. An electric surge burst through him as he strained to see what was going on. Everything around him felt alive: the smallest drafts of wind, each tiny grain of sand, and an increasing appreciation for the weapon at his side.

Despite gunshots and elevated senses, no more signs arose of anything going on. No loud commotion or anyone running from the shack. Fear began to creep through him the longer each perpetual second dragged on. He wondered if anything had happened to his brother, or to a lesser extent, Kody. He caught his breath and drew his gun, creeping around to the side of the shack. He managed to peer into the window.

"That it, you sonuvabitch? And yer supposed to be some kinda badass…you fuckin' pansy."

Adelais fell back, hitting the ground hard, a small spattering of blood flowing from his mouth. He grinned, having taken the bandito's gun with him. The muscular fiend built on decades of meager subsistence towered over Adelais, condescension filling his eyes.

"Like you know the first thing about us," the bandito spoke. "You poor, ill-educated vagabonds hunting people for money. As though your self-righteousness makes you better. You may as well be government-endorsed slavers."

Alejandro marched toward Adelais, dropping a knee into his gut as he mounted him. Alejandro wrapped his monstrous fingers around the back of Adelais's collar, clutching it tight. The bandito pulled his wrists in and his arms close together, clenching Adelais into a cross-collar choke. The blood rushed to Adelais's face, bulging the veins in his forehead. Siggy fidgeted with his gun, unable to get it out of the holster. His fingers kept catching on the leather. Finally ripping it from the holster, he aimed his weapon through the window and pulled the trigger. Nothing but a click.

"Ade! Watch out!" Kody shouted out from behind the doorway, unloading several bullets into a ratty couch and surrounding furniture.

"Adelais?" The bandito spoke. His snarling lips twisted into a sick smirk as he turned to see who fired at him. Adelais reached into his pocket and pulled out a syringe, uncapping it and jabbing it into the bandito's neck. Alejandro recoiled onto his feet, grabbing at the syringe. He fell back, leaning against a table for support.

"Back off, Lehane! Bastard tried ta' shoot me. I got this."

Adelais kicked the gun back and leapt to his feet, planting his fist square in the reeling bandito's face. The momentum of the swing carried Adelais with it, plowing him straight into the bandito and taking them both to the floor. Siggy, unable to hold his weapon, bore witness to Adelais's relentless assault until Kody tried to pull the tyrant off. Looking up, Kody caught Siggy's eye-line.

"Don't just stand there, help me out!"

Finally snapping out of his daze, Siggy made his way into the shack, helping pull Adelais off the bandito.

"Ade, stop! It's done!"

Adelais fought against Siggy as he held him back, giving Kody time to get rope and bind the bandito's hands. The bandito lay restrained, though the rope was largely unnecessary as the man could barely move, much less run. Siggy let his brother go as all the tension he had carried with him finally began to subside. He let out a sigh of relief.

Free and clear of Siggy, Adelais lunged toward the bandito. He caught the side of the bandito's face with a left hook, once more dropping him to the floor before turning around and walking out the door.

"Adelais, what was that for? He's sedated!" Kody asked.

"A, the bastard tried to shoot me. Two, none of yer damn business." Adelais wiped the blood from his mouth and knuckles as he made his way back to the truck.

"The hell was that all about?" Kody asked Siggy, while dragging the bandito to his feet. Kody forced the bandito along back outside to the truck. Siggy followed behind to make sure the bandito didn't try to escape.

"With Ade? Who knows?"

Siggy and Kody, along with their bandito bounty, walked in the grueling afternoon heat back to the truck. Adelais waited in the passenger seat, repeatedly tapping his foot against the floorboard. Kody was the first to speak up.

"Hey, why don't you drive, Sig? I'll keep my eye on our bounty here."

"You sure you'll be all right?"

"Ade beat him pretty good. I mean look at his face—I'm surprised the guy can still see straight. If he can, anyway."

Kody looked over the bandito's face, scrutinizing it with what appeared to be a sense of familiarity while Siggy dropped the tailgate of the truck. He helped Kody load the bandito in before slamming the gate shut and moving up to the driver's seat. The look on Adelais's face made it clear there'd be no brotherly reminiscence down memory lane on the way back.

Siggy drove on quietly back to the bar, checking the bed of the truck every few minutes to make sure Kody was all right. He drove quickly, unwilling to entertain the thought of what would happen if a group of banditos caught them bringing one in—especially one as high profile as a Romero brother.

They made their way back into the outskirts of town—the dozen or so clay and wooden structures barely enough to be called a town—and stopped near the dilapidated building that served as, among other things, the local jailhouse. Siggy looked over to Adelais, finding him absorbed in his own world. Instead, Siggy got out and helped Kody unload the now semi-cognizant bandito. They marched the bandito into the jailhouse. Once inside, Kody turned the bandito over to the acting sheriff as he sat to wait for all the paperwork. He nodded to Siggy, who then headed back out to the truck and drove it on through the town.

The place was rustic: a small, ancestral community built by the people who lived there. The town was quaint and off the grid in the shadows of the mountains, but had the necessities to get by. A small store, little church, a few homes—the essentials. Siggy pulled the truck around to the back of the bar, keeping it as much out of sight as possible as the brothers headed inside. The place was empty, as usual, but they called it home.

"Ade!"

Lorena ran up to Adelais, giving him a bear hug. The impact of her body caused him to reel back under the pressure of her bantam frame. *I dunno know why she even bothers,* crossed Siggy's mind. He continued to watch as Adelais waited for Lorena to let him go.

"Missed ya'," Lorena said.

"Ended up bein' a punk. Nothin' ta' go worryin' about."

"Think it's up to me ta' choose what I think about. And I didn't say I was worried," she teased him.

Adelais sighed, breaking her grasp and pushing her aside to take a seat on one of the bar stools resting behind her. He laid his head down only for a moment before a sturdy blow landed on the back of his head. He jolted up fiery-eyed and turned to Lorena, standing dominantly in front of him.

"Quit treatin' me like I'm your little sister or something! This ain't like me and Siggy," Lorena shouted at him.

"Hey, I'm right here you know! And what does that even—never mind." Siggy shook his head and walked off. He made his way through the bar, to the stairs before the kitchen. He headed down into the basement, where the brothers and their partner-in-crime lived. The basement was good enough for a pair of broke orphans, and more than they had ever had otherwise. Siggy lay down on his bed, closing his eyes, trying to recount his first mission and whether he'd think of it as a success or failure.

Didn't get killed. Didn't get anyone else killed. Caught the bounty. I guess this one counts as a win, he thought, *but all this violence…this ain't how life should be. There's gotta be a way to make it better.*

"Hey, Siggy!"

He sat up, seeing the urban cowboy's Sketchers at the top of the stairs. He waited as Kody made his way down and took a seat on the broken-down bed across from his.

"Back already?"

"Yeah, didn't take long. Looks like they've been looking for Alejandro for a while. High profile, just like you said."

"Maybe I can't fight, but I'm not useless." Siggy lay back down. He licked his bottom lip, his tongue riding the chapped surface from ridge to ridge.

"Nobody gets information better than you. That's the word on the street, anyway." Kody hesitated before continuing. "Speaking of, heard anything on what I asked you about before?"

Siggy canted his head, looking over to Kody from the side of his eye. Kody's attempt at being casual stood out more than his mangled mess of scruffy hair.

"On Lorena's cousins? No. Why don'tcha just ask her about 'em yourself?"

"I have, but it's not like we're living in Tomorrowland here. It's almost impossible to get any good info. And since my van's dead, it's not like I'm getting much further than a few miles without a good bit of cash-money."

Cocking his eyebrow, Siggy sat up. "What's Tomorrowland?"

"Ri—ght. Doesn't matter. Just help me find them so I can get home, all right?"

"Won't promise anything, but long as you keep helpin' out, I'll do what I can. Remember what I told you before, though—Jake left for a reason. If he's stupid enough to come back, it ain't gonna be pretty. Being Lorena's cousin won't protect him from Ade. Or Lorena."

"Just find him, Siggy. Please."

Siggy shook his head and sighed, seeing the resolve in Kody's eyes. The city boy was as lost as everyone else. All so focused on getting to the next day, the next five minutes, so they could get whatever it was they wanted. They didn't see the big picture. They were missing the point. But it didn't matter.

Even if he was only fifteen, if he was the only one who could see what was going on around all of them—so be it. He'd figure out how to fix things and make them the way they should be—he'd be the one to set the record straight.

Damp with sweat, he lay back on his hard burlap sack of a pillow and closed his eyes, sorting out details and planning for whatever would come next.

2. Back Home

"I never would've guessed how much of a difference one person makes."

– The Journal of Charisma Roberts

Same Day: Ann Arbor, Michigan

"I think she's here, Mommy. I think she's here!"

The excited clamor of a little girl's voice accompanied the impatient shuffle of small feet inside the house. A set of tiny eyes peered over the windowsill, eagerly watching Cris's every movement. Underneath a cloudy autumn sky, Cris walked casually along the side of the road, coming up to the house with the rusty station wagon in the driveway. Glancing down, she caught sight of an untied shoelace dancing around her foot at each step. It kept her attention better than the sweater draping itself over her skinny, modestly tall body. She debated if a long skirt was appropriate for fall.

She continued ambling up the driveway and made her way along the grass line to the door, once again filled with the same quiet apprehension she could never quite understand. This place always left her uneasy. She shouldn't be here without him.

The smell of freshly baked cookies drifted into her nostrils as the aroma coasted through the air. She caught it and exhaled slowly. Though the scent brought her only unpleasant thoughts, it inspired the knots in her stomach to loosen up. She arrived at the door just as Tabby, Kody's mom, opened it, welcoming her inside.

"Cris, you made it! Come in."

"Thanks, Ms. Lehane." Cris nodded, forcing a half smile.

"Crissy, Crissy! You're here! Didja bring him with you?"

Kara grabbed her by the hand and drug Cris along into the kitchen before she had a chance to respond or even take her shoes off. Cris looked around, unable to contain her surprise at all the decorations Tabby had already put up. Balloons filled the room, streamers hung from the ceiling, and confetti littered the floor. A few presents sat on the table, a card resting beside them. A picture of a regal little cat with a crown was drawn on the cover of the envelope.

"Did you?"

Kara looked up to Cris, her eyes full of the pleading eagerness of a young child. She brimmed with the joy of an eight-year-old enjoying her birthday.

"Hm? Did I what?"

"Bring him with you!"

"Bring him with me? How would I…Oh, you mean—"

"The kitty! Mr. Bugsby!"

Cris laughed to herself. She imagined what the regal feline would think of being addressed with such an amusing title.

"It's Bixby, sweetie, and no I didn't bring him. He wanted to come, but he needed a bath so I had to drop him off at the kitty salon."

"Aw…but it's my eighth birthday today! He should be here, so we can play games!"

"I'm sorry, honey. I'll bring him next time, I promise. Maybe I'll even let him stay the night as a birthday present. That okay?"

Kara paused in contemplation. "A sleepover?" she asked. Cris nodded. "Hm… I can do that."

Tabby brought a plate of freshly baked cookies to the table. She offered Cris a seat, the latter cordially accepting as she watched the exchange between mother and daughter.

"Kara, go get dressed, okay? Your friends will be here pretty soon, and Cris and I still need to finish setting up."

"But Mo—m!"

"Now, Kara."

"Aw, man."

Cris watched as Kara trudged off to her room, her dejected body reluctantly moseying away. Cris bit her lip, curious how quickly the young girl's spirit would mend, probably at the suggestion of cake and ice cream. She let out a deep breath to try and clear her head.

"How're you holding up?" Tabby asked, meeting Cris's eye line with concern.

"Shouldn't I be asking you that?"

"How I'm holding up? My son's been gone for months, and all I can tell his sister is he's visiting family she's never heard of. I'm worried about him, of course, but he is my son. He was going to venture off on his own sooner or later."

"Plus she's got me."

Geroge poked his scruffy, dark face around the corner, nudging the door shut with his boot as he walked into the room. With his heavy, somewhat muscular frame, he sauntered into the kitchen, carrying a giant wrapped box tied with ornate ribbon. He set it down on the table and grabbed a soda out of the fridge, popping the cap to create a fine, echoing fizz. Cris scooted over, pulling a chair for him to sit down.

"And there's G, who for some reason spends as much time with us as he probably does at his own home. Somehow I manage." Tabby nodded toward G. "But what about you, Cris?"

"I have my sister, who pretty much insists on being my best friend, mentor, life coach, and therapist. And you guys, of course."

Tabby smiled, getting up to check on food in the kitchen. She came back and leaned down behind Cris, placing her hands on Cris's shoulders.

"I know I'm his mom, but that doesn't mean I agree with what he did. I don't care what his reasons were—or what happened between you two and Alma—he shouldn't have left you like he did. If you ever need someone to bitch, vent, or just blow off steam to, I have two good ears."

"Thanks."

Cris reached up, placing her hand over Tabby's. Tabby patted her shoulder as she headed back into the kitchen. Cris and G broke away from the table, heading into the living room to set up for Kara's party.

"Thought you'd be here earlier," Cris said.

"Yeah, well…what can I say? Jeany's a funny lady. We had something to take care of earlier, and she decided that on top of making us late, it'd be funny to roll out while I was in the bathroom. Had to walk back to get the van."

"You're kidding."

"I got way better jokes."

Geroge chuckled as he fumbled around unpacking small speakers he'd left by the door. He carried them into the living room, taking his time to set up a kids' playlist on his laptop. Cris watched him as she put games together in the living room, trying to figure out which Kara would like best. As she watched Geroge, she could never understand the relationship between him and Jence—Jency—Jeany—whatever she responded to—but somehow despite all their issues it seemed to work for them. Before long, the place was ready for a little girl's birthday party.

"I'd say that's an easy day's work, *hermana.*" Geroge tossed his arm around Cris's shoulder.

"Setting up's the easy part. Ever dealt with a house full of eight-year-old girls?"

Cris jumped as her pocket vibrated, immediately catching Geroge's attention. He cocked his head, sporting an accusatory grin. Cris reached into her pocket, shaking her phone at him with a furrowed brow. She broke away from Geroge, stepping aside to check the text she'd received from her sister: *Gotta talk to you ASAP. Looks like he finally came home. Be over there in a couple minutes. Meet me outside. –Em.*

Excusing herself, Cris headed into the kitchen to inform Tabby something had come up. She promised to make it up to Kara and explained she'd come back as soon as possible. She turned toward the door, Geroge catching her on her way out.

"You bailing, *chickarita?*"

"Just for a bit. Don't think it'll be too long—sister stuff."

"Ah, of course. Don't let my Y chrom-y get in the way. We still good for tonight?"

"Should be. I'll text you if anything changes."

Geroge waved a two-finger salute as Cris stepped outside the house. She took a seat on the steps of the porch, texted her sister, and put her phone away as she sat waiting. She started playing with her hair, combing her fingers through chestnut tresses and twisting them about. She caught a whiff of her conditioner as she twirled strands in front of her face and deliberated if Rainforest Radiance was really the right scent for her. She had seen citrusy-scented shampoos recently that looked promising, and considered it might be time for a change.

The wind started picking up, blowing her hair and skirt tails back toward the direction of the road. Ambivalence, given the past few months, had caused her to question much less, and follow the beaten path much more. The whole graduate-head to college-find an amazing job plan didn't play out the way she'd hoped. In its stead, the breath of the Earth was her guide, and she would be its disciple.

She gathered herself up, pushing off her knees, and ambled along the driveway only enough to let the wind lead her. She drifted back and forth along with the sway of the tree branches, blurring her existential line between humanity and the spirits. The trees continued to rustle above, their leaves still green—but not for much longer—as she moved without purpose or compassion toward an unspecified goal. As always, the lukewarm breeze felt cold.

"Hey, wandering lady, want a ride?"

Emma pulled up next to her, as fashionably dressed as she was fashionably late. Her sister lowered her unnecessary sunglasses in an apparent attempt to figure out what Cris was doing.

"Hm...guess that depends. Where are you headed?"

"Ghost hunting."

Cris shrugged. "Eh, good enough."

She opened the door of the old yet classy sports car and climbed in. Emma's car reminded Cris of her old convertible—the one she had promised to lend Alma, which had since gone missing; a promise she had felt too guilty about to report the car as stolen. They headed off down the road and onto the expressway, with no particular direction in mind except to pass the time.

"So you said he came home?" Cris started, trying to reorient herself by fidgeting with the radio. She skipped through the channels, looking for an alternative rock station until Coldplay's "Fix You" lulled her into a pensive dreamland.

"That's what his dad said. Figure we'll give him a day or two to get settled in before we bombard him."

"His dad? What're you..." Cris trailed off. "You don't mean Kody, do you?"

"Kody? No, crazy, I mean Glenn. He's finally home."

Cris looked down to her untied shoes, unable to stop her foot from shaking. She tried to keep her mind clear, listening to the song as it continued to play.

"Look, if this is too much... I get it if you aren't ready to see him," Emma offered.

"No, it's just—you weren't there, Em. He was lying there, breathless and covered in blood. He's dead. We left him for dead."

"You keep saying that, but I'm telling you—he's not dead. The ambulance that *you* called saved him, or brought him back, or whatever. Believe me, I was there. Soon as they called me off that old emergency contact card in his wallet, I was there. He wasn't great, but he wasn't dead."

Cris stared out the window, not focused on any particular thing as they continued down I-94. She gazed out on Ford Lake, wondering how long until it froze over and the winter scenery would finally set in. Was Glenn really alive, and had he come home? Was he the same Glenn who had left on that trip with her only a few months before? Then again, was she the same naïve girl who had just wanted to see some of the world?

Even if the stories about him surviving were true, she couldn't shake the memory of his cold, lifeless body lying on that motel bed reeking of dried blood and orange juice. The idea of him miraculously surviving and coming home seemed farfetched at best. She'd left him for dead. The same way she had left Alma behind. Her recklessness made it all too obvious why Kody had abandoned her. The Dropkick Murphys' humble piano requiem, "The Green Fields of France," played on in the background.

"Crissy, don't stay in your head. It's a scary place in there. Talk to me."

"I'm good, Em. Just thinking."

"That's kinda my point."

Cris brought her hand up to her neck, fingering the hemp-beaded necklace Kody had made for her. She kept her gaze fixed on the leaf-littered roadside as they continued past Belleville, traveling the trails they'd oft ridden so many times before. Driving through nearby towns with her sister remained one of her few treasured pastimes. Along with good music, driving aimlessly was one of the only things that always helped clear her head. She couldn't go back to the party so distracted.

As they drove along, she leaned her head against the window and continued to watch the dissolution of nature. Its death was beautiful, even if depressing. She had never been a fan of autumn.

3. Sketchy Stories

"Far as I know there's no such thing as a noble bastard. Doesn't mean I can't try to be the first."

– The Notebook of Kody Lehane

Outskirts of Los Tios, Mexico

Kody sat on the dirty mattress across from Siggy, trying to ignore the thunderous snoring of Adelais's little brother. Kody had kept most of his belongings in the battered van he had taken from Glenn. However, shortly after reaching the small town he had been sent to by Alexandria Matier, Glenn's former partner, the van had been broken into and most of Kody's things stolen. This left him with little more than a few sets of clothes, a leather duster, and Alma's bag. Among other things, her bag contained a vandalized notebook with "Kody N Alm 4 Ever!" littered throughout the pages.

He remained on the bed, doodling in the margins of his notebook. He sketched a poor rendition of a nervous duck bursting into flames, fleeing from a cantankerous feline. He couldn't explain why a flaming duck would be running from a cat—through a reef of cattails, no less—or why a cat would be chasing a flaming duck, but it didn't seem to matter. His illustrated friends were just ways to pass the time.

He drew his scavenged pencil across the page, twirling lines into letters but never forming words. Thoughts and ideas didn't make sense on paper anymore—they just shifted into shapes until little more than crude pictures remained. Strung together, the images played unceasingly in the theater of his mind in high definition: dead friends dying again, dodging death from evil men. He set his notebook back on the floor, threw on the leather duster, and headed upstairs.

The stairs led up into the shabby bar with a few run-down tables. Beyond the stairway on the right was Lorena's bedroom and the kitchen, both separated by hanging sheets serving as doors. Lorena, sitting at one of the tables, lifted her head from her prayer book as Kody walked by.

"Headin' out on another secret mission?" Lorena smirked.

"Something like that."

"So mysterious. Be careful. Ain't safe walkin' around by yerself."

"I'll keep that in mind."

Kody made his way outside, blinded by the bright desert sun. As his eyes adjusted, he surveyed the small town that fit onto one street, whose name he couldn't pronounce. Despite the sweltering, dry air, the place was quaint and cozy enough, though it didn't have much. In particular, it lacked phones. Still, gazing over the town, the closeness of its community reminded him of home.

He headed around to the back of the bar and hopped into the truck. He sat for a minute, letting his hands adjust to the heat of the steering wheel. Once comfortable, Kody reached under the seat to make sure the shotgun was still in place. He had made the drive a few times before with Siggy, but like Lorena said—going alone wasn't safe.

He headed out onto the dirt road and put in an ear bud, pushing play on Cris's mp3 player. The Kooks distracted him with a relaxed, soft rock rendition "Mr. Maker" long enough for him to get clear of the town and reach a main road. He drove quickly, doing his best to avoid any skirmishes with the local bandito populous or any wily coyotes. By the time Weezer's nostalgic guitar tune "Unspoken" had ended, he reached the outskirts of a slightly larger town unscathed.

He parked the truck outside of a small inn, inconspicuously heading inside. Kody's Spanish was improvisational at best, but Siggy had taught him enough of the basics to get by. Kody did his best to speak with one of the clerks. Unfortunately, he lacked enough points in diplomacy to get it done. With a generous donation to the clerk's private acquisitions fund and a +1 to bribery, however, Kody managed to score his way into the "business center." He wasted no time in picking up the international phone and contacting the one person he could always rely on.

"Ge—roge Evans, at your service!"

"Hey, G."

"Oh, hey, buddy! Gimme a sec." Geroge excused himself in the background. "*¿Qué pasó, brochacho?*"

"Not much, man. How's she been?"

"Cris? Bit depressed as usual. Might perk her up to hear from her one and only. 'Specially since she hasn't heard from you in say…oh, months, and probably figures you're dead and all."

Kody hesitated, staring at the floor. This wasn't the first he'd had this conversation with G, and it wasn't going any better than usual.

"G…I can't."

"Yeah, yeah. Soak up the guilt all you want, man. You're not convincing anyone it's better to leave the lady hangin' like this. At least let me tell her you're all right."

"If she hears anything about me, she won't stop looking until she finds me. This place is way too dangerous for her."

"Then it's too dangerous for you, chief! She's a helluva lot stronger than you, buddy—no offense. You'd see that if you weren't off cowboyin' around, instead of being here and spending time with her proper like you should."

Kody slammed his back against the wall next to the phone, clenching the receiver in an attempt to keep his voice down.

"I'm screwed up! Got it! But I've come too far not to finish this now. Just keep looking after her for me until I get back, all right?"

"Lucky I love you like a brother, man, 'cause you're a real pain in the ass."

"I know." Kody kept his eyes on the ground.

"Whatever, man. Hurry up, stay safe, and get back home before I decide I wanna keep this fine *chica* for myself."

"Thanks. Top of the rock, G."

"Uh huh. Top of the rock, brother."

Kody heard the click of the line disconnecting and set the phone down. He took a breath, leaning his head back against the wall. Small droplets of sweat running down his forehead served as fine reminders the heat was never far off, even in the fall. The leather duster, necessary as it might've been, wasn't making the air any cooler. As a drop of sweat dripped onto the floor, he balled up his fist and slammed it back against the wall. A self-depreciating laugh escaped as he pulled his hand close, nursing sore muscles and bone. Adelais made hitting things look so easy.

Kody looked up, noticing the small crowd of people slowly gathering around him. Their presence quickly reminded him his leather duster—same as the banditos'—only kept him safe so long as he didn't draw attention. Fear of the banditos kept people tolerant of their presence and provided Kody with an effective guise, but a lone bandito causing a ruckus could easily test the limits of that patience. Kody glared back at the crowd, making his way through them until he was outside. He began heading toward the truck, keeping an eye cast over his shoulder as the crowd slowly started to trickle out in his general direction. He picked up his pace, ducking around the corner of a building and creeping his way along its backside.

Maintaining a low profile, he snuck in between buildings and weaved his way through until he made it back to the truck, with only a few people keeping notice of him—none of them interested enough to pursue. He hopped in the seat of the truck and locked the doors. Exhaling a slow, deep breath, he slumped down in the chair, feeling for the shotgun.

"Damn that was close... not safe from banditos *or* townsfolk. Why're mobs always coming after me?" He sighed as he rubbed his forehead. "At least I should have enough constructive credit to apply to ninja school now."

He remained slumped in his seat, equal parts hiding and thinking aloud. "I could take off with this truck right now. Head out and try to make it back to the States. Wouldn't have to worry about any of this bullshit anymore. Could go home and take the world's longest nap right between Cris's boobs, where I belong. No more hunting people all the time, no more people trying to kill me. Just nice, quiet rest and relaxation." He sighed and shook his way out of the jacket to alleviate the heat. "'Course, I'd just be running again. Rest of my life. Leaving Siggy and them high and dry. And I still haven't found Alma."

Kody sat up slowly, peering over the windshield and then out of the windows to make sure no banditos or disgruntled townsfolk had trailed him. With no one in sight, he started the engine and began blasting Fastball's summer anthem, "The Way," from the mp3 player. Not wanting to end up on whatever the local version of the evening news might be, he peeled out of the town before lady luck reconsidered whether he'd escaped one time too many.

4. A Vagrant's Story

"Ain't hard to make even the worst of things sound good—that's why I don't listen much: I trust my gut. "

– The Scratch Pad of Adelais Martinez

Adelais took in a deep breath as he lowered his body against dirty wood grain. His bare chest bounced off the floor, aiding him in lifting his weight an inch above the ground. He struggled to contain the quivering in his arms as he counted the passing seconds. With a sharp thrust of his biceps, he exhaled, lifting his body back off the ground, drops of sweat falling to the floor in the process. He shook the droplets off, drawing another deep breath to continue the cycle.

After a minute of nonstop pushups, he stood up, leaning his back against the countertop to catch his breath. His tongue swayed around his mouth, catching a taste of copper as it made the rounds. He slid the sticky glob around his gums until it reached the front and spit it out, depositing a small stain of crimson on the bar floor. Adelais snorted, smearing the sanguine mark with his boot.

Taking a sip of water from a glass resting on the counter, he turned his focus toward the wall. He flexed his fingers, cracking his knuckles before taking up a good posture. Feet securely in place, he began shadow boxing an illusory opponent, striking out with repeated quick jabs. Dodging one blow after another, he managed to keep his fictitious foe at bay.

Despite maintaining the upper hand on his nonexistent opponent, the momentum of his bloodied swings against the wall left him too distracted to anticipate anything else in his surroundings. The adrenaline fired up his nerves, heightening and amplifying his reflexes.

An imaginary shot rang out from behind him, dropping him to the floor. He remained grounded for a moment, heaving as his muscles ached with bewildered fury. Taking a moment to assess the situation, he realized it was only a past trauma resurfacing once more. He sprung to his feet, striking the wall with a powerful left jab that caught his fist within the foundation.

"Damnit!" Adelais exclaimed, trying to figure out how to remove his hand from its now semi-permanent fixture. As he wriggled around trying to free his hand, he only managed to cut himself. A slow clap echoed from behind. He refused to turn around, focusing on the problem of the moment.

"Gotta say, didn't think ya'd start fightin' the walls. Then again, they were about the only thing ya' haven't hit yet, so why not?"

He ignored Lorena, struggling with the pain of trying to liberate himself from his wooden incarceration. He pulled his shoulder back, but managed only to lodge more splinters into his hand. Ceasing the fight altogether, he shifted his weight to let Lorena by as she came around to inspect. She placed her hands on his, gently coaxing it out of the wall.

"Not every problem can be solved by force, ya' big oaf. Sometimes ya' gotta use a little grace until the situation works in your favor."

"An' sometimes ya' gotta hit shit. What'dya want, Lore?"

"Making sure ya' aren't breaking my bar apart, fer one. My ma left it ta' me—means I gotta take good care of it."

"I'll fix the damn hole."

Adelais grabbed the glass on the counter, forcing the rest of the water down before slamming the glass back on the table. Lorena poured herself a glass from the pitcher and took a seat on a stool next to him. The two exchanged glances, deadlocked, until Lorena's quiet chuckle broke the silence. She offered him a smile, and took up reading from her prayer book.

A sigh escaped from Adelais's lips as he stood around. He rubbed his forehead and walked through the kitchen to the back of the bar. He took a seat on the porch, letting the dry, blistering heat bake his naked chest. Looking out over the sandy rocks, his mind started to drift to places locked away long ago. He remembered trees and a lake, a place full of green. The majesty of a clear blue sky full of clouds. The seat of his long-forgotten innocence. Whatever he had been in the past, he was born in the desert, and with a little luck, he would die there too.

He cast a glance to the woodpile sitting against the wall of the building, wondering what might be living under the stray pieces of timber. He'd nearly been stung by a scorpion before, but it was only a small one, and the incident happened to be one of the better parts of that particular day. He leaned forward and pushed off his knees, getting up to inspect the woodpile. He sifted through the old pieces of debris until he came across a reasonably sized piece of plywood. He pulled it out of the pile and inspected it before taking it back inside.

Lugging the wood through the kitchen and back into the bar, he passed Lorena, who paid him no mind as she continued reading. Gathering up his tools on the other side of the bar, he got to work on patching up the hole he put in the wall. "Didn't mean ta' break yer bar." Adelais mumbled. Lorena closed her book and set it down, sitting up to watch him.

"Never figured ya' did."

"I jes'…" Adelais trailed off.

Lorena continued to watch as Adelais worked to cover up his mistake. Though not overly skilled with a hammer, he managed to accomplish his goal of trying to mend the damage he had caused. He set the hammer down and looked over his work as Lorena spoke up.

"It's hard for ya' here. I get that. None of us got an easy life, and even then, yours has been harder than most. But you're the oldest, Ade. Yer supposed ta' be a role model for Sig an' me. Hell, I ain't that much older than him, yet here I am runnin' our little family. That seem right ta' you?"

Adelais turned around, facing Lorena. He looked her over: an unassuming young woman much stronger and more responsible than anyone he had ever known.

"Ain't my fault ya' ended up in charge 'cause yer ma got herself killed."

Before he could stop himself from speaking, or involving his brain in the matter, the words had left his mouth. Lorena's muscles tensed as she stood. Her hand balled up at her side, holding steady as she took a deep breath. She clenched her fist then slowly released it.

"I love ya', Adelais, but you can be a real ass sometimes."

Lorena grabbed her prayer book off the counter and headed outside. Adelais watched her go, and wandered back out onto the rear porch shortly after. He took a seat and leaned his head against the railing, watching a loose chicken run from a nearby coop.

"Not havin' the best day, huh?"

A hand mussed up his hair as it rubbed his head. He grabbed the wrist and pulled it over his shoulder, flipping Siggy over him and dropping his little brother on his back in the dirt. Siggy lay there for a moment, trying to regain the wind that had been knocked out of him.

"Ya' know better than ta' sneak up on me, little brother."

"Didn't think I could." Siggy groaned as he sat up, rubbing the back of his head. He got back up on his feet and took a seat next to his big brother, making sure to keep a safe distance between them. "Guess that fight with Alejandro slowed you down a bit, huh?"

"Nothin' I ain't dealt with before."

"Yeah, yeah…you're a badass."

Adelais shot a glare at Siggy.

"Just sayin'. Gotta remember some of us ain't like that."

Adelais examined Siggy, who nodded with a brotherly expression that told Adelais he knew exactly what had just transpired with Lorena.

"Mind yer damn business, Sig."

"It's Lorena, so it is my business. Ever think about what happens ta' us if something happens ta' her? Or if she decides she don't want us around anymore?"

"We'll get by, like always."

"Ain't nowhere left for us ta' go, Ade. Can't afford ta' get kicked out again. There's nowhere left. We lose this place, only home for us will be with the banditos."

Adelais snorted, slamming his fist against the side of the railing. He quickly drew his arm back, trying to stop himself from causing any more collateral damage.

"Just sayin', Ade. I like it here. It's quiet, almost peaceful, and we got Lorena. Let's try not to lose our family this time."

Adelais cocked a half-grin, faux punching Siggy's shoulder. He left his hand on his younger brother's shoulder. Siggy returned the gesture by wrapping his right arm around Ade's and placing it on his shoulder. They patted each other on the back, Adelais shoving Siggy off shortly after. The younger Martinez brother freed himself of his older brother's grasp, heading back inside. Rummaging from the pantry echoed out onto the porch as Siggy began preparing a meal.

Looking out over the dusty, sunny afternoon sky, Siggy's words made a kind of sense. This wasn't the home they'd lost long ago, but it was home now, and it might be a place worth fighting for. He just had to figure out how to do it without breaking the whole damned place down.

5. The Brothers Romero

"I got my own mind, thanks. Don't need someone or somethin' else ta' tell me what's right."

– Scribbled in the Margins of Lorena Agramonte's Book of Prayers

Lorena parted the blankets that draped the doorway to the old church as she stepped inside. The building was clearly old, probably the oldest in town, though that didn't say much. Taking small steps, she wasted no time in kneeling before the altar at the front of the chapel. She lit the few melted candles and hummed a small hymn to herself in the ill-lit room. She found herself solitary, but that was hardly unusual. She alone maintained the small shrine. She was no maiden, but she could play the part.

She thumbed through her worn prayer book to the pages she'd read too many times before, ignoring her notes in the margin, and began to read.

Where there is hatred, let me sow love.
Where there is injury, pardon.
Where there is doubt, faith.

Lost in prayer, the strong scent of dirt and life—horses—overwhelmed her as another supplicant took his place beside her. Having not yet finished her prayer, her curiosity got the best of her as she began to steal glances at the newcomer.

"Pay me no mind. Just come to pay my respects."

Lorena quickly averted her eyes. The stranger lit a small stick of incense, leaving it on the altar. Catching the exotic aroma now curling off the font,

Lorena couldn't help but lift her head. She had to catch a glance of the stranger, who traveled far enough to carry incense with him. The small shop they had carried only the necessities of life.

"Where didja get that?" Lorena spoke softly, her eyes leading back to the altar.

"The incense?"

Lorena nodded. The lean man rose. Though no great giant, or even much taller than Lorena herself, he stood more resolute than his kneeling posture implied. He turned and walked back toward the door.

"You aren't gonna tell me?" she called out, turning her head toward him.

"You don't want to know," the stranger stated coldly before walking out.

Sunlight found its way into the sweltering chantry before the blanket covering the doorway fell back into place. Lorena drew a breath, trying to finish her hymns. Starting over from her hymnal, she reached the second verse for the third time, unable to focus on anything other than the stranger. Her concentration was gone.

A resounding yelp came from outside the church. Lorena broke her meditation, put out the candles, and ran into the street to see the town dog on the ground panting heavily. The dog tried to move, but could do little more than wince at the slightest effort. Beside the dog was a large, badly bruised bandito, and next to him, the somewhat smaller stranger who had just left her side. The dog tried to climb back up to its feet when the injured bandito dropped the heel of his boot into the dog's rib cage, making an audible cracking sound throughout the street.

"Stop! Perrito didn't do anything!" Lorena shouted at the larger bandito as she ran up to the dog. "What's wrong with you? Why would you hurt—"

The bandito grabbed her throat and lifted her into the air, pulling her face close to his. He stunk of dried blood.

"Do I look like I've had a good day to you? Shut your mouth, little bitch, before I stuff it."

Lorena gasped for air, looking for help from the stranger standing next to the bandito. He returned her glance disapprovingly. Lorena flailed, clawing at her neck, trying to break free.

"Alejandro…" the stranger sighed, with despondent command authority.

Choking, with darkness closing on her, she launched her desert-hardened foot into the bandito's groin. He dropped her, giving her an opportunity to catch her breath as she lay on the ground next to the dog.

Reluctantly looking up, she couldn't keep from trembling, seeing the malice on the bloodied bandito's face as he began to recover. She tried to scramble away, but his boot came down, crushing her ankle. The scream fought its way up her aching throat, but she refused to let it out. She maintained defiance.

"Alejandro!" the stranger lost his patience.

The bandito, continuing to ignore his comrade, was lifted off his feet and dropped onto his back with the full weight and fury of Adelais finishing the job he had earlier started on the bandito's face. Though smaller than the bandito, but by no means small, Adelais displayed no trouble in dominating his larger, injured opponent. The stranger kicked Adelais off the bandito, dragging Alejandro back to his feet.

"That's enough! My brother's caused enough trouble for one day." The stranger looked down to Lorena, discontented. "I'm sorry about what he did to your dog."

The stranger wrapped his brother's arm around his neck and proceeded to a horse tied up just outside town. Adelais sprung to his feet, ready to chase after them.

"Ade, let them go." Siggy ran up to Lorena and knelt beside her, motioning for Adelais to help.

"Sig, after everything we went through ta' get that bastard, you wanna let 'im walk?"

"More important things right now, Ade."

Siggy tried to help Lorena up, but she refused his assistance, turning to the sickly, dirty dog lying on the ground with flies nipping at its ears. She grazed the dog's underbelly gently with the soft of her hand, causing it to flinch and yelp out. She tried to comfort it as she looked up.

"We can't leave him here. No one takes care of Perrito anymore," Lorena reminded them.

"We ain't got food or nothin' else for it, Lore," Ade responded.

"Ade! Please."

Lorena let out a labored cough, red hand mark still fresh on her neck. Ignoring Siggy's outstretched hand, she took to her feet, wrapping her arm around Siggy's shoulder as they both stood staring at Adelais. They remained for a moment, deadlocked. Lorena's ankle began to give way, forcing Siggy to lean to carry the bulk of her weight. She couldn't walk, but she refused to be carried. Siggy turned away, forcing Lorena to hobble along with him back to the bar. Adelais snorted, picking up the bleeding dog and carrying it closely behind them as he watched the banditos mount their steed and ride off into the desert.

6. The Desert Vanguard

"Time spent talkin' is time lost for doin'."

– Adelais's Scratch Pad

Adelais carried Perrito, the ragged town dog, into the bar and set the stray on the floor. Taking a seat on top of the table, he stared at the dying dog while Lorena, sitting on the opposite table, bandaged up her ankle. The look in the dog's eyes was all too familiar. The last sparks of life before the flame was extinguished.

"Ade, we gotta get 'im to the doc kinda now," Lorena said.

"Dunno why. He ain't gonna make it." Adelais shrugged.

"Don't matter if you believe he can live. We gotta try."

"No truck. The smartass city boy took off with it and ain't been back."

Finishing his sentence, Adelais heard the sound of the engine shutting off in front of the bar. He watched as Kody walked in, stopping in the doorway to figure out what was going on. Adelais waved his hand, shooing Kody away as Siggy came out of the kitchen to look the dog over.

"So…" Kody started.

"Glad you're back. We can go now." Lorena was already trying to get back on her feet.

"It's just a fuckin' dog, Lore." Adelais responded.

"Gotta get my ankle checked out, *Ade*," Lorena said with spiteful emphasis, "so cut the shit and let's go."

Adelais jumped off the table, towering over Lorena, who was still leaning on hers. Glaring down at her, she ignored him and hobbled passed him on her way out the door. Reaching the doorframe, she turned around and returned the glare, shifting her eye line to the dog for a moment before hobbling outside. Siggy began carefully lifting the dog's head, waiting for Adelais to pick up the other half. Pushing his younger brother out of the way, Adelais exhaled as he wrapped his arm around the dog, ignoring its cry. He hoisted it off the ground and carried it outside.

He dropped the dog in the bed of the truck, sitting next to it as the rest of the crew piled into the cab. Adelais dropped his head back against the cab's glass window, watching the skyline recede as nightfall settled in. The cool desert air brought refreshment to the conclusion of a long, hard day.

"You're one unlucky sonuvabitch, dog."

Adelais patted the dog's head. The dog offered no response except to occasionally cry out in pain when the truck bed bounced on the gravelly road. Adelais rested his arm on the dog, keeping its body secure against the warm metal frame.

It wasn't long before they arrived at an unusually well-lit establishment. The main building stood alone along the road, but was sizable enough not to appear out of place on its own. Kody hopped out of the truck first and ran up to the door, pounding on it with little luck. Most folk in the area knew better than to go out or open their doors after dark.

Siggy helped Lorena out of the truck and served as a balancing post for her while Adelais picked the dog up and carried it to the door. A full minute passed after Kody's first knock; Adelais's patience wore thin. He assaulted the door with his free hand.

"Don't break the damn thing! Hold on."

A moment later, the door slowly creaked open to reveal a homely older gentleman, though he possessed no matching demeanor. "What do you want? I have nothing left to steal. Estaban's already cleaned me out."

"We ain't banditos, Doc. Girl over there got her ankle crushed."

Adelais gestured to Lorena, who offered the doc a weak smile as she lifted her leg to show him her ankle. The doc appeared to focus less on the girl and more on the urban cowboy standing next to her.

"And the dog?" the doctor inquired.

"Got kicked a few times. It's probably dyin'."

"And I'm supposed to what? Fix it? I'm not a vet. Last thing I need is to get involved with banditos." The doc continued to eye Kody suspiciously.

"Last thing ya' need is ta' piss me off." Adelais stepped up into the doc's face, nearly hitting him with the dog's head. "Fix the girl, Doc. Don't care what ya' do 'bout the dog."

The doctor, clearly defeated, shrugged and stepped aside, allowing them to enter. The building had a somewhat spacious waiting room beyond the door, with a few beds dressed as exam tables. It appeared to be an improvised clinic.

"The girl can sit on the bed. Set the dog down over there." The doctor nodded to the open floor space near a window. "Don't want it stinking up the place if it dies before I have a chance to get to it."

Adelais dropped the dog near the window and took a seat on one of the empty exam beds, rubbing his palm along the smooth side of the cheap sheets. The soft fabric soothed his torn-up hand. Siggy took a seat next to him, keeping a respectful distance, while Kody stood near the door. They watched as the doc removed the bandage and examined Lorena's swollen ankle.

"Hm. Can't do much. Only have the basics, and not much of those. Like I said before, Estaban's coterie took most of my supplies a while ago."

"Estaban?" Kody asked.

"Yeah, your boss."

"Bos—hey, wait! I'm not a bandito!"

"Mhm. Where'd you get that jacket?"

Adelais looked Kody over, examining the leather duster in detail. It wasn't the first time Adelais had seen it, but like with most things, the jacket hadn't warranted a second look. Until now.

"A friend. Well, not a friend. A friend of a friend. A brother of an ex-girlfriend. It's complicated." Kody confused himself.

"Your ex's brother is a bandito. Not that complicated. If you want me to do anything for the girl—"

"Hi, s'cuse me? *The girl* has a name, 'kay? It's Lorena. Quit talking 'bout me like I'm not here," Lorena interjected.

"Lorena. I can't do much for you unless your bandito friend there gets me some supplies."

"I just told you I'm not—" Kody tried to defend himself as Adelais stood up.

The room quieted down, Adelais's large frame occupying a good portion of it. "Don't got any supplies. What else can ya do, Doc?"

"Nothing worthwhile. No supplies, no medicine, no fixing. If you're that desperate, you could try asking one of Estaban's lackeys, but unless you're looking to die, I don't see the point. It's an ankle. It'll heal. Not great, but it'll heal."

Adelais walked up to the doc and knelt in his face, grabbing him by the cheeks and pulling him close to Lorena's ankle.

"Yer gonna fix this. Tonight. She ain't gonna have no messed-up hobble the rest a' her life."

The doc wriggled his face free, backing up several paces from Adelais. His flushed skin did little to hide the small man's indignation, but the doc wasn't foolish enough to start a fight with a man as stout as Adelais.

"Ade, if banditos took the supplies, then ya' know who prolly has them." Siggy shifted his eyes toward Lorena's ankle.

"Alejandro." Adelais's muscles grew taut as he mentioned the bandito's name, the memory of Lorena being choked out still fresh in his mind.

"Alejandro? *Romero*? Isn't he the one we just—" Kody started.

"Brother got him out this afternoon, just before he did *that*." Siggy nodded toward Lorena. "Prolly bribed or threatened the badge holdin' him." Siggy rubbed his head.

"Don't matter. I'm gettin' the stuff back." Adelais interrupted.

Adelais cast an eye to the dog lying in the corner, still breathing, as he stormed off toward the door. He stopped in front of Kody, who was still standing before the entrance.

"Adelais, you can't do this. Not at night. Banditos have been rolling way too deep lately as it is, and we can barely manage to avoid them during the day."

Adelais grabbed Kody by the shoulder and threw him aside, slamming him into the wall before opening the door.

"Ade, I got hurt—it happens! Don't go gettin' yerself killed over this!" Lorena shouted.

"Fine. I won't go alone." He turned to his brother, calling him out, and wandered outside.

Adelais left the makeshift clinic, leaving the door open. He climbed into the front seat of the truck and felt around behind it until his fingers ran across a piece of warm, broken leather. He grabbed it, and pulled out a set of tangled leather vambraces. He looked them over, testing the strength of each piece as he strapped them to his wrists. Siggy barely had time to hop into the passenger seat of the truck before Adelais started the engine and took off in the direction of Alejandro's shack.

7. Shutters and Boards

"There's nothin' I won't do for my family."

– Siggy's Memory Book

Siggy sat in the passenger seat, trying to see anything beyond the windshield. Evenings were dark in the desert—the roads illuminated only by starlight. A single truck with a set of headlights didn't do much but stand out to every bandito looking for something to raid. Siggy looked over to his brother, once again trying to read the blank slate he so frequently wore.

"Ade, I'm worried 'bout Lorena same as you, but why're ya' tryin' ta' get us killed?"

Adelais snorted, accelerating as the truck started rumbling over the rocky terrain. He was forced to slow his pace to dodge a roaming coyote.

"This is what I mean. What're ya' doin'?"

"I'm drivin'. Gonna find Alejandro, deal with him, and take what he's got."

"Ade, do you even know what we're lookin' for? Or where to find Alejandro?"

"Medical shit! Bandages, pills, I dunno! Can't be that hard ta' figure out. And Alejandro's a dumbass bandito like the rest of 'em. Only two places he coulda gone—wanna make a bet on which one? I'm startin' with the easy one."

Siggy shrugged, watching his brother, trying to remember what Adelais had been like before he had become a monster of a man. He couldn't remember much. Siggy laid his head against the passenger side window as the truck continued barreling along. Resting his head, the excitement of the day finally started catching up with him. After a while, weariness ambushed his sleepy eyelids, and dragged them down to the resting place.

* * *

Siggy's body lurched forward against his seatbelt as the truck ground to a halt. He forced his eyes open, catching a blurry glimpse of Adelais grabbing the shotgun and climbing out of the truck. Siggy looked around, not having any weapon of his own. He scrambled around the truck, trying to find something that would suffice. He felt around under the seat until he finally found his weapon of choice: a Peacemaker he'd received as a gift.

"Heh…"

Without much choice, he grabbed it and got out of the truck, tailing Adelais up to the shanty. He stopped behind Adelais, who turned a severe expression on his younger brother.

"What?" Siggy questioned.

"Shut up." Adelais whispered.

"Shut up? What're you—"

"Yer breathing. Want 'im to hear us?"

Siggy shook his head.

"Then shut up."

Siggy became aware of how rapidly he was breathing but could do little to calm his wiry body. The tension in his nerves wouldn't dissipate. He crept alongside Adelais, noticing the window he had peered into earlier was now boarded up. *Ade guessed right… Alejandro did come back ta' his old shack.* They made their way along to the front door, Adelais stopping to signal for Siggy to wait near the entrance.

Siggy watched as Adelais cocked his shotgun. Adelais reached the front door, lifted his heavy steel-toed boot into the air, and delivered the full force of his massive leg into the center of the doorframe. The feeble door splintered as it broke off the hinges, the remaining portions slamming violently into the interior wall. Adelais took aim as he stormed into the hovel, finding a badly beaten bandito and an unfamiliar associate drinking casually, both reclining on a beat-up sofa. Siggy took his place behind Adelais, ready to provide support.

"You're fuckin' kidding me. Adelais, right?"

Alejandro remained seated, complacent, as he stared at Adelais with amused disbelief. The second man remained frozen, drink in hand.

"Meds. Give 'em up." Adelais demanded.

"You want drugs? Well shit, could've just asked. May not like you, but business is business." Alejandro responded.

"Ain't here fer that shit, and I ain't buyin'. You or yer friends took some meds from a doc not too far from here. Yer gonna give 'em up."

"Or else what? You'll take me back to jail? You barely managed last time, and the odds aren't in your favor now. Huff and puff all you like." Alejandro feigned surrender, raising his arms in the air and waving jazz hands at Adelais. "Please Mr. Big Bad Wolf, don't blow my house down."

Adelais cocked a grin, placing his finger on the cool trigger of his shotgun. He lined up the shot and pulled the trigger without hesitation. Blood spattered around Alejandro's ankle, decorated with new holes. Alejandro let out a terrible, inhumane screeching as he flailed about, clutching at his ankle, trying to hold the blood in. The second bandito jumped up and immediately surrendered, sputtering in fear. He moved slowly toward the door and remained in place, hands in the air.

"Sig, watch the other one."

Adelais tossed the shotgun aside as he walked up to Alejandro's bloodied face, tightening his vambraces and pushing the bandito back into his shoddy couch. He lifted one foot onto the couch, resting the toe of his boot in Alejandro's groin as he leaned in close.

"Meds. Now."

"Uh...uhnder...floor..."

Alejandro gestured toward a latch in the corner. Siggy gasped, finally regaining his breath, unaware he had stopped breathing the moment Adelais pulled the trigger. He couldn't control the profuse sweating in his palms; he struggled to maintain his grip on the revolver as he tried to put his thoughts back together.

Adelais moved over to the corner, lifting the badly disguised floor panel while keeping one eye on Alejandro. Inside lay the assorted loot the banditos must've been collecting: guns, cash, a few bootleg copies of *The Guild*. After digging around a bit, Adelais pulled out some medical supplies. He grabbed up a bag and knelt, filling it with anything looking even remotely useful. He stood, handing the bag off to Siggy, and returned to Alejandro.

"So question is: what do I do with you? Like ya' said, jail won't do nothin'."

Having had a moment to regain some semblance of composure, Alejandro winced as he stood up on his good leg to meet Adelais face to face.

"Listen closely, worthless mutt," Alejandro spoke slowly. "Even violence can only accomplish so much. You're off your leash. You'll be the death of everyone you love." Alejandro smirked as his eyes focused on the door. "You've already been tagged, so do what you will. My boy's on his way back now."

Adelais quickly turned to Siggy, who was now frantically looking around for the second bandito.

"Damnit, Sig! Find 'im!"

Siggy tried to control the nervous retching in his gut, frantically searching for the second bandito. He started toward the door when he noticed a glinting piece of silver in Alejandro's hand. Before Siggy could react, a piece of steel was sticking out of Adelais's gut. Adelais responded with a swift blow to Alejandro's face, falling to the floor with him. Hatred radiated off Siggy's brother, who sat mounted on top of his opponent. Alejandro returned no malice, but instead smiled a sickly, depreciating smile.

"The hell you so happy about?" Adelais asked.

"You think you're some noble soldier fighting a war against the 'bad guys', but you, me, our brothers, we were all raised the same. Only difference is some of us stepped up to make our lives better, even if it made some others worse. Tell me you haven't done the same."

Adelais wrapped his fingers around Alejandro's throat, clutching tightly.

"Ade, stop!" Siggy shouted.

Alejandro brought his arms between Adelais', breaking his grip. He lifted his head enough to meet Adelais face to face. "Go ahead, hero—you know you want to. Just think about what'll happen to that poor little girl and her dog if you don't. I've killed more people than you could imagine to take care of my family. Lives don't mean a thing to me. Just remember the fire you use to smite your enemies will burn your house down too."

Adelais retook his hold on Alejandro's neck, choking the life out of him. Staring into the bandito's remorseless, bloodshot eyes, he lifted his foe's head and slammed it against the floor repeatedly until it cracked, creating a river of crimson. Adelais remained sitting upon Alejandro's desecrated body for a moment, hands soaked in blood. The battle ended, he remained atop his opponent, staring off into nothing.

Siggy grabbed his brother's arm and dragged him out of the shack, rushing the both of them back to the truck. He threw the medical supply bag onto the seat and waited as Adelais stood staring off into the distance, into the dark nothingness that extended before them.

"Ade...what did you do?"

Adelais fell back to the ground, dry heaving. Siggy helped support his brother, noticing a distinguishable stream of red among the sanguine speckles plastering Adelais's shirt. The stab wound was getting worse.

"I...we gotta get you back to the doc."

"Sig." Ade grabbed Siggy's shoulder. "You can't tell anyone."

Adelais vomited into the dirt, heaving the contents of his stomach into desert underbrush. A small scorpion scuttled away at the noise. Siggy patted his brother's back, trying to contain his own nerves and ignore the rancid smell of stomach acid and death.

"Bu... burn it." Adelais gasped in between heaves, loosening the vambraces.

Siggy began to open his mouth, but the look on his brother's face taught him better. Once Adelais was able to support himself, Siggy slowly walked back toward the shack. He looked the hut over. He was a criminal, and his brother a murderer. He agreed to cover up the crime, like a good brother should.

Siggy crept to the doorway, daring only to get close enough to peer inside. Nothing had changed since he ran out. Like a coward. His stomach tossed back and forth repeatedly like a heavy-duty washing machine on the spin cycle. He couldn't shake the disgusting anguish that crept all over him. The taste in his mouth became rancid as he forced the vomit back down. Shaking his head, he clenched his fist and hurried back into the shack only far enough to grab matches, and quickly returned to the door.

He lit the match and placed it near the doorway. He stepped backward, pace by pace, getting away from the hut. This house of horrors was nothing more than a simple assortment of shutters and boards. It was something he never wanted to see again. He watched as it began to burn. The splinters of the door were the first to alight. They soon ignited and took the front of the shack with it. He had seen enough. Sigurd Martinez turned about and walked away from the scene.

He returned to the truck to find Adelais passed out on the ground. He checked his brother's pulse, his heart still beating, and tore Adelais's bloodstained shirt and bracers off him. Siggy used the bloody shirt to clean as much of his brother as he could before tossing it and the bracers into the blaze. Without pulling the knife from his brother's gut, Siggy managed to load Adelais into the passenger seat of the truck. Strapping the behemoth of a man in, Siggy set off for the doc's house, hoping to get back in time to save both of the people he loved. And maybe the dog, too.

8. Arrested Development

"One of the most important things I've learned is that it's nearly impossible to tell when you've lost perspective. Sometimes the brutal honesty of a stranger is what gets you back on the path."

– Cris's Journal

Ann Arbor, Michigan

"Have fun. Call me if you need anything." Emma dropped her sister off at the Diag, the central park of the university campus, in the early evening after Cris's part in Kara's birthday party had wrapped up. She nodded, taking her bag with her. It took only a few moments of searching under the glare of the glowing streetlamps before Cris recognized the musically inclined trio wrapping up an acoustic piece on the far side of the park. She made her way over to the Bards and took a seat, opening her bag to let the furry former kitten known as Bixby onto her lap.

"Sorry for being late. Had to help Tabby finish cleaning up," Cris said.

"It's all good, *amiga*, just gettin' ready to take a break," Geroge responded.

"Cris." Daron, the band's boyishly handsome European bassist, nodded. "A pleasure. We're gonna make a Steaks & Shakes run. Care to join us?"

Cris looked over the regal feline, who appeared disgruntled at being carried in a bag, and shook her head. She took in the scene, enjoying the bright lights and cool breeze of the late-night downtown air.

"I'll be all right. Been a while since I've been downtown. I'll hang out here and watch your stuff."

"Fair enough," Geroge said. "Jeany?"

"I'd prefer shit to that grease, thanks."

"There's that irresistible charm! Love you too, darlin'."

Geroge chuckled as he and Daron headed down the street to the van. Cris let Bixby out of her lap, catching the scent of James & Jonathan's sandwiches drifting in the air. Her stomach rumbled, and she ignored it. For whatever appetite she might've had, nothing seemed appealing. Her thoughts began to wander as she carelessly gazed upon her cat playing in the grass.

The furrlicious fur ball, Allister Theodore Bixby III, Esq., stalked the verdant green he had fallen upon, keeping a watchful eye on the residents of his newly discovered dandelion kingdom. He had escaped the handbag of his handmaiden to explore the free world once more.

The feline liege maintained tight control of his new realm and quickly established his borders. He would not be surprised or overtaken by any wayward waddle-feathers. He'd been forced to retreat from an expedition once before by the annoying civilization of quack-quacks. It was an incident unforgotten, that could never be allowed to reoccur. With time he had grown larger, stronger, fatter. With time, he had become a full-grown cat.

He stretched, readying his kitty muscles. The night air bringing him to life, the regal feline sprinted circles around his area of operations, intimidating anything foolish enough to challenge him. To prove his might, he assaulted a white, flowery sort of plant swaying nearby. A tuft of pollen wafted into his furry, pink nose. Unable to rebel its unusual tactics, he sneezed. His plans were not going as intended. He could not remain undignified in such a manner. Clearly, it was a sign that the inspection of his dominion should be put on hold, until after he had a chance to recuperate. It was time for a catnap. Yawning, the noble meow-meow crawled back into his over-scented handmaiden's lap and rested his fuzzy eyelids.

Cris snapped out of her daze, petting Bixby and making him cozy while she scooted around. She tried to find a comfortable spot against a tree, all the while taking care not to disturb the sleepy cat. Neither she nor the feline himself was fond of his rude awakenings. Watching the small Asian woman with a large personality, she realized how little she and Jence had spoken over the past few months.

"So, Jence—"

"Shut it, princess."

"What?"

Cris recoiled, looking around to see if there were medieval role players dueling behind them, or perhaps some other crazy random happenstance she had missed.

"I'm not one of your fairytale friends," Jence started. "Seen what you do to them—you're the last person standing. You're only here because G decided to babysit you until your runaway boyfriend comes back, and it's getting a little old. Doesn't give you an all-access pass to trample on our lives like you're the Almighty."

"Jence, I never—"

"Shut your mouth? Learn your place? Eat real food?" Jence asked, poking Cris where her gut should be. "I can see that. I know it never crossed your mind—anything other than your own problems seldom does—but for the record, I like Alma. She's the one who got the raw deal out of your debacle—not you. Don't forget that."

Cris closed her mouth, looking over the acoustic guitar lying between herself and Jence. She tried to think of something to say, or to even figure out where Jence was coming from, but she had nothing. Bixby rolled over in her lap, brushing his tail against her leg. She rubbed his belly, startling the feral prince. He gnashed at her hand in retaliation as he awoke. Cris jumped, flinging the cat out of her lap toward Jence as she tried to get away from Bixby's traumatic claws. Jence shifted to the side, moving away from the cat and directing a glare at Cris.

"Are you kidding me?" Jence asked.

"It was an accident, okay? And I don't know what your problem is, but I don't owe you anything. I don't care if you like Alma better, or think I'm trashy, or whatever else. Not that it's any of your business, but yes I slept with my best friend's boyfriend, and I'm glad I did. I'm in love with him. And you know what? It wasn't a one-way deal: Kody slept with me too. He's just as culpable for what happened, and I'm tired of taking all the heat for it, got it?"

Jence scoffed, cocking an eye at Cris while she scooped the cat up by its waist and tossed it back toward Cris. Cris caught the noble feline, who was now calm, though less dignified, being used as an improvised hacky sack, and held him close in her lap as she watched Jence.

"We're going for a little walk."

Cris hesitantly stood up and waited while Jence put the guitar into its case and slung it on her back. She started down the sidewalk, barely waiting for Cris to catch up.

"Maybe I was a little irrational; let me start again. I dislike you, but don't mistake that for thinking I dislike you enough to care about you." Jence led her across the street and past the Diag Deli, the scent of freshly baked pizza wafting in the air. "I don't even think about you most of the time, except for when you're being whiney at G. It's irritating."

"Sorry I'm irritating," Cris replied sarcastically.

"It's *that* pretentious stuck-up attitude I'm talking about. This isn't about you."

Cris looked over to Jence, the latter throwing her arm in front of Cris to stop her from walking into oncoming traffic in front of the State Theater. Cris shrugged apologetically and kept her eyes on the path in front of her.

"I quit the band for a while. When we first got back from the campsite in Tennessee."

"What?" Cris asked.

"Nothing to do with you, princess. It was right after my mom's wedding. She's been married at least...five times now, and yet she keeps going. You could say I'm skeptical, but she swears she's happy every time, so who am I to judge?" They crossed in front of the former headquarters of an old bookstore. "Made me think—can a person be themselves if they restrict their lifestyle to accommodate just one other person?"

"I don't really—"

"Quiet, princess. That's not your line," Jence interrupted. "I'm not one for lifestyle changes. I get comfy, I stay comfy. But graduation screwed everything up. Thteve left for college—didn't so much as tell me he was going until he was gone. Just left me and G. And Daron."

The two continued down the road, passing a large parking structure and small nightclub at an intersection. They made their way through the crowded late-night streets, Cris holding Bixby close for comfort.

"Anyway, it's like I said before—can a woman be herself if she's bound to another person? Especially someone like G...heh, well you should know. More or less the same as dating Kody, I guess, except hairier. So anyway, I left. Left the band, left G."

Jence led Cris across the street to the entrance of the parking structure. They made their way inside the lobby. She hit the elevator button and waited as they watched people far too underdressed for a brisk fall evening pass by outside.

"Why would you—?" Cris started.

"You have a listening problem. You might wanna look to that. I left because the life I made didn't fit me anymore." The elevator opened, beckoning the two ladies and their feline companion inside. They watched the people of the evening get smaller as the elevator ascended.

"Problem was, leaving didn't fix that. I avoided the Bards for over a month, but I still felt out of place—I just had nowhere to do it at. Could've gone back to G at any time, but being with that man... it's like approaching the event horizon. You know you're headed toward something dangerously amazing—something you'll never fully comprehend—but the moment you cross that threshold you can't turn back. Also, there's a whole analogy about getting crushed. He's not a light guy." A small smirk crossed Jence's face.

"Anyway, I did what any smart person would do."

Cris looked over to Jence, eyebrow raised.

"Made a booty call." Jence laughed depreciatingly at herself as they exited the elevator on the top floor. "Might've been a mistake, but I still don't like the idea of restricting myself, even if it is G. And I've known him since I dumped sand down the back of his diaper, if that says anything."

They exited onto the roof, Jence leading Cris over to the ledge of the parking structure. Jence leaned out over the ledge, dragging Cris with her. They stood leaning just over the boundary, overlooking the Michigan Theater and the city itself underneath the bright city lights.

"I've told you before, princess—I dislike you. But that has nothing to do with trying to be a decent person every now and again. I told you that story because even I can be a scrot sometimes and wuss out. But at the end of the day you're still alive, so quit being a whiney priss and get over your damage."

"Jence..."

"Shut up. You might sing well, but you're still irritating. Besides, I get the feeling you're about five seconds away from saying YOLO, and I don't want to get arrested for tossing your skinny ass off this roof."

Jence unslung the guitar, leaving it by Cris as she made her way across the roof of the parking structure to the other exit.

"Where're you going?" Cris called out.

Jence flicked up her middle finger and held it high as she disappeared down the staircase. Cris remained on the cold rooftop, taking in the sight of the city as she mulled over what Jence had said. Looking down at herself, she could see Jence wasn't entirely wrong—she had lost too much weight.

Cris kissed the back off the royal fur ball's head, the august cat returning the affection in kind on her lightly scarred, freckle-stained cheek. Cris jumped at the sound of the rooftop doors opening, Geroge and Daron joining her.

"What're you two doing here? I thought you went to get burgers."

"It was G's turn to buy," Daron said.

"Yeah, well…Jeany kinda swiped my wallet. Again," G responded.

Is that why she ran off so quickly, crossed Cris's mind.

"You two followed us?"

"What? Of course we weren't eavesdropping. That's crazy! We were conducting espionage. It's much cooler," Geroge replied.

"Spying on your girlfriend, huh?" Cris asked.

"Which I'm sure would be all kinds of unethical if you ignore the kleptomania. We happened to spot you two while we tryin' to find my wallet. Anyway, Jeany'll be fine—just gotta give her space."

Cris sighed, unwilling to debate ethics, particularly after Jence's exposition on the philosophy of self-development, or her particular lack thereof.

"So what's the game plan for tonight?" she asked.

"Well, still haven't eaten, so I guess we find something cheap down here," G started.

"Something I'm sure G will be happy to reimburse," Daron added.

"Ri—ght. And then we can go from there," G finished.

Cris nodded, handing G his guitar as the three of them headed for the elevator. They piled in, watching the people grow larger as the lift began to lower. The regal fur ball yawned a whiskery kitty yawn from atop his mobile human throne as the three continued their descent into the night below.

9. Birds of a Feather

"Don't matter how much they seem the same—every day is different for folks who don't waste 'em."

– Siggy's Memory Book

Outskirts of Los Tios, Mexico

The desert sun shone through the window much earlier than Siggy was prepared for, waking him from the precious few hours of sleep he had been able to get the past few days. He looked around the makeshift clinic, still caught in a post-sleep haze and trying to reorient himself from the night before. A body lay passed out on the floor not far from Siggy, covered in a leather duster. On the exam table, Lorena rested with an improvised splint on her ankle. The dog sat staring at Siggy, apparently no better but no worse than it had been before. This left only one person unaccounted.

Siggy got up and looked around, unable to find any trace of his brother. Checking the door, he found a set of shoes missing—steel-toed boots. Siggy slid his own boots on and headed outside. He relished the morning air, not yet baked by the arid heat. Looking around the mostly desolate land, decorated with dull shrubbery, Siggy was unable to find his brother. He did find, however, a set of tracks made by overly large boots.

Trekking along for the better part of the morning, Siggy began to wonder what would cause Adelais to wander so far out into the middle of nowhere. Though they had been raised in the desert, they weren't immune to the perils of living there. The bandito threat in particular had been steadily rising, and he and Adelais were in no small part responsible for that.

Wandering on, Siggy caught sight of a lone blue palm tree looking over a small hill. On the crest of that hill sat a large, shirtless man with innumerable scars. Siggy came up to him slowly and loudly, so as not to alarm his brother and become a potential victim of Adelais's arbitrary violence. Siggy took a seat beside his brother, looking off into the distance.

"What'cha up to?" Siggy asked casually. The two sat in silence for some time before Adelais responded.

"How's Lorena?"

"Dunno. She was still passed out when I got up. Ankle's all patched up, so I figure she's good enough."

The brothers sat quietly, watching tumbleweeds blow by. Little but the fallow air disrupted the silence between them. Farther down the hill, a pack of coyotes pursued a group of roadrunners aggressively. Only the victors continued on.

"How's your gut?"

"Doc patched it up well 'nough. Won't be runnin' any marathons today, but I'll live. Lost my favorite shirt, though."

"Oh yeah… the one Lorena got ya', right? Around Christmas?"

Adelais nodded. "Only Christmas I remember."

"One outta two, anyway."

"Wha'dya… oh. Ya' mean the one where you and ma made those dumbass things fer everyone."

"I think they were bracelets…" Siggy tried to recall.

"The hell were two you thinkin' makin' bracelets fer us?"

"Dunno. Think it was Mom's idea. Was just a kid, after all."

"Yer still just a kid."

Siggy looked up, the fires of the burning shack and smell of melting flesh still fresh in his mind. The crackling of collapsing wood was as loud in his memory as it had been the preceding night.

"I killed 'im, little brother."

"I know."

"Cracked his damn head open like a broken egg."

Siggy looked at his own hands while listening to his brother. He cringed.

"Goddamn banditos. I'd kill every one of 'em if I could," Adelais said.

Siggy clenched his fists, unable to fight the tightness in his chest. "Why? Why'dya always wanna fight? It's the same thing they do!"

"I don't go rapin' families and makin' kids watch while I kill their parents."

"So you figure you'll just start killin' banditos now? It ain't gonna help anything! *They* ain't comin' back. Dead is dead."

Before he could stop them, Siggy caught himself shedding tears. He tried to hide them from Adelais, but his brother caught the change in Siggy's voice.

"Quit bein' a bitch, little brother. I know they're dead, an' I know we can't bring 'em back. But we can kill as many bastards as we can so no one else has to deal with it."

"So you're just gonna keep killin' 'em huh? May as well join 'em if yer gonna act like one—"

Siggy fell back as Adelais grabbed his collar, forcing him into the dirt. He tried to stop sniffling, focusing on catching his breath after the impact.

"Gonna kill me too?"

"Goddamnit, Sig…"

Adelais pulled Siggy up. He sat up, looking to his older brother, confused. Adelais remained expressionless, putting his arm around his brother's shoulder.

"What was I suppose ta' do, Sig? I tried it yer way. Went out and caught the bastard legit. Locked 'im up. Few hours later, he was beatin' on Lorena. If I let 'im go, he woulda ended up killin' 'er. What choice did I have?"

"Maybe you're right Ade, *maybe*. But you're talkin' about killin' all of 'em now. Do you even care that you killed a guy?"

"I ain't soft like you. I dunno if I can even feel sad. Don't have any tears. Just don't."

"We can't keep on like this. There's gotta be a better way than everyone killin' and dyin' for no reason."

"Yeah? Ya' ever find it ya' let me know."

"I…" Siggy stopped himself. "I will."

"You ready ta' head back?"

Siggy nodded. Adelais stood up, helping Siggy to his feet. Adelais began walking off, getting a few paces ahead of Siggy—who was struggling to keep up—before stopping and turning around. Looking back to his brother, Adelais took a knee, kneeling in front of Siggy.

"What're you doin' Ade?"

"Ya' know what I'm doin'. Climb on."

"What? I ain't a kid—"

"Shut up and climb on."

Siggy looked his brother over, concerned about the gut wound Adelais had received the night before. Even after all that, he still didn't seem to slow down. Siggy began to wonder if his brother ran on sheer force of will as he climbed onto Ade's back.

"Rest for a bit, little brother, I'll get us home."

Despite the discomfort and stench of his brother's back, the fatigue from the night before coupled with getting hardly any sleep allowed Siggy to rest his eyes while Adelais carried him. Before long, Siggy's mind began to drift back to his childhood, back to when Adelais was still just his big brother, a kid himself, trying to take care of the family. Though Siggy could feel the elder Martinez struggling to carry him even now, his big brother never quit. Before long, Siggy was fast asleep.

* * *

Siggy woke up to the revving of the truck's engine as Adelais dropped him into the passenger seat of the red pickup, next to Lorena. Kody sat in the driver's seat, messing with the mp3 player, filling the cab with The Fray's sentimental "Look after You." Siggy looked in the rearview mirror to see the back of the truck sink down, supporting Adelais's weight. Next to Adelais lay the dog, resting its head on Adelais's leg.

"Morning, little brother. Heard ya' had an excitin' night. Helped take care a' me and yer brother, huh?" Lorena spoke while Siggy rubbed the sleep from his eyes.

"How much did Ade tell you?"

"That ya' saved the day."

Siggy couldn't remember Adelais ever praising him, even on his best days. He decided not to question whether he was awake or still dreaming.

"You okay, Lorena?"

"More or less. Doc splinted my ankle and said I gotta stay off it awhile. Put together a set a' fancy crutches for me, too. We'll see how long that lasts."

"Glad you're okay."

"Don't worry 'bout me Siggy, I'm tougher than I look. Get some rest— yer the one I'm worried 'bout right now."

"But—"

"Shhh…"

Lorena wrapped her arm around Siggy, gently resting his head against her small bosom as he tried to curl up in the seat. She rubbed his scruffy hair back and forth, nurturing his teenage body like a young child. The feel of her warm cotton dress on his cheek brought a wave of serenity over him. He wrapped his arm around her waist, comfortably situating himself and embracing the rare moment of tranquility. He abandoned his thoughts to the harmonic beating of Lorena's heart. Just once, he remembered what it was like to be part of a family—to be loved. They all rode on home together.

10.Living the Dream

"There's a keen difference between surviving and living."

– The Chronicles of Glenn Radcliffe

Bloomfield Hills, Michigan

Glenn skimmed the page, briefly glancing at the material. He appreciated the artwork—he always appreciated the artwork—and skimmed the page again before moving on to the next. There were any number of things he should be doing, but honestly, what was the point?

"Glenn, c'mere."

His father's voice echoed from the veranda. Glenn chuckled to himself, closing his book and climbing out of the hammock in the courtyard. He took a leisurely stride, walking the marble steps between the koi ponds to the lanai. As he entered, his father, Bernard, was already in a less-than-pleasant mood.

"What c-can I do for you, Father?"

"What are you doing today?"

"R-reading." Glenn offered his father the book.

"*The Other Side of the Mirror?* Do you read anything else?"

Glenn looked away, scratching his thin, newly grown beard. The twenty-three-year-old stared into the fountain back in the courtyard, lanky and disciplined as ever. The ambiance of the splashing water mixed with the fickle remnants of the summer heat was too enticing to waste standing around with his father. He ignored Bernard's audible sigh.

"Boy, try to pay attention. I brought you home so you could get better. Under supervision, since you clearly will not take care of yourself. If you want to waste away into nothing, go do it on the street. If you want to remain here, in the lap of luxury, get off your ass and go out and do something."

"What d-do you suggest, Father?"

"Do you really need me to dictate your life for you? Or is it that it's easier than actually trying to live it?"

"Hm." Glenn smirked halfheartedly, watching the fountain from the corner of his eye. "As you s-stated, Father, I c-clearly will not take c-care of myself. Seems you p-prefer that j-job, in any c-case."

Glenn's cheek burned as the back of Bernard's hand came firmly across it. Glenn recoiled only for a moment before regaining his posture.

"R-right…"

"Watch your mouth, boy, before I reevaluate whether you're worth the upkeep."

"Of c-course, Father."

"Damnit, Glenn, I'm trying!" Bernard threw his arms up into the air. "God help you if nothing else will."

Bernard stormed off into the atrium, taking Glenn's book with him. Glenn stood idly, letting his eyes drift to the koi ponds just outside the lanai. His fingers danced about his hand, restless with nothing to keep them occupied. He clutched his wrist, subconsciously rubbing his thumb against the unruly scar that had failed to take his life—the life regrettably saved by his friends. The life he was now pissing away.

Glenn dropped himself onto a suede sofa that sat in the lanai, sinking into it, resting his head on the arm of the couch. He stared at the ceiling, looking for his familiar wall-crawling fiends, but they were nowhere to be found. They abandoned him with the fear of death. Glenn exhaled, tapping his finger on his nose for amusement, making small mereowing sounds to himself. The excitement of his new hobby quickly died off along with his interest in consciousness. He removed his glasses and allowed his eyelids to relax, waiting for whatever would come next.

* * *

"Wake up, jackass!"

Glenn fell off the couch, or more accurately, was flipped off the couch. Unable to find his glasses, he strained to see who had assaulted him during his nap. As he felt around for his spectacles, he squinted, only able to distinguish blonde hair.

"A-alma?"

"Dreaming about teenage ass? Please, you creepy cradle-robber. Not even close."

He felt his glasses being pushed back onto his face as he looked up and recognized the face of his former paramour.

"Emma? W-what're you doing here?"

"Checking in on you. Not that I care much personally, but your dad asked me to stop by. Been meaning to anyway."

"W-why?"

"Why do you think, dumbass? Cris has been making herself sick worrying about you. She won't admit it, but she's too afraid to come see you. And for some messed-up reason I can't figure out, you haven't come to see her."

Emma grabbed Glenn's hand, pulling him off the ground and sitting him back on the couch. She took a seat next to him, leaning back and getting comfortable.

"Look, I know we've had our disagreements," Emma started.

"D-disagreements?" Glenn's brow furrowed.

"Or I swore hundreds of ugly children on you—whatever. The point is, for a long time we haven't gotten along. But our personal history isn't what's important right now. My sister is, and she looks up to you like a big brother. Right now, she needs you to be one."

"What c-could I provide that K-kody c-cannot?"

"You serious?" Emma sat up.

"I d-don't see how that could be a j-joke."

"Huh, wow," Emma paused. "You've been gone a while. Kody's out of the picture. MIA."

Glenn looked her over, examining her intentions. He watched her, reading her body language, and resigning his eyes to their pleasure. Smooth skin, soft face, well rounded. Complimented by a maize and blue V-neck and not-too-tight jeans. She was more sumptuous than he remembered. His mind slipped to other, more pleasant memories of her—and it showed.

"Hey! Keep it in your pants! That's the last thing I want from you."

Glenn chuckled to himself, trying to recount the number of different ways he'd heard that line before. He took to his feet, glancing back toward the courtyard. He moved close to Emma, taking her hand, and drawing her up from the couch.

"What're you doing, Glenn?"

"Relax, it's n-nicer outside."

He led her into the courtyard, bringing her to the fountain. He stood staring at it, lost in the spraying haze, before he began fidgeting in the pocket of his cargo pants. He pulled out a 50 Euro coin, tossing it into the water. The coin landed amid a collection of others from various nations.

"I c-can't remember…w-when was the last time you were here?" he asked.

"Your dad's house? You brought me here before prom."

"P-prom?"

"You don't remember? I guess that makes sense. Not like we made it to the dance. Glenn, what's this all about?"

He hesitated. Emma looked him over, the bitterness fading from her face. Even though she no longer looked angry, he couldn't believe she'd ever forgive him. Emma nudged him.

"They're just thoughts. Go ahead and speak."

"Everything. I've m-made a lot of m-mistakes. The c-chiefest among them with you."

"I remember. But this isn't about us. Cris needs you. Whatever bullshit excuses you've been telling yourself—like waiting by your pity pond for your life to magically get better—get over them and go see her. Even if it isn't worth much, and even if you don't give a shit about it, she saved your life. You owe it to her to help her get hers back on track, just like she did for you."

Glenn looked up into the sky, staring into the clouds. It was more blue than he remembered. More blue than he deserved. The midnight sun flying high next to its archrival, serving no purpose but to decorate the landscape of the sky. It didn't make sense. Not from his perspective. But wasn't that the point? He took in a deep breath, and expelled it all from his diaphragm, shouting into the sky.

"What're you doing?" Emma jumped back.

"T-trying to make the w-welkin ring. Or become a d-dragonborn."

Glenn reached into his pocket and pulled out a pill bottle, removing a pill from the container and swallowing it. He replaced the bottle into his pocket and turned away from the fountain, looking Emma in the eye.

"W-what happened to K-kody?"

"Ask her yourself."

Emma took a few steps toward the fountain and carefully leaned over the ledge, making sure not to expose too much cleavage. She drew a coin from the water, kissed it for luck, and tossed it back in. Without saying a word, she turned around and headed back into the lanai. Glenn appreciated the sight of her walking away as Emma disappeared from view.

He cast his eyes toward the ground, watching the grass sway in the wind. *Perhaps the dispassionate green possesses a little spirit after all,* crossed his mind. The cool feel of the earth beneath his bare feet was something that never got old. He slowly pressed each toe into the dirt, one by one, the soil climbing into the crevices of his feet.

Raising his eye-line again, he watched Bernard watching him from the atrium. The two men exchanged glances. Glenn shrugged, nothing more to offer, and returned to the hammock to finish his afternoon nap.

11. Dog Saw God

"I could use just about anyone's advice—except my own."

– Kody's Notebook

Outskirts of Los Tios, Mexico

Kody pulled the truck up to the back of the bar, parking and waiting for The Decemberists' lackadaisical "Here I Dreamt I Was an Architect" to finish before getting out. He climbed out of the pickup and went around to the back, grabbing Lorena's crutches out of the truck bed. He moved carefully, trying not to step on the dog Adelais had carelessly dropped on the ground. Kody tried to help Lorena out of the truck, but the lady waited for Adelais to come get his brother, and requested only that Kody leave her crutches. For all their talk of family, he couldn't ever seem to break in.

Kody hesitated heading into the bar, remembering the other outcast of the group. He returned to the poor dog's side and helped it try to stand. The dog possessed little strength, but with encouragement, found the means to move. Kody slowly walked the dog around the bar, bringing it to the small chantry Lorena often visited across the street. He took the canine inside and put together a small bed for it from one of the leftover blankets.

"I bet you wanna come back to the bar, but it's probably better you avoid Adelais—at least while you're getting better. He tends to make things worse." Kody kneeled, looking into the dog's eyes. "You can stay here for now. I'll come visit you, and I'm sure Lorena will too. You like her, don'tcha, boy?"

Kody rubbed the dog behind its ears, petting it and seeing the first signs of life the dog had shown since they found it.

"There ya go. You remind me of a little furry fella I used to know. You're a lot friendlier though." Kody leaned in close. "Just between you and me, I was always kind of a dog person. Stay here, buddy, I'll go get you some food."

Kody brushed the blanket veiling the chantry entrance aside and stepped out into the street. He watched the people going about their day, trying to recount which of their names he could remember. Although he had been in the town for over a month, he hadn't spent much time socializing. He spotted one of the few people he recognized, little more than a child, and made his way over to her.

"Elvia, what'cha up to?"

Kody squatted in the dirt next to the girl, who sat trying to play a guitar much too big for her. She looked up to him, smiling.

"What does it look like? Have you forgotten your eyes today?" she toyed with him playfully.

"Maybe I have! Oh, where'd you go?"

Kody covered his eyes and turned his head from side to side, trying to find where Elvia had apparently disappeared to.

"I'm not a baby, Kody." She giggled at him. "Don't forget, you promised to make me one of your pretty necklaces."

Elvia reached up to touch the beads around his neck, which were now faded by the sun and worn down by the desert sands.

"I will, Elvy." Kody returned her smile. "Actually, I could use your help with something. You remember the dog that was running around here?"

"Perrito?" Her eyes lit up.

"Perrito. I'm taking care of him for now, but the fella doesn't have any food. Do you know where we can find some food for him?"

"Yeah! Momma has some leftovers from supper! Stupid Josue wouldn't eat his. Said it was yucky."

Kody chuckled as the little girl ran inside, smuggling a plate of food out after a few minutes.

"Are you sure Josue won't need this later?" Kody asked.

"That stupid head. My brother don't wanna eat, he don't need ta' eat." Elvia stuck out her tongue.

"Heh. Thanks Elvy."

"Don't forget my necklace!"

"I won't."

Kody smiled and patted Elvia on the head before returning to the chantry. He unwrapped the food and set it on the ground in front of Perrito, waiting to see if the dog would eat.

"Here, buddy, brought you some food. Courtesy of Kara—" Kody paused for a moment. "Elvia."

"Who's Kara?"

Sunlight entered the chantry, illuminating a figure carried by crutches. Lorena took a seat next to Perrito and Kody.

"My sister."

"Didn't know ya' had a sister." Lorena rubbed Perrito's furry head. "She a troublemaker too?"

"There's plenty you don't know about me."

"There's plenty I don't know about a lot a' people," Lorena responded.

"I guess. Gonna go grab some chow."

Kody stood up, nodded to Lorena, and left the chapel. On his way back to the bar, he spotted Siggy moving out of sight of the street and into the shadows, speaking with a conspicuously dressed older man. He watched his young friend with interest. Was it possible he had finally found a lead on Lorena's cousins? In particular, his ex, the missing strawberry blonde? Unwilling to risk messing up whatever Siggy had going on, Kody left the boy to his work and returned to the bar.

The spices filled the air inside the bar, drawing Kody into the kitchen, where Adelais was filling himself a bowl of rice. He brushed past Kody, leaving a pot full of food open as fair game. Kody loaded up a bowl and went back into the bar, grabbing a seat across from Adelais at the table.

"Lorena's a good cook. The hamburger she mixed in with this rice is amazing," Kody said to start the conversation.

"Wouldn't know. Sig cooked. And it's chicken."

"Oh. Huh. Well, I got no beef with the chicken." Kody shoveled rice into his mouth, giving himself time to think. "So, what happened with you and Alejandro? Never did say, and you're sportin' a nasty cut to the gut. Sure you got some kind of glorious war story to tell."

"Shut your mouth, Lehane." Adelais remained curt.

"C'mon Ade—" Kody received an optic rebuke from Adelais. "Adelais. We're on the same team here. Quit treating me like some kind of hitchhiker who just latched on for the ride."

"You are. Ya' got stuck down here 'cause of yer own stupid ass, so you say. Was Lorena who agreed ta' take ya' in, not me. Long as she lets ya' stay, yer gonna be useful. Don't make ya' one of us. And the second she changes her mind..."

Adelais rose, sizing Kody up. Asserting his dominance as the alpha male, Adelais left his bowl and headed out. Kody remained, finishing his rice, and snagging Adelais's leftovers. *You and Thteve would've been the best of friends,* Kody thought. He finished his rice and leaned back in his chair, teetering it back and forth on its hind legs, causing it to creak on the wooden floor.

Bored, he began to retrace the steps of his latest misadventure since he left Cris. The van broke down in Tucson and nearly lost another tire in Douglas, near the Mexican border. Then of course was the border patrol. Good times.

None of it compared, however, to the time he spent in Nuevo Casas Grandes, after getting lost for the third time. Spent a good number of days with a patron not far off the beaten path. Learned a thing or two about patience and self-loathing. There was no making up for his transgressions: leaving the women he claimed to love and leaving his friend to die. He made bastard choices, and there was no changing that. But he could try to make things as right as they could be. If he could figure out what right was. The more he examined it, the more he began to wonder how trustworthy his judgment was.

He sat in his canted chair, twiddling his thumbs. On one hand, Alma, the other, Cris. He did no justice to either one of them. Maybe it was best he removed himself from the equation entirely. He kept his distance with Lorena, and so far managed not to completely screw things up. Even if he wasn't welcome here, and decided not to go home, plenty of small towns were near enough he could find a place and live out a simple life. Might be rougher with the banditos around, but at least not as complicated.

"Why do I keep trying to run away?" Kody thought aloud. "Find Alma, apologize, go back to Cris. It's a simple plan."

Kody repeated this mantra to himself as Siggy walked into the bar. Reading the look on Siggy's face, Kody's stomach immediately sank. "Dude, if you're about to tell me the princess is in another castle..."

"What?" Siggy cocked his head.

"Nothing. How'd your clandestine meeting go?"

"The hell are you talkin' about?" Siggy's eyebrow arched.

"The guy you were all small council meeting with just now."

Siggy scrutinized Kody with suspicion. Returning Siggy's glance, Kody went wide-eyed as he lost control of his chair and fell back onto the floor.

He rubbed the back of his head as he pulled himself up. "Gah! Thought I was gonna die! Honest to God. Thought. I was going. To die."

Siggy shook his head and walked off, heading downstairs. Left with no semblance of respect, Kody picked the chair off the floor and headed back into the kitchen to finish off the rice. It was going to be a long, boring afternoon.

12. Adakias' Shadow

"There are a lot a' things I put off 'cause I get nervous an' make excuses, but lately keep askin' myself—if not now, when?"

– Siggy's Memory Book

Making his way downstairs, Siggy checked to make sure no one was around. He established the area was clear and headed over to his bed, kneeling at its side. *The hell was Kody goin' on about? There's no way he knows about this,* crossed Siggy's mind as he pulled a piece of paper from his pocket. Feeling around for a small box stashed under his bunk, he pulled out the metallic tin and stuffed the paper inside. He looked around once more, pulling out his Peacemaker, and placed it in the tin, closing the container back up. He slid the box back in its spot and lay down on his bed, sorting things out.

"Jake was spotted up north, an' again not too far from here. Can't be too many places he's headed, but why come here at all? If he's runnin', this is the last place ta' go," he thought aloud. He sat up, rubbing his head, "He can't be comin' here. Not now that things are so close."

As he recounted his meeting, his stomach began to rumble. He checked the drawer next to his bed, finding an empty satchel. Siggy hopped out of bed and frantically double-checked the bag. "My jerky's gone! Damnit, Ade!" Siggy slammed the drawer shut and headed upstairs. He ran out onto the hot dirt road, trying to find his brother. With Adelais nowhere in sight, Siggy quickly abandoned his quest for vengeance.

"Prolly for the best. Wouldn't be the worth the hell ta' try an' get 'it back anyway. Prolly stuffed his face 'til he couldn't fit any more," Siggy grumbled to himself.

"Aw, was the little rat finally gonna stand up to his big brother?"

Siggy turned around to see a tall young woman with an antagonizing smirk and under-abundance of clothing standing before him. He sighed, having no good excuse to leave.

"What's it matter, Maite? You ain't Ade's type, and even if you were, I wouldn't set ya' up."

"'Course not. You could try to help out around the town like everyone else, instead of sneakin' around like a little rat, but what would be in it for you?"

The shuffle of crutches beating against the ground not far behind him, Siggy turned to see the blanket of the chantry cast aside.

Lorena hobbled out, injecting herself into the situation. "Oh don't worry, Maite, he's all kinds of helpful ta' people who matter. Kinda like you're s'pose ta' be, right? Instead of interruptin' peoples' prayers by starting fights in front of the church?"

"Lorena, ya' can't stand on your own foot, much less stand up for the boy behind you," Maite responded.

Lorena stood on her good ankle, handing her crutches to Siggy as she stepped up to Maite, face to face. "Didn't ya' say somethin' about helpin' out around here? Must keep ya' pretty busy—well, when ya' aren't already findin' ways to 'make yourself helpful' to the other guys in town. You should prolly get back ta' that."

Lorena turned around and reached up to wrap her arm around Siggy's shoulder, the two of them heading back into the bar. Once inside, he helped her as she took her crutches and hobbled over to a table, sitting on top of it to relieve the pressure on her leg. He took a seat across from her, watching as she rubbed her ankle.

"Lorena, you don't gotta stick up for me, ya' know. I can take care a' myself."

"Wasn't jes' fer you. Can't stand that ass peddler. Always gettin' in our business jes' 'cause Adelais won't take her out back ta' play bury the bone."

"Right…" Siggy trailed off. "Lorena, I need to tell ya' somethin'. And you can't talk 'bout it with anyone else. Got it? Not the city boy, not Ade. No one."

Lorena stopped rubbing her ankle and looked up, giving Siggy her undivided attention.

"Ya' know how I try an' keep an ear to the ground 'bout what's goin' on around here. I heard that Jake might be headin' back. Dunno if he's comin' here, but I dunno where else he could go."

Lorena stared at Siggy, hanging on his every word. Even after he finished speaking, she seemed lost in thought.

"We dunno for sure if he's comin' here, or if it's even really him. Jes' that he could be comin'. We should be careful."

Lorena snapped out of her daze, looking the place over. She examined the bar from top to bottom, apparently trying to figure things out. "We gotta get ready, Sig. There's no way him comin' can be a good thing. Not after all the hell he raised last time. Not after what happened ta' my ma."

Siggy put his hand on her shoulder, trying to calm her down. Lorena remained on the table, fidgeting with her crutches. She ground them against the table, chipping away at the wooden edges.

"Sorry. Little nervous. Got the butterflies, ya' know?"

Siggy got up from table and kneeled before her. He looked up to her, taking her hand into his own. She looked down into his eyes.

"We'll be ready, Lorena. Ade and the city boy can hold their own. And don't worry—I got ya'. I won't let anything happen to you."

"Ya' can't know the future, Sig."

Siggy stood up, holding Lorena's hand. He helped her off the table, leading her on her good ankle. She looked up to him, puzzled, as he wrapped his arms around her waist, supporting and holding her injured side.

"Sig, what're you…?"

"Shh."

Siggy fumbled around in his pocket until he found the mp3 he had lifted from the truck. He placed an ear bud in Lorena's ear and one in his own, the two of them listening to the haunting romance of Iron & Wine's "Fever Dream." He began to sway his hips, bringing her with him as they shared a quiet afternoon dance in the bar. He felt the warmth of her lower back as he slid his hand along the seam of her cotton dress. He managed to control the trembling in his hands as Lorena looked up into his eyes.

"Sig, you're like my brother…" she trailed off.

"I told ya' before—I'm not."

Siggy leaned in slowly, grazing his lips upon hers. Her body quivered in his arms as they touched, and he held her close, unwilling to let her go. After an extended moment, their lips parted. They looked into each other's eyes.

"Can ya' still feel the butterflies?" he asked.

"It's a little weird…"

"Give it time. Maybe you'll like it."

Lorena hesitated a moment before cautiously resting her head on Siggy's chest, being careful to keep weight off her bad ankle. She relaxed her shoulders, exhaling as she closed her eyes. He took on the full weight of her body, resting his head upon hers. The taste of her lips still fresh on his mind, he inhaled, embracing her scent while trying to contain the rapid beating against the walls of his chest. The two continued to rock back and forth, letting the song end. After a period of shuffling together to the breeze of the wind, Siggy chuckled quietly to himself.

"Guess I should get started with dinner, huh?"

"…one more?" Lorena asked without lifting her head.

Siggy smiled, pressing the play button. The couple continued dancing to Death Cab for Cutie's indie dirge, "I Will Follow You into the Dark," as the evening settled in.

13. A Quiet Mind

"Some battles never end—even if you can't win, what's important is that you never quit fighting."

– Glenn's Chronicles

Bloomfield Hills, Michigan

Glenn lay out on the grass near the fountain in the courtyard, keeping the stars as his ceiling. No longer bound by hospital walls, he was free to do as he pleased. As he pleased. What did he please? Hands, his own hands, his exclusive arch-nemeses, rose up before him. They had been the emissaries of his demise. They had drawn the blade that so many times broke his skin. His rotted skin.

He looked down. There was flesh, healthy and strong. Why had he thought it rotted? Oh, right…the mind. T'was his mind that rotted. Was that right? He shook his head. He tried to remember what he was doing here.

He'd traveled with friends to find a comrade long lost, but not forgotten. They, the friends, had promised to help him, and make him whole. He came closer, though not close, and lost himself along the way. How foolish, placing hope in misguided teenagers focused too much on succulent pieces of ass. A mistake he himself made. On one who turned against him. Such folly. How many empires have fallen to the selfsame nonsensical treachery, that of the heart?

And so he imbibed. Drowned out the poison of his thoughts with a finely aged Scotch, adding a strong dose of narcotics for flavor. How sweet the surrender that came with the promise of death. Liberation from a wealth of neglected responsibility. The end of his unattainable journey. At least, that's how he imagined it—how it was supposed to end. Trying to recall anything about his death left him with little but an active imagination.

The hospital staff had told him his stomach had been pumped and his heart restarted. Shouldn't that have brought him a second chance? Wouldn't that clean out his system and purge all of his failures? He had remained idle within the isolated safety of the bland walls as the world continued on. Until his father came.

Removed by a stalwart man ripe with ambition, it was impossible to say he was his father's son. But the credentials were good enough for the man, Bernard, to take him home after the long months of hospitalizations. So home they went. Like church and state they remained, constantly antagonizing each other yet bound by lineage. His father's convictions a perpetual slight. The elder Radcliffe never understood infirmity. Nor did the younger.

To the tunnels of blood under his hands' flesh he stared. He followed them down to the wrists, one particularly unbearable, marred by clean skin. It was a lie. The other, the scar-stained tissue, openly told the secrets he couldn't keep. It's how the not-Roberts girl knew.

Too much noise breeds too much noise—the price of a quiet mind is inflated. Around and around he looked, remembering his knife's delight at the taste of his wicked flesh. But that blade was since abandoned. He rose to his feet, his bare feet, and wandered into the house. Dark as always, but his eyes needed no guide—he was raised here. He found his way into the kitchen and drew the sharpest blade from the drawer. Dull blades are no one's friend.

He slammed it on the counter, staring at it. It wasn't *his* blade, it wasn't the same. Was this really something he wanted to do? Why would *want* matter? Since when did desire play into the mix? What *did* he desire? He took the knife in both hands, grasping its handle tightly. He examined his wrists, the guiding lines he'd left himself in case he ever forgot. It was time to take the knife to its purpose.

He took a deep breath, arching his arms back and stabbing the blade into the wall. Slowly, he let the handle go, the knife remaining in place. His fingers grew taut clutching at his wrist. He ran each finger over the scars, remembering the catharsis that bleeding brings, and with it, the chaos of letting go. He clutched his wrist until it cracked.

"Gah! D-damnit!"

He shouted at the knife, clearly at fault for tempting him without a clear resolution. He grasped the handle and pulled it out, slamming it on the counter. He hovered over it with his head in his hands.

"F-fucking fuck…"

The strawberry blonde forced her way into his mind, reminding him of her siren's song. The lone piece of salvation in a damned world, no matter how transient or ultimately disastrous. But she was gone, and here he remained—unwanted, damaged goods.

A light flicked on in the kitchen. Glenn rose to see his father standing in the doorway. The two locked eyes, possessing no adequate words.

Bernard stood for a moment before walking over to the counter, seeing the knife laid out before them. He looked over to his son, who refused to meet his father's eyes. Glenn left his gaze focused on the knife, perfect for the awkward tension rising between the two.

Glenn jumped, feeling the strong pat of his father's hand on his back as the man stood next to him. Catching the scent of orange juice, he heard his father leave a glass in the sink. The unfamiliar feel of his father's lips against his forehead caught Glenn completely off guard. He kept his eyes on the counter, examining a small part of Bernard's arm. Scar-stained. After a moment, his father walked back to the hallway and turned off the kitchen light. The two exchanged glances once more, Glenn staring into his father's eyes, before the man disappeared beyond the frame.

He remained, staring at the blade. It lay bare, next to his mottled arm, once again resting on the counter. His muscles knew their art by memory, and yet, stood fast. A distraction had broken his chain of thoughts. Gleaning a new chain, he caught a fractured memory, a simple fleeting image. It wasn't of violent intimacy, or furtive seduction, but only an honest moment. His head resting in her lap, her soothing his thoughts and giving him a quiet mind. Her fingers so gently drawn through his hair.

She had vowed to help him. Inebriated as he might've been, he had sworn his love to her. His closest act to nobility, short of saving her life. She had brought beauty to his grief, and reflected the possibility of calmness in his dark. If he proceeded any further, he'd lose that gift. More importantly, if he proceeded any further, he'd break her heart. He closed his eyes, exhaling slowly through his mouth. He placed the knife back into the drawer.

Keeping his fists clenched tight, he headed back out on to the veranda. He made his way to the moonlit fountain, taking a seat on the ledge. A cool evening breeze blew by. He dug his hand into his pocket, pulling out a small pill bottle and swallowing one of its contents. He leaned back, looking up the midnight sky. Always he'd been waiting, trying to find the one who'd save him. A search that never produced. Maybe there was a reason it had always failed.

Drips and drops splashed into the fountain as a light rain began to come down. Cold beads trickled onto his face, gliding down the sides of his cheeks like the tears that never fell. He chuckled, thinking of his missing Cinderella.

Mumbling a quiet litany to himself, he hummed Modest Mouse's melancholy "Bankrupt on Selling" as he awaited his body's verdict between insomnia and medicinal intervention. He might've won the battle for the evening, but there was still a long war ahead. He chuckled to himself as he watched the stars become blurry.

"Heh...I'm so f-fucked."

14. Nothing Gold Can Stay

"Some days are just terrible, horrible, no-good, very bad days."

– Lorena's Prayer Book

Outer Region of Los Tios, Mexico

Lorena climbed out of the uncomfortably firm bed she inherited from her mother. She stretched in front of her window as the sun began to rise, careful to keep on her good foot and letting the first light of the day warm her skin.

She lowered her torso down to her knees and extended her legs, resting her injured ankle on top of the strong one. Finishing her stretch, she proceeded to do push-ups until she could no longer lift herself, and then brought her knees to the floor to do a few more. After completing her push-ups and the remainder of her cautiously executed exercise regimen, she found a comfortable summer dress and slipped it on. She glanced at her crutches lying on the wall, continuing without them. Walking softly, she brushed aside the blanket that served as the door to her room.

She stepped out into the bar, still empty as expected, and crept midway down the stairs to check on her boys. Three sets of feet, all dangling at the edge of their beds, accompanied by a harmony of monstrous snoring and man-stink told her everything was in order. There sat three additional empty beds, though Lorena had no use for them.

Lorena returned to the top of the stairs and grabbed her prayer book as she exited the bar. She limped across the road, keeping an eye out for scorpions and rattlesnakes, having come across them before at first light. She brushed aside the chantry blanket-door to find her dog sleeping on his side in the corner. She smiled, seeing her Perrito finally able to roll around. She lit the candles and began reciting her hymns.

As she proceeded through her recitations, her dog growled at the imaginary terrors dancing around in his head. The dog rolled over in his sleep—apparently hitting a sore spot on his ribs—and jerked himself awake. He lazily climbed to its feet, sauntering his way over to Lorena and licking her face mid-chant. She gave the pup a stern look before noticing the plate Kody had left him yesterday was empty.

"Perrito, are you feeling better?"

She pulled the dog close, hugging him and rubbing his head. Though she had no way to be certain, she was sure she could see a smile in the dog's large dark eyes. Lorena stood up, brushing aside the chapel door, motioning for Perrito to walk through ahead of her. Instead, the dog stayed by her side, and the two walked through together.

Lorena wandered down the street, watching the early risers go about their day. A few neighbors tended livestock, some townsfolk washed clothes, and others made linens and crafts or tended to whatever small crops they could maintain. A local hunter appeared to have only recently returned, skinning a pair of freshly killed coyotes.

Lorena returned to the bar, inviting her dog inside. She walked the dog to her room and tapped the floor next to her bed gently with her sore foot, indicating where he should lie down. Perrito followed her instruction, continuing to pant well after the walk had ended. Lorena herself sat on her bed only for a moment before her stomach rumbled. She got up and left her room, heading to the stairs.

"Siggy! Breakfast!"

She stood and waited, repeatedly tapping her good foot against the wood grain. Waiting too long, Lorena carefully marched down the stairs and over to Siggy's bed, pulling the thin blanket off him to reveal his lean, naked body. Though she'd lived this scene so many times before, an unexpected warmth overtook her. For what might've been the first time, her cheeks turned flush. Looking at Siggy from the corner of her eye, she did her best to toss the blanket back over him. Still not awake, she walked over to his side and lightly slapped him on the cheek.

"Siggy, time to get up and get breakfast started."

Lorena received little more than a groan. Being persistent, she amused herself finding different ways to pester him until he finally kept his eyes open long enough to pay attention. She practiced poking him in various places, tapping his forehead, and even tickling his feet. Reluctantly, Siggy climbed out of bed, tossed on some clothes along with his blue kerchief, and ambled up the stairs to start breakfast. Lorena started back toward the stairs, stopping in front of Adelais's bed. She hesitated for a moment before making her way back upstairs.

Lorena took a seat at the bar, finally able to rest her foot, and began walking her fingers along the wooden counter, waiting for breakfast. As she played with her rough hands, she heard clumsy fumbling as the scruffy-haired city dweller made his first appearance of the day.

"Morning, stranger."

"Hey." Kody nodded, taking a seat at the table.

"Always avoidin' me. Over here."

Lorena pulled out a chair sitting next to her. She sat waiting as Kody failed to make a move of any kind. Done with her hand-game, she stood up and hobble-dragged him over, sitting him down in the chair next to her.

"Sleepy?" she asked.

"I guess. Don't sleep well."

"I get that." Lorena nodded. "So, let's talk cousins."

"Sure. I have a few on my dad's side, although I haven't seen them in forever."

"We're not talkin' 'bout yours. Ya' didn't really tell me why you're lookin' fer mine. Jes' because we haven't said anything don't mean none of us haven't noticed ya' wearin' Jake's jacket around."

"I just need to talk to Alma, that's all. Don't care about her brother. Besides, I found his jacket at his old place when I was looking for her."

"Okay. So ya' know that Jake's a bandito, right? Or was, anyway. Ran off after bringin' down a world of hurt on us. Walkin' around wearin' that thing is an insult ta' every decent person here. Ever wonder why Ade don't like you?" Lorena took a breath, changing subjects.

"Back to what we were talkin' about: I dunno what'cha see in Alma. Love my cousin, don't get me wrong, but she was always kinda a flake. So, say those crazy siblings're out here. Mebbe Jake gets dumb and tries ta' hide out with the one or two people he didn't piss off yet. Then what? Gonna bring him back here and cause even more trouble fer us?"

74

Kody sighed. "I don't care about Jake, or what Alma was like when you knew her. All I care about is finding her so I can work on finding a way home."

Lorena leaned toward him, sticking her finger in his face. "People not carin' 'bout anything but themselves is how everyone else gets hurt. Ya' better know what you're doin'. We can't afford any mistakes."

"Breakfast is ready!" Siggy interrupted their conversation.

They piled into the kitchen, each grabbing a plate and serving their own food. Trudging up the stairs partially dressed in no particular fashion, Adelais found himself at the end of the serving line. Lorena waited for him to load up his plate before looking over his bandaged abdomen. They all took a seat at the table, enjoying Siggy's fine breakfast cuisine together.

Kody and Siggy finished first, taking their plates to the kitchen before heading downstairs to get ready for the first patrol of the day. Lorena remained at the table with an empty plate while Adelais continued eating—his plates tending to be much larger.

"How you feelin', Ade?"

Adelais nodded, chewing emphatically to illustrate talking wasn't the best idea while eating. Lorena chuckled to herself, and took her plate into the kitchen. She checked the chore chart and found today was her day for the dishes. She scrubbed them clean without much trouble, humming Iron and Wine's "Fever Dream" as she washed. She received Adelais's plate just as she finished the others and rinsed it off. Putting the dishes away, she went back into the bar and carefully knelt to look at Adelais's waist.

"What're you doin' Lore? You ain't no nurse."

"Ain't an idiot either. Jes' wanna make sure yer okay."

She unraveled Adelais's bandages, knowing full well he'd never remember to dress them himself. She walked back into her room to grab fresh bandages and filled up a basin of water in the kitchen. She came back into the bar as Kody and Siggy were coming up the stairs.

"You two headed out?"

"Just a quick patrol," Siggy responded.

"We'll stay out of trouble." Kody met Lorena's eyes as he spoke.

"Good. Stay safe. Both of you."

Lorena's eyes lingered on Siggy as they left. She returned to Adelais, kneeling and looking over his wound. She wiped it with a clean cloth, gently inspecting his skin to make sure it was clear of any infection. She re-wrapped his waist and secured his bandages.

"This ain't a small cut. Ya' got lucky, Ade. Ya' gotta stop doin' this ta' me."

"I did it *for* you. Say I left Alejandro alone, what woulda happened ta' ya'? Think he woulda jes' fergot ya' brought him down in the middle of town?"

"And what? I'm not s'pose ta' protect myself?" She looked up to him.

"Nothin' wrong with that." He shrugged. "Just sayin'...did it fer you is all," he muttered.

"I know ya' did. So that mean we gotta worry 'bout Alejandro comin' back here fer you, or fer me?"

"He ain't comin' back."

The look on Adelais's face told Lorena to leave the subject be. Curiosity wasn't going to win her any favors today. Adelais stood up and walked to the front door, stepping outside the blanket.

Having finished her work for the morning, Lorena went through the kitchen to the back porch, taking a seat to rest her ankle. She dangled her feet in the sand, dragging her toes across to draw pictures. The warm dirt grazed softly along her heels as she played around, trying to decide what to make. Her toes worked their way along the sandy ground until eventually a crude puppy with a party hat, eating a chicken was born. Examining the funny-looking chicken, she stomped him out of existence and began anew.

While playing in the sand, she heard a faint commotion on the other side of the bar. She pulled herself up one of the support pillars on the porch, and leaned over the railing to see if she could find anything. She searched around, but found nothing out of the ordinary.

As she started to sit back down, several banditos ran up from both sides of the building. Limbs shaking with adrenaline, she escaped into the kitchen and slid open a fake panel built into the wall, placed there by her mother as a precaution against bandito raids. While it wasn't able to protect Sarita, Lorena had found success with it in the past. She began to close herself off inside when her dog howled nearby.

Abandoning the hidden room, Lorena hobble-ran to her bedroom, coming upon a bandito with a drawn knife encroaching on her dog. She slammed her body into the bandito, tripping him over the dog and causing him to fall face-first into the wall. She grabbed her dog by the neck and dragged him back to the kitchen.

She managed to push the dog into the hidden room before hitting the ground hard on her back, violently tackled by a bandito entering from the back porch. The force of the blow bounced her head off the hard wood floor and knocked the wind out of her. Trying to regain her focus, she remained dazed as the bandito climbed on top of her. She struggled, managing to force the bandito off her and knee him in the groin.

As she tried to regain her feet, two more banditos grabbed her wrists and ankles, holding her down. She tried to scream, but as soon as she opened her mouth, a knotted gag was tied around her head, muting her voice. She tried to flail about, but couldn't free herself from the banditos' grasp.

The injured bandito got back on his knees and pulled out a knife, cutting her dress open down the middle. He grabbed at her chest and began fondling her breasts. Her heart pounded fiercely against the walls of her ribcage, the weight of the bandito pushing down on her making it nearly impossible to breathe.

She struggled, trying her best to squirm free. Thrashing her body about, she attempted to escape the dirty fingers clawing all over her. Her waist stung at the snapping of a cotton waistband as her underwear was torn off.

She closed her eyes, trying to focus on the burning tears streaming down her face as a disgusting, sloppy tongue wriggled its way around her body. Working herself free of the gag, she bit the closest bandito, buying herself a temporary reprieve, before feeling foreskin and sticky dampness on her inner thigh. She forced her eyes shut, trying to fight her way free.

Amid the chaos, multiple shots rang out, dropping the banditos all over her onto the floor. She lay still, shivering and naked, covered in blood mostly not her own. With unremitting trembling, she opened her eyes long enough to see the immediate threat had passed, and scrambled back to the hidden panel, concealing herself in her safe room with the dog.

She slid back as the panel slid opened, screaming out in response before she realized who had opened the door. Siggy stepped inside the room, closing the door behind him and putting his gun away. She embraced him, clutching him as she tried to control her shaking. He held her only for a moment before taking off his shirt. He offered it to her along with his kerchief.

"I'm so sorry, Lorena, but ya' gotta do what ya' can with these quick as possible. Ade and Kody are holding 'em off, but we gotta get outta here."

She wiped the tears from her face, improvising with the clothes Siggy gave her. She hid behind him, leaning on him for support, as he listened for movement on the other side of the panel. Unable to hear anything herself, she debated whether it was worth the risk to re-enter the fray. Siggy cautiously slid the panel open, checking the scene. Catching a glimpse over his shoulder, she saw her three assailants dead on her kitchen floor. Siggy turned back to her.

"I know yer scared, but I promise—no matter what, I won't let anyone hurt ya'."

Siggy pulled her close, giving her a kiss on her forehead. He took her hand and slowly led her out of the hiding spot. The duo moved surreptitiously to the bar, where Kody and Adelais stood guarding the door.

"They gone?" Siggy asked.

"Dunno… don't see 'em. Like they disappeared…" Adelais trailed off, peering out of the window. It took him a moment to notice Lorena, banged up and half-dressed, hiding behind Siggy. "Ya' okay, Lore?"

Still dazed and trying to find some semblance of balance on regaining control of her body, she looked to Siggy, who subtly shook his head.

"I took care of her," Siggy replied.

"Good. Dunno what these bastards are up ta', but no way in hell I let them touch one a' mine."

"Adelais, look around." Kody maintained his watch. "They came straight here. They didn't even touch the pelts in the street."

"Shit, they were after us." Adelais thought aloud.

"Him, actually."

Lorena fell into a chair near the bar, violently shoved from behind. She sprawled out on the floor as she looked up to see a bandito wearing a burka standing behind Siggy. Adelais and Kody both fell to banditos storming the front entrance of the bar, leaving Siggy alone to fight the small tyrant. "R…run," was all Lorena could manage with her scratchy voice.

Siggy spun around to face his opponent, reaching for his gun. The vicious bandito threw a punch that launched Siggy into the bar, producing a deafening cracking sound as the wood broke on impact. Grabbing one of the many knives littered on the floor, Lorena lay waiting as the bandito approached Siggy.

The bandito drew close, allowing Lorena an opportunity to stab the knife deep into its calf muscle. As she lunged, the blade clinked on metal and slid against the boot, landing little more than a graze on the leather. The surprised grunt emitted from the bandito was enough to catch Adelais's attention, causing him to abandon his current target in favor the bandito attacking his brother.

The menacing bandito reached out with both hands, grabbing Siggy behind the head and pulling him close. The bandito whispered something to Siggy, but Lorena couldn't hear it over the rest of the conflict. She climbed to her feet and grabbed at the bandito's arms, but a swift elbow to the gut knocked the wind out of her, dropping her back to the floor. All she caught was Siggy's response as the bandito spun him around and held him in a half choke with one arm as it pulled the knife from its boot with the other:

"Ya' betrayed him. What'dya expect? But we can stop the fightin'—"

The bandito loosened its grip enough to cut Siggy's throat, forcing the blade so deep into his neck it caught on his jugular on the way to the carotid artery. The bandito dropped Siggy to the floor and headed out through the kitchen doorway.

Lorena watched Adelais barrel after the burka-covered bandito, but the bandito Kody had been fighting launched itself onto Adelais's back, dropping him back to the floor. Kody and Adelais fought the remaining bandito while Lorena crawled over to Siggy. She lifted his head, watching him bleed out. She tried to stop the blood, but she accomplished little more than bathing her hands in it before Siggy's neck ran dry.

"Just keep breathing..."

Lorena nurtured him, her tears once again flowing and decorating both the sanguine floor and lifeless cheeks. She thought she could hear muted punches being thrown in the background, but it was impossible to tell. She jumped at a hand landing on her shoulder, quickly turning her head to see Kody kneeling down beside her.

"Adelais."

Kody called out to him. Lorena heard little more than one-sided punches landing against what she assumed to be bone. Kody called out to him again, and once again, no response. Lorena heard shuffling of some kind and a conflict between Kody and Adelais, but Siggy never left her sight. A heavy thud hit the floor behind her; Adelais must've finally realized what had happened.

"Ade..."

Adelais carefully picked up Siggy's body, taking him from Lorena. She fought to hold onto him, refusing to let go, but Kody restrained her and unlatched her fingers, allowing Adelais to take his brother. Covered in blood, sweat, and bleeding still, Adelais walked out the front door, carrying his brother with him.

15. The Value of a Miracle Is...

"Most times I'm a perfectly rational person. Unfortunately, it's the few times I'm not that everyone seems to remember."

– Cris's Journal

Ann Arbor, Michigan

The pads of cantankerous cat's paws landed on hard cement inside a large building. He knew little of the place except for the loud noises the hairy man and colorful woman continued to make. In *his* presence. On purpose. His handmaiden had odd friends.

The august cat yawned, licking chunks of turkey from his teeth. Enjoying his leftovers for only a moment, a furry appendage attacked from above! He swiped at the dangling calamity, taunting him from all directions. He jumped after it, but it always remained out of reach. He slinked back, prowling and biding his time until just the right moment. He struck, nipping the furry appendage, and yowled out as teeth released their grip on his tail.

His mysterious foe defeated and disappeared for the moment, the meow-meow continued to explore his new environment, perchance he might find a stronghold. He needed a good place to prepare his revenge against his feathered nemeses. Instead, however, he caught a familiar scent—sweet and bitter, like that of an old friend—and decided to investigate.

"It's funny. If you started playing with your fingers instead of your dick, maybe we wouldn't sound like foreplay."

Cris listened to Jence criticize the Bards' rehearsal as she sat in an unsteady chair in a practice space downtown. Specifically, Cris listened to Jence and Geroge go back and forth over his handling of his guitar.

"Uh, Jeany? How do you play a guitar with a dick? If that was even kinda possible, I'd honestly give it a shot because damn, that'd be a hell of a show."

"It's easy. Pull it out of my bag and use it like a bow. I can show you if you'd like."

Geroge stopped to consider the possibilities.

"Mm, maybe later. Think I'm doin' all right."

"You're dry-humping that thing so hard the wood's starting to warp."

Cris intervened, trying to keep the peace. "Hey! You guys finally started booking some small shows! Shouldn't you be a little happy about it, and maybe focus on finding a full-time replacement drummer instead of bickering all the time?"

"I'm done here. You want him, princess, you can have him."

Jence stared icily at Cris and began to disconnect her keyboard. She quickly and carefully separated and packaged all the cables, blowing her prismatic hair out of her face as she got everything together.

"Jeany, hey, hold on. Don't get your butt floss all twisted up. We're all friends here," Geroge said, trying to clear the air.

Jence, only a bit taller than the equipment itself, grabbed her bag and her keyboard and stormed out. Geroge unslung his guitar and took a sip of water from his water bottle, some of it getting caught in his man-boy beard. Though he had put on some weight over the summer, Geroge was still mostly muscle.

Looking at her reflection in the glass door, Cris could see she still hadn't regained the weight she'd lost after Kody left. She pulled a bag of cherry Twizzlers out of her bag and began munching on them, waiting for Daron to arrive.

"Huh. Cris, you're a chick. What'dya figure Jeany's deal is? Is she cracking under the pressure of impending stardom? Can't handle all the fame? Or do ya think she misses her burly courtesan?"

"G, you guys have booked a couple shows locally. I'm not trying to crush your bubble, but I don't think the Bards are as famous as you think they are. And as far as Thteve... I don't know. It's hard having the people you care about far away. Even more so if they left abruptly without even telling you..." Cris shook her head, catching herself getting trapped in her pensive dreamland.

"Could be, *señorita*. Could be." Geroge nodded, drawing his fingers through his beard as he considered the possibility.

"Uh huh. That reminds me—why do you keep speaking Spanish to me so much lately?"

"Uhh... no reason."

Cris eyed Geroge suspiciously, and stood up to stretch her legs. She wandered around the practice space, looking it over while trying to find her furry little friend. The space itself was fairly large; as best she could tell it was an old warehouse renovated for some project that probably got cancelled. According to Geroge, the place wasn't that expensive for an afternoon practice session. If they paid for it at all.

"G, have you seen where Bixby went?"

"Nope. Not a clue, milady. Not sure why you brought a cat to a rehearsal anyway."

"Because either someone watches him or he stays with me. I'm not taking my eyes off of him again. You remember what happened last time..." Cris trailed off.

"Hey, got it." Geroge stopped to think for a minute. "Doesn't look like D's gonna show. You wanna give it another shot?"

Cris looked over to Geroge, who was still leaning on the wall near his guitar. She shook her head, to which he responded by picking his guitar up, slinging it, and waiting for Cris. He walked over to her and took her hand, leading her back toward the improvised stage with the microphone.

"C'mon, *chica*, you were born for this and you know it. Don't be shy."

"I just don't like singing without—"

"Don't say the K-word. Music sweetheart, we're focusing on the music."

"But—"

"What do you do when your guy disappears chasing his ex across country? Do what the wise man said: Make good art. Now, from the top. You want Florence or Adele?" Geroge considered the options. "You ain't gettin' Adele. Except maybe 'Rolling in the Deep.'"

"No. 'Shake it out,' please."

"Still think it sounds weird acoustic, but make it work."

Geroge started playing inspirational power chords, tuning them to Florence + the Machine's "Shake it out," adjusting it for a single acoustic guitar. Cris took to the microphone, doing her best to match the vocals of Florence Welch. She focused intently on her singing, trying to remember to maintain proper posture and form. Though she had no audience, something about being center stage seemed… off. She pushed it from her mind, recalling the last time she had sung and the joy it had brought. She tightened her grip on the microphone, belting out the chorus. She began dancing with the music, shaking her butt just a little as she finished.

"Not bad, *chica*. Not exactly Ms. Welch herself, but not bad." Geroge set his guitar down and applauded. Cris laughed to herself, giving Geroge a light shove.

"Uh huh. But thanks. I think I needed that."

"Kinda figured. Up for finding that cat of yours who likes to disappear all the damn time?"

"Crap! You're right! Bixby?"

Cris put the microphone back and began running around the practice space, trying to find the regal feline. She checked around the Bards' equipment, the bathroom, and even the maintenance closet. The cat was nowhere to be found.

"G, what am I gonna do? I think he's gone!"

"Wouldn't worry too much. That fur ball always shows up eventually."

"That he d-does. In his own t-time, in any c-case." Glenn closed the door behind himself, clean-shaven and holding the inconsiderate kitty in his arms. The cat nuzzled him, and he returned the gesture in kind. "I m-missed you t-too, Allister."

"Oh my God!"

Cris stared at Glenn, through him, seeing the resurrection of her greatest horror manifest. Her head spun, muddled, unable to form words or remind her to breathe. She flashed back to her dreams, seeing him illuminated in sizzling lighting, drowning in freezing oceans, falling off a cliff. She flashed back to the motel room, hands covered in dried blood, smelling nothing but orange juice. She had cried for him so many nights, wishing and praying for anything to get him back. And here he was, awakening her from the nightmare. Her lip bled as she realized she was biting it. She wiped the blood away with her trembling hand.

"Uh…I think that's Cris for 'I'm happy to see you.' Welcome back to the land of the living, man," Geroge shook his hand.

Glenn nodded, returning the gesture. He walked up to Cris, set the cat down, and embraced her. "I-it's all right, C-charisma."

"I don't even—" Cris finally remembered to breathe.

"You d-don't need to say anything. You saved my life. The least I can do is r-return the favor."

"What?" She looked up into his eyes.

"K-kody's missing, right? We're going to find him."

Cris and Glenn sat, discussing everything that had happened after she had abandoned him and how she had been managing to get by the last few months with help from Emma and Geroge. As they talked, seeing Glenn reminded Cris of what her life had been like before her summer had fallen apart; it reminded her of what she had been. She buried herself in his chest, ignoring the escaping stream of tears. Even as the humble not-so-kitten prince clawed at her ankle to beg for his regal treat, Cris felt no pain while embracing Glenn.

He lifted her chin, looking into her blurry tear-filled eyes, and for the first time in quite a long time, smiled. Cris finally started getting her sniffles under control, and realizing Geroge was still watching the two of them, tried to hide her blushing embarrassment as she sat up.

"Whew, okay, so…embarrassment aside, what do we do? I tried to find Kody on my own, but all I ever got were dead ends."

"Before everything h-had happened, I was tracking Jake. I w-was to get the information on his wh-whereabouts in Laughlin, but I s-suspect that's no longer an op-option. I suppose the first c-course of action is d-determining the best st-starting point on where to find K-kody. Any ideas?"

Cris shook her head. Glenn reached into his pocket, pulled out a pill from his pill bottle, and swallowed it whole. Cris cocked an eyebrow, but Glenn's reserved smile implied that whatever his new medication was, he wasn't concerned. He continued.

"I suppose we c-could go to N-nevada, and start th-there. I'm sure my father w-would be overjoyed to f-fund me getting out of the h-house."

"Actually…" Geroge opened his mouth. "I kinda know where the Kod-man is. He's safe…sorta, down Mexico way."

Cris whipped her head toward Geroge, causing him to raise his palms defensively.

"Woulda said somethin' sooner, chaste Penelope, but he made me swear. Said he didn't want you gettin' hurt. I'm sorry. But if we're gonna go find him anyway, may as well start in the right place."

Cris turned to Geroge, trying to restrain herself. Glenn winced as Cris's nails dug into his leg.

"You knew this whole time!" she said.

"*Chica*, look—"

"Don't. You should probably leave now." Cris relaxed her grip on Glenn's leg, breathing slowly.

"I guess that's fair, but anyone else know where he's at? He's like a brother to me, in case you forgot. I ain't leavin' him hangin', and you ain't leavin' without me."

Glenn intervened, consoling Cris as the all-too-eager feline continued to brush himself against Glenn's leg. Glenn nodded to Geroge.

"We all want to find K-Kody, so I suggest th-that remain our f-focus."

"I can work with that. I don't have a good number for him or anything, but I'll see what I can shake out. Catch up with you guys in a bit."

Geroge shook Glenn's hand, gathered up his gear, and headed out. Glenn picked up the cantankerous cat, carrying the feline with him as he examined the practice space. Cris stood staring at the ceiling, taking slow, deep breaths as she tried to compose herself. The day held more surprises than she ever could've guessed. Looking at her situation, she now had a starting point, and a plan. If there was a time to take action, this was it.

She clutched the beads around her neck, watching Glenn as he walked around the practice space. For the first time in quite a while, nostalgia brought back happy memories. For the first time in a long time, she could breathe without the heavy weight of guilt. For the first time in a long time, she was ready to take action.

16. (The Worst Day Since) Yesterday

"The more I learn, the less I know."

– Lorena's Prayer Book

Outer Region of Los Tios, Mexico

Lorena lay in her bed for a good portion of the day, Perrito always at her side. Her stomach rumbled, though she couldn't tell if she was any kind of hungry. Shuffling and other noises kept echoing outside her room—she'd figured they were Kody. He was the only one left. Either way, it wasn't worth getting up to check.

"Lorena, do you mind if I come in?" Kody said outside the door.

She caught him peeking his head in, though she paid him no mind. He gradually brought the rest of his body into her room. Like her, he looked like one giant pincushion. Yesterday hadn't been particularly kind to either one of them, and the developing scars and bruises ensured they wouldn't forget any time soon. Kody sat at the foot of Lorena's bed, staring at the wall.

"I didn't know him that well, but Siggy was a good man."

Lorena barely lifted her head as she replied. "Have you heard from Adelais?"

"Not since he took the truck. He probably needs some time. How're you holding up?"

"My…brother just died. And I—my brother just died."

Kody nodded. The two remained in silence, neither fully aware of the other. Perrito brought his head onto the bed, staring at Lorena with puppy dog eyes. She patted him and invited him onto the bed. The dog took a spot next to Kody, who began petting him as well. After a few minutes of comforting and being comforted by the dog, Kody took to his feet.

"I don't know about you, but sitting around just messes with my head. I'm gonna try to clean up the rest of the bar. As much as it can be cleaned, anyway. Some townsfolk already helped… uh…*deal* with the kitchen. I'll be right outside if you need me."

Lorena grabbed Kody's wrist as he moved to leave. He turned back to her, but no words left her mouth. Her gaze lingered on him. Kody nodded. She released his wrist, and he continued toward the door. Kody paused for a moment, observing her crutches lying idly against the doorframe, and brought them to her bedside before heading out into the bar.

Lorena took a deep breath, trying to calm her nerves. She reached for her crutches, and fumbled around with them, trying to stand up. She started slowly, hobbling back and forth from her bed and catching herself on Perrito a few times. Once she got a feel for walking with them again, she dressed and redressed herself. She tried a number of different shirt and pants combinations, uninterested in any of her dresses. Nothing felt right. She ended up wearing what she was wearing.

She made her way into the bar, nodding to Kody as she and Perrito made their way outside. Reluctant at first, she looked around, checking every possible avenue of approach. She saw no sign nor heard any indication of banditos, but that didn't mean they weren't there. The town, other than the bar itself, had been left untouched.

She and Perrito made their way to the little chantry. A mare stood tied up outside the entrance. She looked around, trying to find someone who could've ridden it. Perrito, being but the clumsy dog he was, carelessly wandered into the church, leaving her no choice but to follow.

"Perrito, get back he—" she whispered after him.

Sitting in the same spot near the altar as when she had first met him was the stranger, Alejandro's brother. Wide-eyed, she froze dead in her tracks, fighting the urge to run. A nauseating contingent of guilt developed within her at the thought of whether to leave Perrito to his own fate, as he so willingly wandered into an assured death trap.

"Pay me no mind. Like I said before, I come only to pay my respects," the stranger said.

"Perrito, come over here now!" Lorena commanded in her quietest voice.

"You come to the church and do not pray?"

The stranger turned his head to meet her. He moved aside, making a space for her where she had been the last time they met.

"I'm a bandito. I make no secret of it. But not all of us want needless bloodshed. I'm alone, and have no interest in harming you. If you wish to pray, I'd welcome your company. If you'd just as soon leave, that's fine too."

Lorena remained near the door, refusing to move. Perrito, now being petted by the stranger, rested comfortably on his blanket bed. He left Lorena no option if she wished to keep an eye on her dog.

She left one of her crutches in the doorway, holding the door-blanket wide open as she apprehensively approached the already lit altar. She felt her back pocket to make sure she still had her small knife, just in case. She knelt before the altar. "Why're ya' here? You ain't from here. Bet there're plenty of churches between here and wherever ya' *are* from."

"Nostalgia. My brother just died, and this was the last place I saw him."

"Alejandro, the…" She thought carefully before insulting the bandito's deceased brother, Siggy coming to mind, "the man who did *this* ta' my leg." She lifted her ankle.

"Yes. My brother was overly aggressive. Probably why he was killed."

Lorena nodded, ignoring the small trembling her body refused to cease.

"There was a raid on this town yesterday. Several banditos were killed, and if I'm not mistaken, one of yours too?" the stranger lifted his head to meet her eye-line.

Lorena tensed up, instinctively reaching for her back pocket. As her fingers edged their way to the grip of her knife, she remembered where she was and suppressed her anger. "How do ya'—?"

"Not all banditos work together, but we still talk."

Lorena hesitated, staring into the flame of the candles.

"I lost my brother, Siggy."

"You lost a brother too. My condolences. If you don't mind my asking…"

Lorena couldn't be sure, but it sounded as if the bandito's voice began wavering.

"What do you believe happens to them when they die?"

"I dunno. All I know is I loved my brother, an' now he's gone." Lorena's eyes began watering, but she did her best to hold back the tears. Looking over to the bandito for the first time, she saw the subtle glistening on his cheek. "Are you... are ya' crying?" she asked.

The bandito wiped his cheek. After a moment, he turned to her. "Alejandro was a bastard. But like you, I loved my brother."

Lorena finally managed to relax, the trembling in her body starting to subside. "What's yer name?"

"I am Arturo Romero, of the infamous Romero family. Yours?"

"Lorena."

"I wish I could say it was a pleasure, Lorena, but you see our circumstance."

Perrito wandered over to Lorena, taking a seat next to her. He nudged her, waiting to be petted.

"Arturo, most banditos are nothin' but violent bastards. Why're ya' with 'em?"

"I was born into it. I was told since I was very small that I would be a leader of the bandito clan. It's my role in life, so I accept it. As to the violence...well, a dog's only as good as its owner, wouldn't you agree? If the owner is kind hearted, then you have a good mongrel like your dog here. However, if the owner is cruel...well, I think we all know."

"So the current 'owner' of the banditos..."

"Is senile, but dangerous. There are those of us, kin leaders, who have been trying to convince Estaban to change his ways, but he's been doing this much longer than most of us have been alive. To live this kind of life as long as he has...he's everything anyone has ever said."

Lorena sat quietly, listening to Arturo's story. Her stomach left her feeling uneasy; something she couldn't describe reminded her of Siggy.

"So yer a peaceful bandito? But banditos kill people."

"I am a bandito, so yes, I kill when I need to. Aren't there times when you would—"

A loud car pulled up outside, blasting LMFAO's dance mix, "Party Rock Anthem," as the engine cut off. They both turned toward the entrance of the chantry to see a bright-red convertible parked outside the bar. The mare tied up near the chantry's entryway began fretting, causing a ruckus.

"Seems it's my time to go. Viaje is getting upset. I wish you health and safety, Lorena, and truly, I regret what happened to your brother."

"I—I'm sorry Alejandro was yours."

89

Arturo excused himself and headed outside. Lorena, with Perrito's help, rose to her feet and grabbed her crutches. The two of them exited the chantry, watching Arturo ride off.

"Oh my God, is that you, Lauren?"

Lorena redirected her attention to a buxom, short-haired brunette who ran up squealing and started hugging her. Hearing the commotion, Kody ran outside to help Lorena.

"Uh, crutches. Careful please. An' my name ain't Lauren, it's Lorena. Also ow, an' who the hell?"

As Lorena spoke, she looked past the strawberry brunette semi-accosting her to the rough-rugged man with the stubbly face still sitting in the passenger seat putting out a cigarette. Her least favorite cousin.

"…aw shit."

Kody, standing baffled on the steps of the bar, watched Lorena. He stood, apparently waiting for some sort of sign to either help or stay out of the way. Receiving none, he spoke up.

"Lorena, what's—"

The girl hugging Lorena slowly turned around to face Kody. He recognized the beaded hemp necklace he had made her still tied around her neck. "Huh. You changed your hair."

"You gotta be shittin' me." The hazel-eyed half-Mexican sighed. "Why the hell not?" Alma

rubbed her forehead. "Hey, ex-honey bunny, how ya' been?" was all she had to say.

17. His Forgotten Seat of Innocence

"Heard a sayin' once—'the good die young.' Only sayin' I ever believed."

– Adelais's Scratch Pad

Unknown Region, Mexico

Adelais awoke at dawn in the driver's seat of the truck, to the sound of a rattlesnake finishing its skirmish with some unfortunate prey. He had already used up a full tank of gas, and checking the gauge, was coming close to finishing off another. Having made this trip once before, he knew to bring several containers, which lay resting in the bed of the truck. He looked back, making sure the containers were still secure under the tarp he had tied down, along with his brother's body.

Continuing his drive, at about mid-day he finally came upon the remains of a ghost town in a fertile mountain valley. On the way in, he passed the only sign that still stood—one of the few structures not charred to ash. He drove along the broken-down road until he could make out the small lake hidden by a dense thicket of trees. Only a handful of houses remained.

Taking the truck through the pocket-sized forest, he reached an old, dilapidated cabin that had long ago succumbed to the ravages of nature. He remained in the truck, cutting off the engine and taking a minute to look the place over. "Good ta' be home," he muttered.

Adelais climbed out of the truck, wasting no time in heading into the cabin. He paused in the small doorway, surveying the long-abandoned cabin. A few pieces of assorted rustic furniture lay strewn about, either tossed around or simply disturbed by wildlife. The dusty air left no kind impression in his lungs, discouraging an extended trip down memory lane.

He rummaged through the small closet near the door, trying to find something to protect his torn-up hands. He came upon a pair of mismatched gloves, apparently meant for a lady, and made do. As he pulled them off the shelf, a small, beaded bracelet came along with them, caught on part of the glove. Adelais scoffed, tearing the bracelet off the gloves and sticking it in his pocket. He reached behind the door, feeling for and grabbing his shovel before heading out back.

He wandered into his backyard, a mix of sandy dirt and overgrown vegetation. It wasn't overly large, but held enough space for the two person-length mounds of dirt marked by crude, handmade crosses. Staring at them, he estimated the yard could hold at least two more. He knelt, rubbing the shoddy etching on the wooden crucifixes.

"Roque and Aimée Martinez..."

A crop of honey-colored flowers swayed in the wind around the markers. Their golden petals danced with the breeze. Adelais leaned in, taking in the scent of his home. For a moment, he recalled what it had been like to be nothing but a boy. He exhaled and broke a flower off at the stem, keeping it with him.

Putting his mother's gloves on, Adelais went to work digging a hole next to his father. With a mighty plunge, he broke the earth with his shovel. As he dug, he drew slow breaths, relishing the cool mountain air grazing his skin. His body had long ago abandoned the woodland scent of home, but it hadn't forgotten.

After digging for some time, he took a seat under a nearby tree, pulling the gloves off as he sipped from a bottle of water. He leaned back on the rough bark, exhaling while he pressed his hand against his abdomen. He lifted his fingers up to see only small spots of red. That particular wound was healing. He pressed his hand against his abdomen again, laughing quietly to himself. He couldn't tell if the pain in his gut was any different from the ache all over the rest of his body. He stood and continued his work.

Finally reaching an adequate depth, he tossed the shovel aside and headed back for the truck. He untied the tarp, scaring off the animals that had been poking around, and picked up his brother's stiff, rotting body. The stench overwhelmed him, forcing Adelais to hold his breath and keep his eyes off his brother as much as possible. He quickly moved to the hole and dropped his brother in.

"I think I'm supposed ta' say somethin' here, but I dunno…I ain't much of a thinker. Was always your job." Adelais slid his hands into his pockets, feeling the bracelet. He pulled it out, playing with the beads. "Never got ya', Sig. Spent all yer time playin' with shit instead of fightin'. If you were any kinda smart, you'da learned how to take care of yerrself a long time ago instead of always makin' me have ta' do it."

Adelais picked up the shovel and began tossing dirt on top of his brother, into his grave. "Wasn't enough I had to bury *them*, was it? Puttin' my own baby brother inta' the ground…still takin' care of yer dead ass." Adelais's grip on the handle tightened as he filled the hole. Looking at his brother's face again and again, he stopped shoveling. He snorted, glaring at the corpse. "What gives you the fuckin' right?" Adelais threw the shovel down, gripping Siggy's bracelet so tightly his knuckles cracked. Adelais ripped the bracelet into pieces, throwing beads and pieces at Siggy's body.

"Ya' know what? I'm so goddamn sick of this, always cleanin' up after yer messes. Ya' can't just die and leave yer shit for me ta' fix. Clean up yer own fuckin' mess fer once!" Adelais grabbed the gloves off the ground and threw them at Siggy's face.

He paced around in a circle a few times, trying to breathe and keep his hands steady. He dug his hands through his hair, ripping out several strands as they caught on his fingers. He stopped in front of the open grave, staring at the abomination that used to be his brother. "Ugh, ya' know what? Fuck this." Adelais kicked the shovel into the grave and walked off, back to the truck.

As he held the truck door open, he noticed an aged man wearing a satchel and dressed in skins off in the distance, watching him. Adelais set his yellow flower in the truck and stomped off toward the man, still trying to calm his nerves.

"The hell you starin' at, old man?" Adelais said.

"Nothing much," the old man replied, smirking.

"Ya' think this is funny?"

"I thought you'd be more respectful with your dead."

Adelais grabbed at the older gentleman, ready to shove him onto the ground when the wizened man evaded his grasp and grabbed him by the bicep and collar. The older gentleman shifted his weight and dropped Adelais onto the ground, mounting him. Adelais stared up in disbelief at the old man, who sat on top of him, until the old man stood up, offering his hand. Adelais took it and pulled himself to his feet.

"Guess you just lack respect in general. Said the general." The wizened man chuckled.

"Lucky shot…"

"Wanna try again?" the older man waited, but Adelais made no move. "Good boy. Now, we both have a problem. You've been off killing my lieutenants, and my lieutenants have been killing off you. You all. Your friends. Not *you*. Bunch of dead bodies doesn't help anyone. Community can't thrive if everyone's dead, can it?"

Adelais looked up into the sere, well-groomed face. "Who're you?"

"Pay attention son, I'm the grandfather of all this modern desert. But we can graze over the hype, for now." The older gentleman brushed Adelais off.

"Estaban?"

"And you just skipped to the head of the class. I don't like wasting my time, so listen up: some of my lieutenants have become a problem. Since you've already made it your mission in life to snuff them out, I want you to do it for me."

"I ain't doin' shit fer you. I ain't a bandito, and yer the reason my brother's dead."

"Zero for two. Yes, I sit high atop my proverbial castle. Guess what? Castles have great views. Especially the bastion. Seriously, you should see my bastion." The old man took a breath. "You've done solid for work for me already, whether it was your intent or not. So fickle, intentions. Because of that, I'm gonna make you this offer: I'll give you a list of names, you make the people those names belong to as ambitious as your brother over there," the old man nodded to the open grave. He continued, "When the list is concluded, I'll personally adorn and deliver the fine man responsible for your loss. With a decorative ribbon, if you like. Oh, and I'll make sure no one else you love dies bloody. Believe it or not—I hate bloodshed."

Adelais stood staring at Estaban, unable to tell whether he was talking to one of the most powerful men ever to rule the land, or a senile old fool. His expression must've betrayed him, because the old man began to lose interest.

"Forgive me. I've been living this life a long time. Thought the wrinkles gave it away. Take your time and consider my offer, but bring me your response by week's end. I'm sure you know where to find me. But if you forget, just ask for directions to the Hacienda."

Estaban took Adelais's arm over his shoulder, and with surprising strength walked Adelais back to the red pickup. Estaban unslung his old leather satchel, pulling out a piece of jerky, and handed the bag to Adelais as a gift. Taking a seat in the truck, Adelais watched as the old man walked off and waited at the edge of the town. Before long, a black SUV pulled up, with two well-armed banditos getting out to help the old man in. Adelais drew a piece of jerky out of the bag and took a bite as he waited for the pain in his body to subside. It wouldn't be long before he'd be ready to travel once again.

18. Your Ex-Lover is Dead

"Don't expect the unexpected—that's just stupid. Expect the expected, 'cause that's probably what's gonna happen."

– The Diary of Alma Grey

Alma stood next to her cousin, locked in an apparent staring contest with her former snuffle bug, Kody. The two exchanged an extended glance, tension stagnating the air between them.

"Well betrayal bear, you just gonna stand the—"

Alma was brushed aside by her hobbling cousin, who crutched her way over to the convertible.

"Are you crazy? The hell're ya' doing here?" Lorena shouted at Jake.

"Back off, Lore. I ain't here 'cause I wanna be. You can thank that pain in the ass over there." Jake dismissively waved his hand at Alma. "But since I *am* stuck here, where're the men of the house? Got business with them."

"You sonuvabitch." Lorena leaned on the edge of the convertible, getting in Jake's face.

"A fine dead bitch at that. Just like your mom. I'm sure they're off frolicking together in some majestic whorehouse in the great beyond. Now—big dude, lots of muscles, likes to hit things. Where's he at?"

Lorena shifted her weight to one side, holding her body up with one crutch while balling her fist. She swung a strong right hook, catching and shifting Jake's jaw. He reeled back, shaking it off, apparently unsurprised.

"He's off buryin' his brother. You'd best be gone before he comes back ta' do the same ta' you."

Lorena jerked her dog by the neck, indicating for it to follow her as she hobbled back inside. Jake leaned back, readjusting his jaw, and pulled out a cigarette. He lit it as he watched the unhappy couple.

"What? That nonsense don't interest you two. Carry on with the show." Jake waved his hand like a maestro and kicked his boots up onto the dashboard.

Alma sighed, rubbing her temples with one hand as she took a seat on the hood of the car, turning back to her brother. "You ruined my entrance, ya' know. Imagine—of all the possible things that could happen, I run into this douchebag here. Maybe karma's going my way, maybe I get some kind of payback. I dunno. But no—it's still all about you, huh Jake?"

Jake shrugged, cracking a wry smile. "It is what it is, sis."

Alma pulled herself off the hood and followed Lorena's trail toward the bar. "I'm not done with you, Kody. Not by a long shot." Alma knocked him out of the way as she proceeded inside.

Entering the bar, Alma found Lorena sitting at a table, holding her head in her hands. She walked up behind Lorena, placing her hands on Lorena's shoulders. Lorena jumped back, causing Alma to jump back before they each recognized what had happened. Alma started rubbing Lorena's shoulders, trying to ease the tension. They exchanged pleasantries and discussed trivial matters for a few minutes before Lorena cut to the chase.

"What're you doin' here, Alma?"

"My mom died. I don't really wanna get into it, but you're the only family I got left, so I wanted to check up on you and make sure you were okay. Haven't heard from you in I don't even know how long."

"Uh huh." Lorena sighed. "Well, my life's nothin' worth showin' off right now. My foster brother jes' died, the other one is out buryin' him, and ya' brought back the one person who's damn good at making things worse."

Alma watched her cousin's stern expression, trying to hold it all in. Failing, she burst out into laughter.

"Uh, what?"

"Heh, sorry. It's just—" Alma tried to calm herself down. "It's just that's exactly it. As soon as I found out Jake was alive—thanks for not mentioning anything about that all these years, by the way—all I wanted was to find him. Now that I have…I can't get rid of him! He's a giant pain in my ass!"

"Yeah…guess I don't see how that's funny." Lorena looked to her cousin only for a moment before her gaze wandered to the floor. "Life ain't easy down here, in case ya' missed that part. Might've told you about him at some point if he wasn't busy screwin' everything up. By the time he finally left, all we wanted to do was forget 'im." Lorena blew stray hairs out of her face as sweat trickled down her forehead.

"I hear ya'. And I'm sorry about your brother. I shouldn't have laughed. Just been so stressed lately…it just came out."

"I'm gonna go lie down. There're some extra beds downstairs. Sorry ya' gotta share with the boys, but it's all I got."

Alma tried to help Lorena up, but her cousin brushed her aside and struggled to get up on her own. Mounting her crutches under her arms, Lorena hobbled off with her dog into her room. Alma meandered along, exploring the bar. She wandered into the small kitchen, caught off-guard by the bloodstained floor. Walking back into the bar, she noticed more and more of the sanguine speckles and splatters sparsely scattered about.

She approached the top of the stairs, looking down before making her approach. She reached the bottom step, turning on the light and looking around the small basement sleeping room: three beds on either side, across from each other. In the middle, on one side, was Kody's, and across from his was a bunk with scattered books and trinkets. On the far end was a bleak bunk with nothing but a few sets of clothes, many of them bloodstained.

Alma invited herself to Kody's bunk, rummaging through his things that turned out to be her things. Digging through the things in her bag, she found an old bandana, the vandalized notebook, and a pair of her red, polka-dot underwear.

"Huh. Well isn't this interesting…"

She closed up the bag and headed upstairs. She stood around in the bar, leaning on a table looking out the window. Daylight started to fade as the sun began its descent. She walked outside, noticing the red convertible was gone, yet for some reason Kody remained. She took a seat on the front steps of the porch, waiting for the sun to set.

"So, where's my car, Kody? Decided you wanted that, too?"

"It stood out sitting in the middle of the road. Jake moved it. Haven't seen him or the car since. And for the record, isn't that Cris's car?"

Alma chuckled to herself. Kody took a seat next to her, but a firm shove kept him at an appropriate distance.

"Lehane, Lehane, Lehane…you have more important things to worry about. Where do we begin?"

"The beginning's usually a decent place."

"Sure, smartass. Go ahead, enlighten me."

Kody filled Alma in on everything that had transpired since they had parted ways, omitting the parts about Glenn. She maintained only marginal interest, trying not to yawn through most of it. The formalities out of the way, Alma jumped into her key subject of interest.

"So Kody, enough about the boring misadventures of the drama llama—it's 20 Questions time, and I want honest answers." Alma turned to face him. "Tell me, what was it about Cris that you just couldn't resist? Was it her tight ass? Her amazing tits? Fresh cherry? Or just the fact that she was unattainable for most, yet had a mad hard-on for you?"

"Take your pick. They're all fine features."

Alma cocked her eye. She watched him with a furrowed brow, rubbing her tongue along her teeth.

"I screwed you over, Alm. I know it. What I did to you was the single most fucked-up thing I have ever done, and hopefully will ever do. I had feelings for Cris, I knew it, and I lied about it. Tried to hide them, tried to pretend they weren't there, and all I ended up doing was getting drunk and screwing her. I was wrong, and I'm sorry. So if you want your revenge—"

Alma cocked her arm back and slugged Kody with a strong jab to his face, dropping him back onto the porch.

"If I want something, I'll take it. *That's* what I took away from your little experiment. Don't get all humble with me and act like you've learned some grand lesson, because you haven't, Lehane. Not a damn thing."

Alma launched onto her feet, contorting her face into a vicious mien. As she looked down on him, the fear of a little boy still dwindled in Kody's eyes. Breaking her posture, she started cracking up, laughing at him. He sat up, keeping his distance from Alma and nursing his injured cheek.

"Don't be such a baby about it. You're fine."

"I deserved that. That and—"

"Shut up. I know it. Just because I'm not taking your head on a pike doesn't mean we're friends. We're not. Especially if I actually find a pike."

With dusk having settled in, Alma took a couple steps toward the door. Turning back to Kody, she smirked and shook her ass, shaking her head as she continued inside. She headed downstairs and took the bed closest to the stairs, side opposite of Kody's. She took her pants and bra off, climbing into bed. Kody came down the stairs shortly after.

"Better not catch you trying to sneak a peek. This is a strict no-fly zone."

"Might wanna tell that to the flies." Kody remarked as he stripped and climbed into his bed.

"Yeah, yeah," Alma mumbled as her eyelids became heavy, weary after a long day of driving. Before she could rest, one question still sat on her mind. "Hey, Lehane."

"Yeah?"

"What happened to Glenn? You didn't say anything about him."

"It's late, Alm, we'll catch up tomorrow."

"Kody, answer my—"

"G'night."

Kody cut her off. Alma tightened her fist, tempted to carry out her plan of pummeling Kody into submission until he cowered to her every whim, but it was already late. And she'd need something to do tomorrow. Putting her plans for dominating her ex-lover on hold, she closed her eyes and retired for the night.

19. Mad World

"In a land without contractions, it is do or do not. There is no 'don't.'"

– Glenn's Chronicles

Ypsilanti, Michigan

In the middle of the dingy apartment lay a considerable pile of dirty clothes. Glenn stood near the door, listening to somber candidness of Third Eye Blind's "Slow Motion" on Geroge's sound system and doing his best to avoid any lingering odors while waiting on Geroge to pack a bag. To his interest, Glenn couldn't help but notice most of the clothing strewn about the place was female. Geroge came out of the bedroom without a shirt, still pulling up his pants and trying to fix his belt.

"It's only one b-bag, what could p-possibly be keeping you?"

"Not a lot of space, man. And looking at what happened last time you guys went all *Fear and Loathing* across country, thinkin' I might wanna plan this one out."

"It happened one t-time. The likelihood of a s-similar series of events—"

"Save the old fogey philosophy, man. Did my time and failed that class proper. Not lookin' for extra credit after the fact."

Geroge took a seat at his improvised laptop desk, uploading new music onto his mp3 player. Glancing over at Glenn, he changed the song on the attached stereo system to Blue October's optimistically hopeful "Inner Glow."

"Heh, sorry 'bout that. This better? Should only take a minute."

Glenn shifted his eyes, intentionally disregarding Geroge's comment. Glenn paced around the apartment, taking a seat on the futon and considering what preparation he himself might've forgotten. His mind wandered only for a moment back to so many days spent alone in his own ill-lit abode. It wasn't that long ago he and Kody sat together in a dingy apartment, waiting to seek out something greater. It was impossible to tell whether those were better times.

Geroge finished with his mp3 player, dropping it in his pocket, and pulled a shirt out of the pile. Slipping into the shirt of questionable cleanliness, he tossed a few more clothes into his bag and zipped it up, heading for the door.

"All right, ready to go, man?"

"A-always."

Glenn rose to his feet as the bedroom door opened. In its frame stood a smallish, nude Asian woman, confidently fending off blonde-and-black-striped sex hair.

"No goodbye kiss?" She pursed her lips.

"Uh, Jeany…we have a guest."

"He want one too?"

Geroge sighed and shook his head, rushing over to give Jence a kiss before pushing Glenn out the door. The two made their way down to the Bards' van, Geroge taking the helm.

"Sorry about that. She's been more than a little needy lately."

"Apologies are all m-mine. Sorry to have left her w-wanting."

Geroge looked over to Glenn curiously before checking the back to make sure his guitar was present and cased up. He started up the engine.

"Okay, I know Jeany and I have an unorthodox relationship of sorts, and it's not exactly a one-man-one-woman kinda deal, but that's not cool."

"T-this seems like a c-conversation you should be having w-with her."

Despite his words, Glenn showed little interest and kept his eyes focused on the road outside. Geroge watched him, likely trying to dissect him, but his thoughts were elsewhere.

"Ohh, I get it. This ain't about Jeany at all, is it? You're just pickin' fights. My bad, man, been kinda defensive lately. Got a lot goin' on. Don't worry, your good ole' pal G'll take care of ya."

Glenn looked back to Geroge, who put the van in gear as they took off out of the parking lot. Watching the roads, they passed the expressway leading to Cris's house. Geroge continued down a back road for some time until they reached a rundown house with a For Sale sign in the front yard. Glenn recognized it instantly as Geroge parked on the curb.

"Wh-wh-what're we doing here?"

"Chickadee's been on your mind for a while's my guess. Guy's intuition, ya' know? She ain't been here that I've heard of. Even when her ma died not too long ago."

Glenn opened his door, stepping outside. He looked over Alma's house, seeing the place had been cleared out—probably for some time. Maintaining little interest in a place that was no longer a place he knew, he sat back on the curb, falling into the grass. He inhaled deeply, remembering the last time he had rested there.

"Meroeeow."

Glenn made the sound with his mouth, playing with his lips to form different shapes. He smacked them together, making bubbly popping sounds, and stared off into the ravine of the deep blue sky. He canted his head, trying to change the shape of the scene, but he couldn't turn a world that was already turning. Instead, he rotated to its rhythm, seeking a synchronicity with the earth mother.

"Glad you're having fun over there, buddy, but uh… we gotta get goin'. The lady's waiting."

There was a lady somewhere, true. And in this somewhere she would surely be waiting, if she was not ambitious and self-serving. But the lady, his lady, was not the same as the one the bard mentioned. Or was she? He could never tell.

Piercing; were there eyes in the ceiling? A malevolent nimbus, circling above. Crackling divine wrath through the heavens; heat bolts, loomed in congress, cowered in the skies above. Storms defined his life; they brought no trepidation. His strength came in assimilating the fury of fallen fears. Glenn shook his head, pulling a pill out of his pocket and swallowing it. He climbed to his feet, and sat once again in the seat of the van.

Glenn fiddled with Geroge's mp3 player, hooked into the van's speakers, as they took off down the road. He scanned through the songs, going back to Blue October, this time playing a more pessimistic track, "The Answer."

"Interesting choice," Geroge commented. "So which is it? Zoloft? Wellbutrin? Flintstones Kids?"

"W-would you know the difference?"

"Not a bit. Just makin' conversation."

"Hm."

The two men rode on in silence, listening to the rest of the album on their way. Before long, they arrived at the home of Cameron Roberts to retrieve his daughter. They both got out of the van and began their walk to the door. As they neared the steps of the porch, Cris came running out from around the side of the house, bag in hand.

"Whoa, *chica*, what're you—"

Cris grabbed Geroge's arm and dragged him back to the van, tossing her bag inside. Glenn, not overly interested in the situation, pivoted back to the van.

"Hey, jackass." Emma's voice caused Glenn to turn, seeing her waiting by the side of the house. "You better take care of her this time, or I'll do a hell of a lot more than toss your ass off of a couch."

"N-noted."

Emma disappeared behind the side of the house, leaving Glenn no reason to linger a moment longer. He returned to the van and the three of them took off. Cris leaned in between the two front seats to explain, Bixby climbing out of her lap to perch comfortably on Glenn's scraggly mess of hair.

"Sorry about that. Dad wasn't thrilled about me leaving again, especially after last time. So Emmy and I had to…improvise. I'm eighteen now though, so nothing he can do about it."

"Enough dicking around then, let's get our asses in gear and go find your boy." Geroge cranked the engine and floored the pedal, peeling out of Cris's neighborhood. He turned up Franz Ferdinand's indie rock party song, "Take Me Out," as they headed out, one last thing to take care of before heading south of the border.

20. Let Sleeping Dogs Lie

"Know ya' can win, or know when to run. Anything else gets ya' killed."

– Adelais's Scratch Pad

Outer Region, Los Tios, Mexico

Adelais drove past the makeshift clinic as he finished his last piece of jerky. After so many pieces, the rations tasted raw in his mouth—little more than bitter meat. But they kept him fed long enough to make it back home. Not far from the town outskirts, Adelais drove on.

Finally reaching the bar, he parked the truck in the back, next to a large heap of several old blankets. He walked past, lifting one of the blankets, and trudged inside through the kitchen. He headed straight to the basement, finding a young brunette woman sitting in the bed next to Siggy's, reading.

"The hell're you?"

"Alma. You're Adelais, right?"

"Yeah. Car outside yers?"

"Yep."

"Huh."

Adelais trudged over to his bed, stripped naked, and collapsed.

* * *

A small hand shook him, but wasn't worth getting up for. He waited it out, and the hand eventually stopped, allowing him to fall back asleep. A moment later, the hard sting of a crutch hit his spine. He forced his weary eyes open; Lorena stood before him.

"Glad yer back."

She hobbled to his bedside, inviting herself onto it. She wrapped her arms tightly around him, squeezing as if he might never return. Adelais struggled to break her grip, the tightness of her embrace hurting his gut.

"Oh, yer stomach. Sorry."

Now awake, Adelais had a moment to look around. He looked to Siggy's bed, empty, and then to the empty bed Alma had been resting in as his eyes came to meet Lorena's.

"Who's Alma?"

"Oh, my cousin."

"Yer cousin." As they spoke, Adelais could see the reservation in Lorena's eyes. He took a deep breath before asking. "He here too?"

Lorena looked away before answering. "He's upstairs. Been comin' an' goin'."

Adelais took to his feet, brushing Lorena aside. She hobbled up, grabbed him by the shoulder and, using his injured gut against him, forced him back down. She took a seat beside him.

"You've been runnin' yourself ragged fer days. You ain't in any shape ta' fight. We can deal with Jake soon enough, but ya' ain't goin' anywhere right now."

"We wait too long, Lore, an' there won't be a soon 'nough to deal with."

Lorena leaned back on her hands, cocking an eyebrow. She looked at Adelais, then around the room. Her gaze lingered on the bed full of trinkets before bringing herself back to him.

"Ade, I know how much trouble he is. Ya' know I do. But there's a lot more goin' on than normal. Maybe best we wait and sort things out fer once. Figure out some kinda plan."

"And how do we do that, Lore? Only one ever good at that is rottin' dead in his hole."

The hurt in Lorena's eyes silenced him. He hesitated, gruffly patting her on the back and giving her a minute to recompose herself.

"'Tween Kody, Alma, and Jake—like 'im or not"—Lorena turned to Adelais—"we could probably put somethin' decent together."

"Soon as Jake gets involved, all we're puttin' together is our own funeral."

"Just this once, Ade, listen to me without fightin', 'kay? We're both tired, and I don't have it in me ta' go back and forth with ya'. Ya' have such an issue with Jake, work it out with him straight. Then we can talk."

Lorena grabbed her crutches, helped herself up, and headed back upstairs. Adelais checked around his bed, looking for some kind of weapon. Unable to find any, he turned his attention to the thud of heavy boots hitting the stairs and waited as Jake approached.

"Lookin' for your sharpies?" Jake smirked, holding out a knife.

"An' here comes the bullshit."

Jake raised his hands. "Hey, wasn't my plan to be here. I hate here."

"So leave."

"Will soon as I can, believe that. And I'm sorry to hear about little man. Not sure what kinda brain damage made you think goin' after the Romeros was a good idea—I mean, seems obvious at least one of ya' would get popped tryin' to pull that off—but I hope you ain't plannin' anything like that again."

Adelais picked up a nearby chair and threw it at Jake's head. Jake narrowly dodged the chair, watching it splinter as it crashed into the wall. The debris hit him in various places, a piece catching underneath his boot, causing him to slip and fall onto the floor. Adelais stomped over, dropping his knee into Jake's chest.

"I'ma say this slow so yer dumb ass don't miss a word. We. Ain't. Friends. This entire goddamn mess is yer fault. Lore is the *only* reason I ain't killed yer ass yet, and that don't mean I ain't gonna change my mind. So shut your fuckin' mouth 'bout the things ya' don't understand."

"Get off my brother, big man!" Alma shouted from the top of the stairs. She ran down the steps, pushing Adelais off Jake and helping her brother up. Jake cracked a provocative grin at Adelais, kicking Adelais off himself as he got free. Adelais, regaining his footing, lunged for Jake. His fingers made contact with Jake's shirt as he fled upstairs, but Adelais couldn't get a grip with Alma jumping in his way. He snorted, grabbing Alma by her shoulders.

"Get outta my way!"

"Adelais, enough!"

Lorena watched from the top of the stairs, letting Jake through. "Let her go, now." Lorena spoke slowly, through gritted teeth. The two stared each other down, Alma taking the opportunity to break Adelais's grip and free herself, heading back upstairs. The man himself remained on the stairs.

"Get rid of him, Lore. 'Less ya' want him puttin' more blood on yer hands." Adelais threatened. Lorena crutched her way to the head of stairs, shaking her head.

"Get outta my house Ade," she muttered. She moved aside, making way Adelais. He remained on the stairs, staring up at her. She raised her voice.

"What, ya' deaf now? If you're gonna start beatin' up on women and tryin' to run my house, then yer no better than a bandito. I want ya' outta my home, now."

"Lore, I've lived—"

Perrito came to his lady's defense, bearing his fangs at Adelais. Jake and Alma lined up behind Lorena, staring down at him. He slammed his fist into the side of the stairwell. He tore his hand away from the wall, the wood bloody and splintered, and stomped his way up the stairs and through the bar.

Heading out through the kitchen into the early evening, he passed Kody, who stood gazing beyond the back porch. Adelais stopped in front of his truck.

"Goddamnit…I ain't Sig. I can't get all touchy-feely. Second I do, the banditos'll kill us all." Adelais pulled something from the pickup and turned back, looking to Kody. He approached the urban cowboy. Standing in front of Kody, he held out a goldenrod flower.

"Uh…thanks Adelais, but I don't really think about you—"

"Shut up, smart ass. It's fer Lore. Ya' been workin' with me long enough ta' know we can't fuck around out here. We sit back thinkin' everything's all right, the people *should* be livin' get killed. Ya' wanna be part a' the family, then it's time ya' earn yer place. Make sure she stays safe 'til I get back."

Kody nodded, taking the flower. Adelais climbed into his dirty red pickup, and looked over the hand-drawn map resting in the passenger seat. He looked over the few places that took in vagrants, and examined the route to the Hacienda. Slamming the truck into overdrive, he took off into the night.

21. The Night Will Go As Follows

"Life's pretty easy, as long as you can keep your heart out of it."

– Alma's Diary

"Well, *that* was some shit. If you'll excuse me…" Jake said.

"Where're you going?" Alma questioned.

Jake walked out of the bar, leaving her and Lorena standing around with little to do. Lorena took a seat at one of the tables, staring into nothing.

"Lost 'em both…now what?"

"I vote we get shitfaced. I mean, this is a bar, right?" Alma spoke up.

Lorena sighed. "S'pose ta' be. Almost impossible ta' get any alcohol, and it's not like we'd want the people it'd bring in."

"So where's a real bar then?"

"Next town over. But Ade took the truck."

"Still got my car." Alma smirked. Kody entered through the kitchen, kneeling next to Lorena. He set a flower before her. "He left this for you." Lorena looked up to him, then down to the flower. She shook her head. The three of them remained in awkward silence, Alma watching Kody intently with a furrowed brow.

Lorena slammed her fist on the table, knocking over a glass of water. As Kody reached up to comfort her, she smacked his hand away and took the flower. She hobbled off to her room with her dog. Alma scoffed, heading for the kitchen. As she reached the door, Kody caught up to her, stopping her.

"You heading out?"

"Why not? Nothing going on here. Bored as hell, and seems like a good of time as any to get wasted."

"You gotta stop hanging out with your brother."

"Don't remember that being any of your business." She turned to him, scrutinizing him, "speaking of, why the hell're you all up in mine?"

"You can't go out there by yourself. You don't know how dangerous this place is, especially at night."

Alma paused for a moment, considering her options. She stood with her hands on her waist. "So you're offering to come along, huh?" She tapped her fingers against her hips. After casually looking around the bar, she redirected her attention to him. "Better than drinking alone, I guess—long as you stay outta trouble."

Kody ran downstairs, grabbing the leather duster and heading back up. He and Alma headed out the back door, Alma tossing the blankets that covered the convertible into the back seat. She hopped in the driver's seat, kicking on the engine.

"C'mon, bucko, don't got all night." She beckoned, waving Kody to the passenger seat. He climbed in, and they took off. Alma cranked up the radio, playing Black Kids' infectious dance song, "I'm Not Gonna Teach Your Boyfriend How to Dance with You."

"You gotta admit—it's catchy." Alma grinned.

"Funny. You know a loud radio in the middle of the night makes us a moving bandito magnet, right?"

Alma shoved Kody, turning the radio down to avoid any potential issues. Ignoring her violent tendencies, Kody directed Alma to the next town while avoiding any bandito stomping grounds.

"You used to be fun. What happened?" Alma asked.

"Spent the last couple months looking for you and trying not to get killed."

"Still don't get that. For all the time you spent looking for me, you didn't say much."

"Yeah, well...made more sense in retrospect." Kody shrugged.

"The master of half-assed plans...now *that* sounds more like you." Alma stuck her tongue out.

They reached the next town, parking the convertible on the outskirts and covering it with blankets to avoid drawing any attention. They wandered the streets with Kody leading the way, following the sound of loud music and louder drunks. They made their way inside a small but surprisingly busy bar, Alma managing to snag a table in the corner. She headed up to the bar and grabbed the first round of drinks.

"So, you owe me an explanation, Lehane. What happened to Glenn?" Alma took a swig of her drink.

"It's gonna take more than one drink to get me to talk about that."

"You were never a hard ass, sweetie, don't start tryin' now."

The two exchanged glances, waiting to see who would fold first. Alma took another drink, coming up with a far better solution to their situation.

"All right, wanna-be cowboy, I'll give you a chance to prove yourself."

"Huh?" Kody cocked his head, coughing on his drink as he tried to take a sip.

"You're a new man, all badass-like? Got it. Then we'll settle this the best way any dispute can be settled in a bar—darts."

"Alm, c'mon…"

Taking another swig, Alma got up, dragging Kody out of his seat and carrying their drinks over to a vacant dartboard. She pulled the darts off the board and handed him three.

"It's real simple. Three shots, high score wins. See the outer ring? It's worth double. Inner ring is triple. The bull's-eye is twenty-five and fifty points respectively."

"How do you even know this? You're not old enough to go to bars," Kody asked.

"Like you said—hanging with my brother too much."

Alma stepped up first, backing up to the throwing line. She closed one eye, lining her shot up, and flicked the dart. She struck a triple in the five region.

"A five? You sure you've played before?" Kody chuckled.

"That's a fifteen, hun. You're up."

She backed up, making space for Kody as he moved forward. He cocked his arm back, whipping the dart forward. It bounced off the board, dropping to the floor.

"Ouch. How am I gonna compete with that?"

Alma grinned, stepping up to take her second shot. She loosened up and let the dart fly, striking the narrow spot on the one region.

"Hm, well, we can't all be pros like you now, can we?" Kody chided her as he stepped up, taking a deep breath before sizing up his target. He kept his arm close to his body as he threw the dart, striking the eighteen region. "Huh."

Alma took her place, remembering the fundamentals Jake had taught her. She steadied her breathing, holding her breath while she lined up the last shot. She tossed the dart, striking the double bull's-eye.

"Ooh, sorry honey. I think you might be done here."

"How much is that?"

"Double bull is fifty, which gives me a grand total of sixty-six to your eighteen. Good luck."

Alma finished off her first drink, watching Kody's poor form. He lined up his arm, looking the target over. He brought his arm back. "Don't choke!" Alma shouted as he threw the dart. She watched it fly. The dart landed on the triple twenty. She scoffed.

"Oh that's such…beginner's luck. Good job, Lehane." Alma offered him a celebratory hug. "C'mon, it's a show of good will." He eyed her suspiciously, but she moved in toward him regardless. She wrapped her arms around him, not appreciating the fine scent of dirt and sweat that coated him. He gradually returned the gesture. She slid her hand down to cop a feel, breaking the embrace shortly after.

"Uh… thanks?" Kody stammered.

"Mhm. So, as the winner, I guess I'll let the issue go and you can buy the next round."

"How does that even work?"

"I bought the last one."

"So?"

Alma stared at him expectantly. Defeated, Kody walked up to the bar to buy the next round. Alma returned to her seat, watching him with a big smile. Kody received the drinks and reached into his pocket, before becoming flustered and getting into a minor dispute with the bartender. Alma worked her way up to the bar.

"Problem, hun?" Turning her attention to the bartender, she said, "Don't worry about my friend. This one's on me."

Alma pulled out Kody's wallet, paying for the drinks. She left a generous tip for the bartender, nodding politely to Kody as she picked up the drinks and took them back to the table.

"Good will, huh?" Kody said sardonically.

"I thought so. Although since I had to buy the drinks—"

"With my money!" Kody interrupted.

"I think you'll be telling me the story now. Unless you consider your wallet a generous donation, that is. Drink up, and get to talkin'."

Kody shook his head. Alma watched, amused, as Kody forced his first drink down, and began telling her about what happened to Glenn. He explained how he and Cris had found him, and how they were forced to run off, leaving him.

"Are you shittin' me? He was bleedin' on the bed, probably OD'ed, and you two just left him? Kody, c'mon, honey…there's no way you did that! Not to Glenn!"

"Didn't have a choice. He was gone, and the crowd thought we did it. They were gonna take us in, and there was no getting out." Kody took a sip of his second drink. "I'm sorry. I know you two were close."

Alma took a minute to digest the information, finishing off her second drink. She looked away from Kody, watching the other drunks in the bar. Thinking the situation over, she turned back to him.

"I can't believe you did that. I mean, I guess I shouldn't expect much, but to be completely honest, I didn't care all that much that you slept with Cris."

Kody looked up, raising an eyebrow.

"Not saying I'm fine with it, asswipe. What I mean is I've had time to think it all over, and I used to do you dirty all the time, we both know that. So how can I really be *that* mad that karma finally paid me back? What really pissed me off was Cris. I expected so much better of her. But this isn't anything like screwing around with someone. You left our friend for dead. That's something I can't forgive, Lehane."

Alma rose from the table, walking to the door. An arm grabbed her, Kody spinning her around.

"Alm, wait."

"Back off, Lehane!"

Alma ripped her arm away from Kody, shoving him and stepping back. As she started to walk off, a loud crack rang out from a splintering chair as Kody hit the floor hard. She caught sight of a small cut across his face. One of the larger drunks had apparently stepped up to defend her honor.

"Stay away from the lady, bandito. You're all alone here." The burly drunk took a swig as he moved toward Kody.

"Thanks, but he's not dangerous, just stupid."

Alma tried to placate the larger drunk as he kicked Kody in the gut. Kody curled up into a ball, trying to protect himself. Alma tried to break it up. "Hey! I said—"

"Banditos start trouble, we put 'em down."

"Well, he's not a bandito, so leave him alone!"

The drunk ignored Alma, continuing to kick Kody as others started joining in. Alma jumped into the fray, slamming her elbow into the large drunk's nose, producing a violent cracking sound. She grabbed one of Kody's hands, pulling him up and trying to force her way through the increasingly thick crowd. The exit blocked off, she tried to make her way through as a hand grabbed her from behind. She clutched Kody tightly, trying to free herself, but was pulled through the crowd by the hand that had her. The stubbly man dragged her outside—Kody along with her.

"You fuckin' idiot. If there's nothin' I taught you, it's how to not get caught in a damn bar fight." Jake scolded his sister.

"What're you doing here?" Alma asked.

"It's a bar. The question is what're *you* doin' here? This place is way too dangerous to be goin' off on your own. And don't try to say this little bitch dressed up like a bandito…"

Jake kept his eye on Kody, who was still reeling and bruised on the ground.

"That's my goddamn duster!"

Jake lifted Kody up enough to pull off the jacket, and dropped him back onto the ground. Jake put his duster back on, visibly content.

"All right, school kids, where'd you leave the car? It's time to get you fuck-ups home."

Alma picked Kody up off the ground, helping him walk as she guided Jake back to the car. She tossed Kody along with the blankets in the back seat, finding Jake in the driver's seat as she pulled out the keys.

"Uh-uh." She shook her head at Jake.

"Sad to say I'm more sober than you, little sis. Get in."

Jake snatched the keys away from Alma, starting the car and taking them home.

"How'd you even get here? Figured you'd be off doing something shady."

"Don't think her name was Shady," Jake smirked as he lit a cigarette. "'Sides, drink first, then business. Calms the nerves. And I lived here for a good while, sis. Know this place pretty well, including all the ways to get around."

Jake put on the Eagles' classic "Hotel California" as they rode back to the bar. He pulled the car in front of the porch and kicked his sister and Kody out, taking off. Alma walked Kody into the bar, with his arm wrapped around her shoulder, dragging him along down to the basement. Setting him down for a moment, she noticed him passed out as she laid him out on his bed.

She took his shoes and socks off, looking his face over. She turned it from side to side, noticing a black eye starting to develop. Carefully, she took his shirt off, drawing her hands across his chest. She felt some tenderness on his warm, swollen skin.

"You idiot...what're you doing out here, trying to play cowboy...it's amazing you haven't already gotten yourself killed."

Alma went upstairs into the kitchen to get some rags. She dampened them and brought them back down. She laid one across the tender parts of Kody's face, and a few on his ribs to try to bring the swelling down. As she finished dressing his wounds, she looked over her own body, noting the scrapes and cuts she'd gotten in the bar fight.

"Mom would be so proud."

Alma lifted Kody up, pulling his blanket out from under him and covering him with it. She yawned, looking over his bruised scruffy head. She smiled to herself, mussing his hair and playing with it for a moment, before she drew her hand across his face. She shoved him over to the side of his bed, making room for herself, and laid down next to him. She rested quietly as he began to stir. She could feel his neck crane down, trying to see what was going on.

"Alm? What're you doing?" Kody asked groggily.

"Shut up."

She adjusted herself, snuggling up to him and placing her head on his chest. She felt its warmth—tougher than it used to be, yet not as fragrant. There was something of a man amongst this boy. For a moment, she rested and listened to his heartbeat as he continued to stir. His arm found its way around her shoulder. As she lay there, embraced, she tried to get cozy, but it just wasn't the same. He wasn't her snuggy bear anymore.

She tossed his arm aside, got up, and returned to her bed. Sliding under the covers, she took her bra and pants off, lying down and staring at the ceiling. Another unfamiliar ceiling. Too many things crept through her mind, including her last moments with Glenn. She closed her eyes.

She gently drew her fingers across her stomach, walking them one by one. She shivered as they slid down her abs and crossed her pelvis. Convinced she heard something, she froze as she cast a furtive glance toward the stairs. Seeing nothing, she took a moment to relax herself, certain it was only her overactive imagination. Gradually, she continued as she comforted herself to sleep.

22. Down by the River

"Got to learn to lighten up. Load doesn't get any lighter by keeping everything heavy."

– Cris's Journal

Ann Arbor, Michigan

Cris ran down the short, rocky driveway, hopping the guardrail. She waited on the other side, catching Glenn as he tripped over the metal beam. The feline of questionable noble heritage flew out of Glenn's jacket, landing on the pads of his furry paws as the duo caught their breath on the way into the park.

"Why...did we decide...it'd be a good idea...to sneak into Gallop Park...after dark?" Cris said in between breaths.

"B-because...I wanted to see this p-place again...be-before we left. I like rivers. And we...h-had some time until G-geroge...finished up whatever...he n-needed to do," Glenn replied.

"Uh huh. Next time... decide to go sightseeing during the day. When it's not trespassing."

"I'll k-keep...that in mind."

Cris knelt, patting Bixby as she forcibly placed him into a cat harness. The regal feline nipped at the leash, but found no success in liberating himself despite his apparent displeasure. Cris offered the leash to Glenn as they started walking.

"Is that n-necessary? I c-can't imagine Allister is fond of that c-contraption."

"Guess my parenting style is a bit more harsh than yours, huh?" Cris teased.

"He's a c-cat, not your c-child. You didn't b-birth him." Glenn cocked an eye as they continued.

They stopped at a small bridge overlooking the Huron River. The sound of the rushing waves helped to alleviate the tension in Cris's body. Breathing deep, she took in the calming scent of the water. She stood by Glenn as he freed Bixby from the feline torture device, allowing him to play in the nearby grass.

"Remember the last time we hung out by a river?" Cris asked.

"Hm, in the w-woods. N-no, wait—the park near Texarkana. I recall you being manically d-depressed, me having a near ps-psychotic break, and B-bixby being assaulted by a raft of d-ducks."

"Good times." Cris smiled.

Glenn nodded, watching the river. He seemed lost in it. Cris followed his line of sight, watching traffic pass on the bridge crossing the river. The same bridge she had gone over nearly every day for four years back in high school. For some reason she couldn't quite place, it reminded her of Kody. She sighed.

"I can't believe G knew where Kody's been the whole time and never said a word. I thought I could trust him," Cris said.

"You believe you c-can't?"

"Of course not! He lied to me!" Cris looked over to Glenn, furious.

"He ch-chose not to t-tell you something. Something he swore to p-protect for the sake of a friend. C-can't be easy."

Cris cocked her head to the side, keeping an eye on Bixby as she looked Glenn over. From her peripheral, she could see the royal cat nearly fall into the water as he stalked the riverside.

"T-think about it, Ch-charisma," Glenn said, receiving a sharp jab from Cris's elbow shortly after. "C-cris. I knew you and K-kody had feelings for each other well b-before either of you ever admitted it. It was fairly obvious. Yet I c-chose not to tell Alma for your sake. You c-could say I'm a t-terrible person or a g-good friend, but either way, I'm still me. G-good and bad."

Cris cast her gaze back toward the flowing river, catching a glimpse of their reflection in the moonlight.

"As I'm sure E-emma has said to you—life is v-very much a-about one's own p-priorities. For e-example, who do you think sent K-kody to your room that night?"

"What?" Cris turned to Glenn, furrowing her brow. "You were involved in that? So you know about..." she trailed off.

"Alma t-told me, b-before she disappeared. We all have roles to p-play. I h-helped facilitate your situation, and in return, h-helped myself."

Cris stood up, looking over Glenn to make sure she could still see Bixby, who was rolling around in the grass. "What're you talking about? How did you—" Cris paused for a moment as the realization struck her."You and Alma."

Glenn chuckled, taking off his glasses to wipe the lenses before putting them back. He remained focused on the moonlit river. "At first I j-just wanted to find J-jake. But spending time with Alma... something about that g-girl, whether it's our mutual p-past, or just her..."

"Glenn, what happened between you two?"

Glenn pulled out his pill bottle, popping a pill as he went over to pick up Bixby. He began walking a trail near the river, motioning for Cris to follow.

"After Alma c-caught you two, she c-came on to me. She found out about J-jake and t-trashed my room. I overd-dosed. So you see, we all make d-decisions we're not p-proud of, even if we stand by them. Was my intervention in th-these relationships a g-grand and noble gesture? D-doubtful. But I followed my heart, j-just as you followed yours." Glenn brushed branches aside as they made their way along the trail.

"We might need to rethink this whole follow-your-heart thing. Seems like jumping into things only gets us in trouble."

Glenn turned back to her, looking over his glasses. "I d-disagree. It might not always end c-conveniently, b-but I'd say we grew. I d-don't regret my actions. D-doesn't mean they're 'c-correct' or easy to j-justify. More imp-portantly though, Kody left to find Alma. Given fate's f-fascination with the boy, I'd say you have b-better things to worry—"

"Hey, who's over there!" a voice shouted out from behind the brush.

Cris followed Glenn, who began running through the trail, fighting through branches. Heavy footsteps pounded the ground behind them, picking up the pace. Glenn darted off the trail, holding Bixby close to his chest in one hand while grabbing Cris's wrist with the other. The two circled around another path and doubled back, making their way back to the entrance. They found a hiding spot behind the brush in the parking lot, and waited.

Bixby, his royal catness, observed the situation from his man-perch. His keen feline senses tingling, he wriggled his way from his man-friend's grasp. He leapt to the ground, searching for their feathery assailants. Surely the mangy quack-quacks had returned to cause more chaos, but no such calamity would be allowed on his watch.

His cantankerousness scoured the area. He searched until convinced any cowardly water-squeekers that may have been in the area had fled. Being a righteous king, he sought to sooth his subjects.

His eminence sauntered over to his handmaiden, allowing her an opportunity to stroke his sovereign fur. He reverberated with her touch, allowing a rare glimpse of his charity. He allowed her a few moments of comfort before continuing.

The monarchial fur ball moved on to his man-friend, climbing his way up his subject's side to show his feline affection. Looking to his man-friend's face, his majestic chicken-stained tongue chaffed the man-friend's skin. Salty. Satisfied that justice had been served, the imperial feline returned to his perch, maintaining an ever-vigilant watch in case his fluff-brained nemeses decided to return.

"Think we're clear?" Cris asked, staring at the cat on Glenn's head.

"There's a vehicle p-parked off in the d-distance. We should wait a bit until it leaves."

"Right." Cris paused for a moment. "So you think Kody found Alma and that's why he hasn't come back?"

"I c-can't say. What I d-do know is that you said he left to f-find her, and no one has mentioned her c-coming back. It'd be wise to assume he may have accomplished his g-goal."

Cris sat next to Glenn, watching the sweaty fur ball try to claw his way out of Glenn's hair. She reached over and gently handled him, letting the cat rest on her lap.

"And Jake, too," Cris said.

"We b-both have reasons to find them as soon as p-possible."

"Well, for what it's worth... thanks."

Cris reached over and kissed Glenn on the cheek. He smiled, not letting her distract him from his lookout.

After watching the vehicle for a few minutes, Cris turned to Glenn and asked if the vehicle seemed familiar. Both of them continued looking closer, until Cris finally recognized the license plate. Geroge sat in the driver's seat, playing a game on his phone as he waited.

"We're smart," Cris said sarcastically.

"It was f-fun," Glenn replied as they climbed out of the bramble.

The two snuck out of the park, making their way up to the van and climbing inside. Glenn took the window seat while Cris sat in the middle. She looked up front, watching Geroge play the air-banjo to Panic! At the Disco's old-timey "Folkin' Around" while she waited for him to notice they had returned.

"Oh, hey. Didn't think you two were comin' back," he said.

"Ran into some trouble, but it's all good," Cris replied. Leaning forward, she said, "Sorry about earlier."

"No sweat, chickarita. I'd probably be more than a little steamed if I found out someone was holdin' out on me like that. Reminds me—Daron can watch the fur ball until Tabby and Kara get back from their little Cedar Point birthday-holiday. But we need to haul ass if we're gonna catch the last flight out."

Geroge started up the engine. Cris handed Bixby over to Glenn, letting the two have a moment as they headed out.

"Don't worry, we'll only be gone for a little while. Bixby's in good hands," Cris said.

"I'm not w-worried. He left me, and then I, him. It's our way, ap-pparently. But as the f-fox said, 'W-we are responsible forever for w-what we have tamed.' We'll meet again."

Glenn smiled, patting the little prince as the feline purred himself to sleep. Cris shifted around next to Glenn, laying her head on his shoulder. She closed her eyes, his arm wrapping around her as she exhaled, careless. Before long, sleep took her.

23. Bittersweet

"Few things in life are worth their cost. Stick with the things that are."

– Jake's Scribble on a Dirty Napkin

Outer Region of Los Tios, Mexico

Jake sat on the hood of the car, listening to Oasis' "Wonderwall" as he watched a scorpion scuttle from an overturned rock to a burrow across the unimproved road as the sun rose. It had been a long time since he'd been this far south, and he'd hoped it would be a lot longer before he returned. He stuffed his hand in his pocket, pulling out an old clinic ID badge. He looked it over, turning it about again and again. Holding it left a longing, like the end of a beautiful lie—bittersweet. He used the edges of the ID badge to pick dirt out of his nails before flicking it to the ground.

He lit a cigarette and leaned back, enjoying the drag. The smooth burn always faded too quickly, like every fine moment. He inhaled slowly, ingesting the nicotine and letting the smoke dance about in his lungs before shooting it out his nose in a divided stream. He was grateful for the fact he couldn't smell well—from what he could pick up, the place smelled like shit.

He slid off the hood of the car, taking the keys and heading inside the bar. He raided the kitchen, snatching a loaf of bread and taking it to the counter top to enjoy his spoils. He grabbed a seat and started chowing down, ignoring the thumping of crutches hitting wood behind him.

"Mornin'," Lorena said.

Jake nodded, never turning his head.

Lorena continued. "Ya' gotta help me find Adelais."

He laughed, choking on his bread as he turned around to face Lorena. He held a finger up, indicating for her to wait as he finished trying to swallow. He poured himself a glass of water from the pitcher on the table and took a sip, helping wash the bread down.

"Sorry, sweetheart, I'm still kinda sober. You're gonna have to run that by me again."

"I'm not kiddin'. Adelais was outta line last night. I know that. But he wasn't wrong. All a' this, everything that's happened—ta' include Siggy—is because a' what you started. You're the one that brought the banditos this far out an' put us on their map. You owe it to us ta' help any way ya' can."

"Lore, kiddo, I don't owe you shit. I *might* owe Estaban, but that'd be between me and him. An' I got no idea why you think I'd wanna go lookin' for your roid rage boyfriend anyway. S'pecially after he went and got boot marks on my nice shirt. Sorry, but you got the wrong cousin."

Perrito appeared behind Lorena, growling at Jake.

"What, that your personal attack dog now? You train it to bark at people ya' don't like?"

"Jake, I took you inta' my home even after all the shit ya' caused. Yer gonna help, one way or the other."

"Don't think so, cuz. What I'm gonna do is find myself a nice quiet place to relax, full of alcohol and fine *senoritas*, until my sister is done dickin' around down here. Then I'm gonna get my ass outta dodge, 'cause I fuckin' hate this place."

Jake got up and walked past Lorena on his way to the kitchen. Perrito continued to growl at him, barking as he walked away. Turning about, Jake leaned into the dog's face, returning the canine's slobbery snarl. The ambitious hound snapped at him, bathing him in foul dog breath and clipping his nose. In retaliation, Jake punched the dog. Perrito chomped back at him, latching onto his hand. Jake dug around in his pocket for a knife while Lorena pulled Perrito off him, freeing his hand before the dog managed to do any permanent damage. Spitting at it, Jake kicked the dog in its ribs, collapsing it onto the floor.

"Perrito was defending himself! Ya' had no right!"

"Fuck you and that dog. Hope y'all rot."

Jake turned around and headed back out the door. He ambled across the street, digging into his pocket with his good hand as he went. He leaned back against the small chantry, lighting up another cigarette as he stared off into the sky.

"This fuckin' place…it'd look better as a pile of ash."

He nursed his hand as the nicotine swelled in his blood. Closing his eyes, he lost himself as it coursed through his body on some unknown mission, ravaging his arteries along the way. It was never strong enough to take him, but the little bit it brought him closer to death always made him feel more alive. The moments never lasted long enough.

His eyelids slowly rolled back, reintroducing him into the bullshit world. He fished the keys out of his pocket and headed back to the car, starting it and disappearing into the desert once again.

24. The Red Cliffs Exercise

"Survival isn't always about strength or smarts—a lot of times, it's about luck."

– Lorena's Prayer Book

Lorena dropped her crutches, kneeling to Perrito's side. She examined the dog's ribs, still on the mend from its last bandito encounter.

"C'mon, puppy, yer gonna be okay. You're a tough doggy."

Lorena tried to lift the dog, but couldn't support both her and the dog's weight on her bad ankle. She hobbled without her crutches to the stairs and called for Kody. Receiving no response, she made her way downstairs to find him wrapped in rags.

"What happened?"

"Bar fight. He's an idiot, but he'll be fine. What's up?" Alma sat up groggily.

"I need ta' move Perrito back inta' the church. Yer brother busted his rib."

Alma scoffed, shaking her head. "Any guy here that isn't totally worthless?"

Lorena cast her eyes to the side for only a moment. "Can ya' move him?"

"Yeah. Gimme a minute. There a bathroom down here?"

"Under the stairs."

Lorena returned upstairs, nursing the dog while she waited for Alma. She pet Perrito, humming an old lullaby to the dog. Before long, the strawberry brunette made her way upstairs, and picked up the puppy, following Lorena to the chantry. Lorena rearranged Perrito's blankets to form a soft bed for the dog to rest. Alma carefully set the dog down in the middle of the bed.

"Why not just keep him in your room?"

"It's too dangerous in there the way the bar's been lately. Besides, it's quieter out here, and he'll be out of sight."

The two women walked back to the bar, sharing the rest of the bread Jake left on the table. They each took a piece, with Lorena breaking off a bit for Kody.

"What's the deal with you two, Alma?"

"Me two who?" Alma raised an eyebrow.

"You and Kody, dummy."

Alma coughed up a piece of bread, beating her chest with her fist until she could get it back down.

"There's no me and Kody. There hasn't been for good while now. Long story short—we didn't work out."

Lorena tilted her head as she listened to Alma. "Taking pretty good care a' him for someone ya' don't care about."

"So, I'm a caring person." Alma leaned forward, taking a large bite.

As they spoke, a door slammed shut outside, followed by heavy footsteps in the kitchen. Lorena jumped, fighting the instinct to hide behind the bar counter. She looked up, Alma staring at her as if she was a mad woman while a man came in from the kitchen.

"Hey, Deebo. Didja come back for my bike?" Alma teased.

Lorena looked past Alma, seeing Adelais staring down at her. She stood and hobble-ran up to hug Adelais.

"Kick me out yesterday, welcomin' me with open arms today. The hell's wrong with you?" Adelais said.

"Ya' were being an ass, so I treated ya' like one. Doesn't mean I'm not glad to see ya'."

"Sit down, we got a lot ta' figure out and almost no time ta' do it. Where's Jake and the city boy?"

"Gone and resting. Kody got inta' a fight last night."

"Get him."

Adelais pushed Lorena off and took a seat on top of one of the tables. Lorena looked over to Alma, motioning toward the stairs as she took a seat near Adelais.

"Ade, about what happened last night—" Lorena started.

"Ferget about it."

"I ain't apologizin', dumbass. I'm glad yer home, but if ya' pull shit like that in my house again, yer gonna have to find a new place ta' live. Already lost Siggy ta' senseless violence. Not gonna lose you the same way."

Adelais sat in silence, breathing heavily through his nose as Alma helped Kody up the stairs. The urban cowboy's voice carried into the bar as the two made their way up.

"I can walk, Alm. I don't need you to carry me."

"You're an idiot. God knows if I let you try to walk on your own you'll end up falling down the stairs and killing yourself."

Adelais watched the two, cracking a grin as a small chuckle came out. Lorena lifted her head, smiling. Alma dropped Kody on a bench and took a seat at an adjacent table.

"All right." Adelais pulled a piece of paper out of his pocket. "I talked ta' Estaban."

They all fixed their gaze on Adelais.

"He gave me a list. People he wants dead or delivered."

"Ade, what the hell?" Lorena interrupted.

"Lemme finish. Jake's the reason the banditos are out here in the first place. Estaban says we give 'im Jake, he'll leave us alone."

"Are you serious?" Lorena looked up to him.

"Wait, what? How does Jake have anything to do with this?" Alma asked.

"He didn't—of course he didn't tell ya'. Who tells everyone the ways they fucked up?" Adelais paused. "He got Estaban's daughter killed. Sarita—Lore's ma—too. Almost got all of us killed. Banditos came up here lookin' for him, and he ran like a little bitch. Sarita..." Adelais looked glanced toward Lorena, "She uh, 'kept 'em busy' while the rest of us hid."

Lorena kept her eyes cast to the floor.

"But these days ain't nothin' worth anything here 'cept us, so Estaban agreed to leave us alone if we give 'im Jake."

They all sat quietly for a minute, looking at each other while avoiding eye contact with others. Kody picked up a piece of bread and began munching it down.

"Ade, I still don't get how you and Estaban... why wouldn't he jes' kill ya'?" Lorena asked.

Kody spoke up in between bites. "He's a leader. No reason to kill an asset. Makes more sense to use your enemies than kill them."

Alma cocked an eyebrow. *"Dynasty Warriors,"* Kody replied as he finished chewing.

Adelais chuckled, nodding. "Prolly easier to make me do stuff than use his own boys. Plus we know Jake. He ain't the only one on this list, but he's at the top."

"Okay, here's an idea—no." Alma stood and crossed her arms while clearing her throat. "Jake's my brother. I thought he was dead until a couple months ago. I'm not giving him over to anyone—don't care how much of a shitbag he can be. Got it? If us being here is a problem, we'll leave."

"Estaban decides he don't wanna be friends no more, or thinks Jake's gonna rabbit, might be all of us ends up dead," Adelais countered.

"Then we all leave now. Problem solved."

"And go where, Alm? This is our home," Lorena asked.

"Dunno, don't care. We'll figure it out."

Lorena looked up to Adelais, seeing kindred thoughts in his eyes. They both turned to Alma, who took a step back as she furrowed her brow.

"You gotta be fuckin' kidding! We're not doing this! I will *not* let you take my brother. You'd murder him to save your own asses."

"Alma, I don't wanna kill Jake," Lorena spoke up.

"Then don't!"

"But he's responsible fer too many deaths already, and if givin' him ta' Estaban can stop all this—"

Alma glared furiously at Lorena, breathing heavily through her teeth. She turned to Kody, who had just finished his bread. "What about you? You wanna kill him too?"

"Little bit. He's half the reason I'm down here." Kody leaned back, wincing.

"Fine." Alma stormed toward the basement. "I'll grab my shit and go."

"Hold up," Kody interrupted. "Don't like Jake. Not at all. But I'm not on board with murdering anyone, indirectly or otherwise. Even if I was, and even if we give Jake to Estaban, he's still a bandito. No guarantee he wouldn't backstab us anyway."

Alma looked back to Kody with unexpected reverence in her eyes. Taking a moment, Alma turned her glance to Lorena and Adelais. "So we're not giving Jake up. Find another way."

Adelais shook his head. Lorena understood his frustration—the two newcomers hadn't lived under bandito martial law for any real period of time. They couldn't understand what it was like to live in constant fear and persecution, and then be offered a chance for some kind of peace. Even a thinly veiled one was still an option worth considering.

"Look, we can figure something else out," Kody started.

Lorena took a deep breath, listening to Kody as she caught the faint scent of something… cinder. She looked around, unable to see anything in the immediate area. She stood up, trying to figure out what the smell was.

"Lore, what is it?" Adelais asked.

"Do ya' smell something?" Lorena asked, looking around more frantically as the smell became stronger. She peeked her head into the kitchen, not seeing anything. Coming back into the bar, she heard a shrill yowl from outside. Lorena rushed outside the front door to see the chantry and surrounding buildings immersed in flames. The air singed with burning, toasting her nostrils while the heat baked her lungs. The town glowed a bright, ignited orange. Whimpering until he collapsed in front of the burning church lay the immolated corpse of her dog, Perrito.

25. Remains

"Whoever said 'fire is the source of life,' was a little confused."

– Kody's Notebook

"No!" Lorena shouted.

Kody jumped to his feet, wincing from the pain in his ribs. He was quickly overtaken by Adelais, who rushed to grab Lorena. Adelais pulled her back into the bar, trying to restrain her as she fought to get to her dog.

"Lore, the dog's gone. We gotta get outta here, now."

Adelais threw the combative Lorena over his shoulder. He carried her through the kitchen out to the truck. Kody rushed outside the bar, trying to figure out what happened. Most of the town had already caught fire. He focused his gaze on a home burning just down the street. Alma followed close behind him, trying to drag him back to the truck.

"Kody, what're you doing?"

"There's a little girl that lives here! I wanna make sure she's okay."

"That's sweet, really, but if she could've made it out, then she made it out. We gotta go."

"I'm not leaving anyone behind again!"

Kody broke free of Alma's grasp and ran across the street, to the outside of young Elvia and Josue's home. As he got there, the roof was already on fire. He whipped the door open, burning his hand, and catching a face full of smoke for his trouble. He called out for the children, but couldn't distinguish sounds over the immense crackling of the flames. Kody dropped onto his stomach, knocking the wind out of himself as he hit the dirt. Once he caught his breath, he crawled into the home, keeping himself as low to the ground as possible.

Kody tried to find Elvia, but couldn't make anything out with all the smoke. He accomplished little other than burning his eyes. Grabbing around blindly, he tried to find something, but had no success.

"Huh... help..."

He thought he heard someone coughing out through the blaze. He scrambled further in, toward the source of the voice. He felt around, grasping at what he thought to be a foot. Pulling on it, he felt a small jerking response. He pulled the limb closer, trying to get the person out, but found himself too lost and confused to navigate the smoggy inferno. He wrapped his arm around the leg, trying to bring the person with him as he searched for an exit. He tried to shout, but only managed to fill his lungs with more smoke. Something caught his ankle as everything went dark.

* * *

Kody coughed violently, rolling over on his side. As he tried to inhale, his stomach lurched, leaving him on all fours, vomiting. He struggled to breathe while his lungs and throat adapted to the burning pain that now came with each breath. He leaned back onto his feet, helping clear his stomach and regain his sense of gravity. After a minute, he managed to sit back and look around. Nightfall had settled in, the air still full of smoke.

"You stupid jerk."

Alma, covered in soot, sat against a tire of the truck, teary-eyed.

"Alm...what happened?" he gasped.

"You damn near died, you fucking moron. What the hell were you thinking?"

He caught his breath, looking around some more. He was sitting behind the bar. Adelais walked out of the ruins, scavenging what little remained of the burnt-out hovel of a bar. Lorena sat nearby in front of a small, freshly dug mound. Kody looked around, trying to see if he could find Elvia anywhere.

"The little girl...she okay?"

Alma looked up, confused. "Little girl? Your arm was wrapped around someone, but I don't think it was a little girl. Couldn't really..." she trailed off.

Kody took a moment. "They okay?"

Alma shook her head. Kody lowered his, catching sight of what used to be his shirt. The little fabric that remained hung off him like a poncho carelessly draped over a burnt log. Kody sat up, trying to sort everything out in his head when Alma tackled him back to the ground. She pulled him up, wrapping her arms around his shoulders.

"Thought we weren't friends."

"Just like a boy to believe everything he's told. Friends or not, doesn't mean I want you dead. Lost enough people already."

"Help me up."

Alma stood, helping Kody to his feet. He wandered around to the front of the bar, surveying the damage. Little was left of the town other than charred building frames and smoldering ruins. Kody walked over to Elvia and Josue's house, supported by Alma. In front of the building lay a small body. Judging from the location and drag marks in the dirt, Kody guessed it was Josue. The smell alone would've made tolerating or keeping anything in his stomach impossible, if he hadn't already liberated its contents.

He looked inside the wreckage of the house, seeing two more bodies in a charred rocking chair next to the scorched remains of a guitar. A small child held by an adult. *Elvia and her father.* Kody let Alma go, cautiously making his way into the remains of the building. He stopped in front of the two bodies, still resting in their chair, and pulled a knife from his pocket. He cut the necklace from his collar and laid it around Elvia's neck.

"I didn't forget."

Kody fell to his knees, weeping before the two bodies. He remained there for some time, until Alma helped him up and they walked back to the truck together.

"Adelais, I don't...what happens in this situation? Do we bury them?" Alma asked.

"I'm prolly the wrong person to ask."

Adelais finished loading up the truck with the few items he managed to salvage from the bar. Lorena sat in the passenger seat of the truck, staring off vacantly. After some time, she spoke up.

"I dunno. If it was jes' one person, then yeah. But..." Lorena trailed off.

"Do we know what happened?" Kody asked.

"If I had ta' guess, fire started in the chantry an' burned through the town," Adelais answered. "I'd bet banditos."

"I thought you and Estaban—" Kody held his tongue.

"I dunno…he said some banditos workin' fer 'im were 'causin' trouble. Could be they heard about our deal. Could be Estaban changed his mind. Hell, could even be Jake."

Alma shot Adelais a dirty look, but quickly dropped her head. Kody had considered the possibility as well.

"What now?" Alma changed the subject.

"Now that my home's gone?" Lorena spoke up. "We go somewhere else. The closest town ain't too far away. Guess we start there, an' figure things out after that. I won't let 'em keep takin' away everything I love."

Kody stood up on his own as Alma let him go. She climbed into the back of the truck and helped him up onto the tailgate. They made space near the cab, moving their scavenged personal effects aside. Alma dug through a bag Adelais had salvaged and pulled out an old jacket. She handed it to Kody. He looked it over for a minute, eventually recognizing it.

"I took it when I left. Don't ask."

Kody nodded and pulled it over his patchwork-stained skin. He wrapped his arm around Alma's shoulder, holding her close as they waited for Adelais to start the truck. Kody rested his head on hers and closed his eyes, thinking back to only a few days ago when he had played with Elvia in the street. He thought of Glenn, and whether his old friend would ever forgive him for always failing to save the people he cared about. As his mind began to drift, Kody wondered if his sister had had a good birthday.

26. Between Dead Men

"A perk of having no expectations is that you can still be surprised without all of the disappointment."

– Glenn's Chronicles

Outer Region, Los Tios, Mexico

The cab stopped in the smoldering daylight ruins of a small desert town. Glenn looked to Cris, who seemed to be thinking the same thing.

"G, are you sure this is where Kody's staying?" Cris asked.

"He said it was some one-horse town outside of Los Tios. Don't see the horse, though. Hey, cabby, how many towns like this around here?"

"None, now."

"Huh."

Glenn stared at the singed ruins. Adjusting his glasses, he thought he caught sight of something, but he couldn't be sure. He paid the cab driver and got out of the cab, proceeding on foot. He thought he heard some discourse between Geroge and the cab driver, but he continued. Glenn walked up to the town, looking it over. Smoke still rose from the ash.

"This j-just happened."

Cris caught up to him, looking around.

"What? Are you saying this town *just* burnt down? As in…well, now?"

"Within the last d-day, at any rate."

Glenn continued wandering around, noting the ash falling from the sky like desert snow. He came upon a small burnt-out house with a charred corpse laid out in front of it. He stopped and watched as a group of vultures picked at the remains of the crispy body. Cris walked into him, looking over his shoulder to see what he was looking at. Catching sight of the vultures and the body, she turned away.

"It-it's nature Cris. It's what h-happens in the real w-world."

Glenn leaned forward to take a closer look at the body, causing Cris to fall forward and do the same. He ignored the unseemly nausea in his stomach growing from the stench of decay.

"Glenn…oh my God, Glenn!"

"W-what?"

"Is that Kody?" she asked.

The vultures craned their necks up at the noise, flying off. Cris ran up to the body and looked it over.

"Glenn, he's dead!"

"W-what? Why do you think it's K-kody?"

Cris picked up a small beaded necklace that rested on the charred body, undamaged by the fire, and held it up to show Glenn.

"It's Kody's necklace." She pulled her own out from her shirt. "Same as mine."

Glenn looked over the necklace Cris held in her hand, and glanced back toward the body. He turned and searched the village as Geroge finally caught up with them.

"You don't care?"

"I d-don't think that's Kody."

"What?

"The necklace is unsc-cathed. A little dirty, but not b-burnt. Look at the b-body. It's small and laid out. Someone p-placed it there. Maybe the ne-necklace, too."

"Who's playing puppet master with the leftovers?" Geroge asked. Glenn glared at him. "Uh, sorry. Not used to this kinda thing."

"Hush. L-listen," Glenn said.

As they quieted down, the faint sound of shoveling carried from a distance. Glenn looked over to the remains of a large wooden structure and made his way over to it, Cris and Geroge following behind. They found their way around it only to run into a bright-red convertible.

"C-cris, isn't that your—"

"My car."

"Hey, *chica*, how and why is your car down here?" Geroge asked.

"Alma had to have brought it. I left my keys with her mom."

"Wait, wait, wait…you're tellin' me the Alm'ster's here?"

Glenn ignored them, continuing past the car. He wandered into a row of freshly dug mounds of dirt. Each had stones to mark the new graves. At the end of the row was a man in a leather duster piling dirt onto the latest mound. As Glenn approached, the man stopped digging. Drawing closer, a shot fired off as the man now pointed a handgun at Glenn.

"Back the hell off. Next shot won't be a warnin'."

"J-jake?"

"The hell're you? Estaban start a book club?"

Jake looked Glenn up and down, apparently thrown off by the glasses and khakis. He squinted, lowering his gun to examine Glenn. "I know you?"

Glenn reached into his pocket for his medication, unable to mitigate his trembling. Swallowing a pill, he placed the bottle back in his pocket. "I sh-should hope so. I spent the last de-decade or so looking for you."

Jake took an extended moment to examine Glenn, cocking his head to the side as he did so. After a moment, he spoke up. "Lot of folks have. S'long time to look for someone. Ain't very good at findin' are ya?"

"No b-better than you are at hiding, I suppose. B-but here I am, and here you are."

Jake hesitated as he looked Glenn over, putting his gun away. As the two made eye contact, Cris and Geroge came up behind Glenn. Jake cocked an eyebrow.

"Atticus?"

Glenn nodded. Jake laughed to himself and made his way up to Glenn. Glenn threw his arms around Jake, the latter reluctant and pulling himself away. Unable to break Glenn's grasp, Jake rode it out, giving Glenn a small pat on the back.

"Uh, not fan of sausage parties or anything, so you can let go now," Jake said.

"S-sorry… it's j-just… if you k-knew…"

"Had it rough, lots of troubles. Major tearjerker, I'm sure. Bet you've seen your fair share, but it's been a while, Atty. We've all been through some shit."

"I s-see that." Glenn motioned to the mounds.

"Oh, these ain't mine. Just watchin' 'em for a friend."

"And my car?" Cris stepped up.

"Borrowed it." Jake paused, giving Cris a once-over. "So that makes you the slut. Little skinny, but not bad."

"Excuse me?"

"My little sister's words." Jake sighed, taking a swig from his water bottle in the hot sun. "'Bout time for a break anyway. May as well trade stories."

They all sat in the shade of the burnt-down bar, Glenn explaining the extent of his investigation and Matier's involvement in the matter. Jake filled in the gaps about what happened after he and Alma found each other.

"S-so you two went to g-go see your m-mother."

"Found her rotting in her own filth. Guess she'd been sick or somethin'. Alma was pretty torn up, but you see how we live down here. One more stiff don't matter much to me, even if she did squirt me out forever and a day ago. Ended up taking that chick's car"—Jake nodded to Cris—"and headed down here. Alms wanted to see our cousin."

"And M-matier assumed you'd end here. A logical c-conclusion, based on your h-history."

"Uh huh. So you're lookin' for my sister and her chump ass boyfriend?"

"He's not her boyfriend!" Cris interrupted, "Or a chump!"

"Yuh huh. Whatever. Why don'tcha get off your asses and help me finish buryin' these folks, and we'll go find 'em. They ain't here, but there's only a handful of places they coulda gone."

Jake stood up, handing Cris the shovel as he went back for the last body. Glenn tagging along behind Jake, they came back around the bar to a bloodstain trailing down the road.

"Never mind. Coyotes took care of that one," Jake said to Glenn. He shouted past the bar, "Hey slut! Finish burying the dead kid and we'll head out."

"Jake, the girl's name is C-cris. I know she and Alma h-had their issues, but she's like a s-sister to me. C-could you please—"

Jake waved his hand dismissively as he and Glenn continued to search the charred town for bodies.

27. Rising of the Midnight Sun

"The only thing life promises is death; start lookin' at yourself as a dead man and you're already one step ahead of the pack."

– Jake's Dirty Napkin

"You all right, chickarita?" Geroge asked casually, as he leaned back in the passenger seat of Cris's convertible. "Been a long day. Lots of excitement."

Cris sighed, watching the sunset in the northern Mexican desert. She couldn't stop from biting her lip as the contemplative soliloquy of Aimee Mann's "How Am I Different" played through the car's speakers.

"I just thought...I don't know."

"That the Alm'ster would be the one MIA instead of your not so Don Quixote?"

She scoffed, turning to him. "I'm still a little mad at you, you know."

"Yeah, yeah. We can hash it out after we find our missing boy wonder."

She forced a halfhearted smile. Geroge shared a similar expression, unruly hair sprawled out over his head on its march down the sides of his face. Looking back to the dashboard, Cris tried to ignore the town's overwhelming stench of burnt decay as she played with her hands on the steering wheel.

"Ugh!" escaped Cris's lips. "I've been worried about him for months, months! Crying my eyes out in between being depressed and dysfunctionally optimistic. I had no idea whether he was alive or where he was at, yet he's been down here the whole damn time living it up. Making secret phone calls to you, hanging out with Alma, and not saying a word to me…this is bullshit!"

She slammed her fist on the steering wheel, inadvertently hitting the car horn and scaring herself back into her seat. She dropped her head into her hand, frizzy mahogany split ends falling into view. She brushed them aside, looking over her sand-covered clothes and trying to ignore the sticky sweat gliding along every crevice of her body. Geroge cocked his head back as he spoke up.

"It's definitely not a happily ever after. So what? Like most of us, Kod's an idiot sometimes. But can you tell me the genius part of *your* plan? Ya' know, the masterpiece that ended up with you sleeping with your best friend's guy?"

Cris exhaled, refusing to make eye contact with Geroge. He continued.

"Not judging. Painting you a picture. Breaking hearts leads to broken hearts. Maybe your life's messed up right now, but so are a lot of people's. What else would you expect when you do that much messin' around? We all got shit to make up for, lady friend, it's just a matter of suckin' it up until the debt is paid and we can make a half-assed effort to keep it that way."

"You know, for a pep talk, that kind of sucked."

"Wasn't s'posed to make ya' feel better, sugarplum. Just get your head outta those pretty clouds you're so fond of. This is life, not your own personal dustland fairytale."

Cris changed the song and lifted her head, observing a tumbleweed drift by in the distance. Looking past that, she stared into the explosive tapestry of stars illuminating the early evening just beyond the mountain ridge. She reclined her seat, getting a better view of the night sky.

"So you agree with Jake. You think I'm a harlot."

"Harlot ain't the word he used, mon lady frère. And like I said—not here to judge. You know how Jeany and I live, so believe I'm not big on getting into your ass about the choices you make. Just that you understand the consequences don't disappear when you get tired of 'em. Gotta deal with them until you get back to bein' golden."

"Like I don't know that."

Cris sat up, climbing out of the car to put the roof up. Geroge got out to help her, and they both secured it as they climbed back in.

"I think you're learnin'."

"Good for me, I guess. Achievement unlocked."

"Heh," Geroge chuckled. "Guess all that prodding you to check out Steam finally paid off. But as for the issue at hand. The whimsical Alm'ster…"

Cris glared at him, to no effect.

"Don't have an answer for ya'. Those two were cookies 'n cream before you tore that Oreo apart. But you love him and he loves you, and Spike loves Buffy loves Angel loves Cordelia, so who knows? I think there was some guy love in that little chain too… lost my point."

"Yeah, I see that. Thanks G. Very helpful. Goodnight."

Cris rolled over, doing her best to get comfortable in the reclined driver's seat. She shifted up and down, trying to find some sort of compromise for a good resting spot. Fidgeting tirelessly, she clasped her fingers around her necklace as she retired her eyelids and waited for morning.

* * *

The two long-estranged friends sat on the burnt-out porch in the middle of the night, sharing a cigarette. "Atticus, you're one crazy motherfucker, you know that?" The scruffier of the two, Jake, kicked back, relaxing while keeping an eye out for scorpions. "Spend that much time lookin' for me… I mean, don't get me wrong, you're an all right guy an' all, but we were like seven."

"Tw-twelve-ish, actually. And you w-were my only friend."

"Man, I forgot how weird you rich kids are. Can't even make friends." Jake laughed to himself.

"I su-suppose. Still, you never d-did tell me why you di-didn't come home."

Jake finished his cigarette, flicking it back into the bar before digging into his pocket and pulling out another.

"J-jake, you really sh-shouldn't."

"Or else what? The rubble'll burn down?" Jake lit the cigarette and took a slow drag, inhaling the bittersweet nectar of cancerous death. "I didn't come home 'cause there was no reason to. The past is kinda fuzzy, but some bullshit cliché about gettin' found. Don't remember if I was floatin' or washed up or what, but it don't really matter, does it? Ended up livin' with a junkie family that didn't give much of a shit about what I did. Taught me how to get by without school or any of that Cleaver family crap. Eventually got tired of them and moved on. Enough of a hist'ry lesson for ya?"

He flicked the ash from his cigarette, waiting for the smoke to drift out of his lungs before turning to Glenn. His unkempt, unsteady friend nodded. He offered Glenn another cigarette, but his friend instead pulled out a pill bottle and started to unscrew the cap. Jake held out his hand, to which Glenn handed him the bottle.

"The fuck're these?"

"K-klonopin."

"K-pins huh? They business or pleasure?"

Glenn adjusted his glasses, his hand starting to shake visibly.

"R-required. I overd-dosed on my other meds a few months ago. I tolerate these b-better and they help k-keep me c-calm."

"You OD and the doc gives you klonnies. That's some funny shit. Good old American medicine. Well, I know you dunno this, but I actually used to work for a doc, so here's my medical advice."

Jake stood up, careful not to drop his cigarette from his mouth, and rocked his arm back, heaving the bottle off into the distance. He took his seat once again, offering Glenn another cigarette. Looking at him wide-eyed, Glenn's shaky hand took the cigarette.

"Relax, man. Those things weren't worth sellin', and if you really need 'em, you can get way better drugs out here. But check it out: you're worried about OD'ing again, right?"

Glenn hesitantly nodded.

"A' course. Every junkie's nightmare is OD'ing. Or not getting a fix. But check it out: Among the many glorious things I've done in my life, kicking this shit was the least interesting."

Glenn cocked an eyebrow as he placed the cigarette between his lips. Jake tossed him a lighter, watching him light up.

"We're all gonna die, Atty. Every one of us motherfuckers has an expiration date. And since, like me, you've already kicked on death's door, you understand that better than most the other pansies running around here."

"Th-that's been the p-problem. With limited exceptions, I don't c-care anymore. Whether I live or die, or d-do anything at all, it d-doesn't matter much. N-not like it used to."

Jake took the cigarette out of his mouth and put it out on his boot, tucking the butt behind his ear.

"Atticus, shut the fuck up. Whatever you're worried about, it ain't that important. You bitch about not carin', but if you don't care, there's no reason ta' bitch about it."

"J-jake, it's not that—"

Jake took to his feet, lifting Glenn by the collar of his shirt. He pulled Glenn's face close to his own, and threw him back onto the ground, knocking the cigarette out of his mouth. He watched as Glenn landed on the ground, the wind knocked out of him.

"Look around, man. This town's dead. Burnt to the ground. Every man, woman, and child that wasn't lucky enough to get gone has shuffled off. Maybe that makes them the lucky ones. Dunno. What I do know is that so far today, it wasn't us. But it will be soon enough. Maybe come morning, maybe come the mornin' after that. Tried to take yer own life, Atty, so what could you possibly fear that you ain't done yerself?"

Glenn cleaned himself off and picked himself up. He opened his mouth to reply, but formed no words, instead catching Jake's fist in his gut, dropping him to the ground once again.

"I've probably talked more today than I have in the last month, 'cause ta' be honest, you're the only person who asked. But words don't fix nothin'. Words don't change nothin'. We live until we die, like every forefather that fucked our ancestors into existence before us."

Jake pulled the butt out from behind his ear, placing it once again between his lips and lighting the remnants as Glenn drew heavy breaths, trying to recover.

"Take a deep breath, take it all in, and look around. We told death to piss off, and for today, we're still here. Get outta your goddamn head about it."

Glenn stood up, shaking, and smacked the cigarette out of Jake's mouth. Jake laughed it off, hitting Glenn upside the head. Glenn recoiled, rubbing his head before looking up with fury in his eyes. He charged Jake and tackled him to the ground. The two lay there, Glenn pinning Jake on the ground.

Jake hocked a loogie into Glenn's face, causing Glenn to fall back. Jake picked up his cigarette and lit it for a third time, puffing it only once before mounting and pinning Glenn to the ground. The two stared each other down. Jake pulled off Glenn's scratched up glasses, tossing them onto the charred porch. Smiling, he took the lit cigarette and put it out on Glenn's cheek.

He held Glenn's face in the dirt as the cigarette cauterized his cheek, ignoring the cries of pain while the tip sizzled. When the cigarette extinguished in Glenn's face, he removed it, chucking the cigarette aside and freeing Glenn. Jake returned to the porch, picking up a bottle of whiskey he had salvaged during his evenings out, and took a swig. He offered some to Glenn, who kept his distance.

"Your loss."

Jake kicked back, taking another swig. Glenn picked up his fallen cigarette, lighting it and taking a puff. He stared Jake down. Jake sat laughing at him, sloshing the whiskey around. Glenn rushed toward him, slamming Jake's back into the porch, and returned the favor by forcing his own cigarette into Jake's face. Though Glenn's form was sloppier, it was far more commanding. Jake shoved Glenn off, dropping the whiskey bottle in the process.

The two were once again staring at each other, each with a circular burn mark on his face. Glenn was the first to make a move, picking up the whiskey bottle and taking a drink for himself. He then handed it back to Jake, who continued to drink.

"Now you're startin' to get it. Flesh is just flesh, brother. Body is slave to the mind."

Glenn looked to Jake from the corner of his eye. "You're insane."

"I'm not hearin' any complaints, ya little pussy."

Jake punched Glenn on the shoulder, passing the whiskey bottle. Hearing the howl of a coyote off in the distance, Jake stood up and howled back into the humid desert night—the two friends reunited at last.

28. Ms. Brightside

"Know the difference between sex and love."

– Alma's Diary

Los Tios, Mexico

Alma climbed out of the truck's passenger seat, heading into an old rustic inn with Adelais. Pooling their money and selling off the bits of salvage they didn't need, they had enough to afford two rooms for a couple of nights. The two went their separate ways, Adelais heading to his room while Alma headed to hers. Closing the door behind her, she landed on her stomach, sprawling out onto the freshly made king-size bed. She closed her eyes, finding only a moment's reprieve before Kody entered the room.

"Any luck?" he asked.

"We sold the rest of it. Even had to hawk Lorena's crutches. But we made enough to get by until the end of the week, at least."

"Good. We have a few days to sort everything out."

Alma rolled over onto her back, staring at another ceiling. She waved her hand slowly in front of her face, letting it drop back onto the mattress. She alternated kicking her feet back and forth.

"Bored?" Kody asked.

"Just a bit. I'd head back home—or somewhere, I guess—right now if I could find Jake. You?"

"Same. Sans the Jake part."

144

Alma stopped kicking her feet and sat up. She watched Kody, who sat slouched near the door with his head rolled back onto the top of the chair.

"Why *are* you still here? I mean, you said your whole deal was to find me, and you did that, so shouldn't you be running back to wonder tits by now?"

Kody chuckled as he raised his head. "Wonder tits? Really? She used to be your friend, you know. Anyway, I tried calling G, but I couldn't get ahold of him."

"Uh huh, that's great. But it doesn't answer my question. You're the only one of us with an out who isn't taking it. Why?"

Kody sighed, casting his eyes to the side. After a minute, he took a deep breath and shrugged. "I guess I don't like the thought of leaving people behind. Ever since Glenn...we should all go back together."

Alma scrunched her lips together, bringing them to one side. She squinted, carefully observing Kody. He looked at her only momentarily, averting his gaze to some bad motel art they'd both spent more than enough time examining. Bringing her finger across her chin, Alma devised a plan to test a theory. She interlocked her fingers, stretching her arms out in front of her body. She then raised them over her head to stretch her abs. She arched her back, keeping a keen eye on Kody as she did so. She caught him subtly sneaking glances at her before turning away.

"I knew it!" she exclaimed.

"Huh?" Kody's eyes widened as he reeled back.

"Heh, nothing." She laughed to herself. "How're your burns? Feeling better?"

"I'll live." Kody eyed her suspiciously.

"Good. I'm bored." She looked around the room, putting together an idea. "Gonna go take a dip in the pool."

"There's a pool?"

Alma got up and headed through the lobby of the small inn, pulling an abandoned tarp off the ground as she got outside into the bright afternoon sun. Small creatures skittered and scattered as the tarp came off the ground, exposed to the harsh light of day. Alma continued behind the inn, with Kody following close behind.

She dropped the tailgate of the truck, carefully lining it with the tarp as she looked around for a nearby hose. Glancing at it, Kody followed her line of sight and handed it to her, turning it on shortly after. Alma hopped out of the back of the truck, closing it up and leaning against the side of the tailgate as she waited for it to fill. Once full, she killed the hose and stripped down to her bikini underwear, hopping in the newly improvised truck-pool.

The waves of faucet water washed over her sweaty legs. She sank slowly into the truck-pool, the water coolly creeping its way inch by inch along her spine, all the way up to her neck. Eventually remembering Kody had followed her out, she turned to him. He watched her awkwardly.

"You can stop staring any time now. Really, it's okay."

He shook his head and turned it back toward the motel, apparently debating whether to go back inside.

"There's plenty of room in here, if that's what you're wondering. Promise I won't try to drown you. Wouldn't wanna mess up my new pool."

He walked over and pulled his shirt off, wincing as it touched his mild burns. He looked around and hesitated as he dropped his pants.

"What're you so shy about? No one's around, and it's not like I haven't seen your boxers or their fun surprise before."

He climbed up onto the tire and dipped a toe into the truck-pool, pulling his foot back as soon as it touched the water. Alma reached up and grabbed his ankle, forcing his foot into the water and pulling him down with it. Kody cringed as he adjusted to the relatively cool water of the truck-pool.

"See? Isn't that better? Finally a bit of relief from this crazy heat. And tell me that doesn't feel good on your burns."

"Kinda stings a little."

"Oh hush, you big baby."

Alma laughed at him, splashing water at his face. He tried to dodge before retaliating, splashing her and soaking her hair. The two played back and forth for a few minutes, soaking everything in the immediate area, including their clothes lying on the ground. After a while, they took a break to kick back and relax. They sat next to each other, resting their heads against the back of the truck's tailgate.

"I think this is the first day that hasn't sucked since I got here." Kody turned his head to Alma.

"I noticed you've been Mr. Tightpants lately. Just need to loosen up a bit. If there's one thing I've learned from my brother, it's that life is too short to spend stressed all the damn time."

"Not a bad philosophy."

"I didn't think so. Wake me up before I bake?"

"Sure."

Alma closed her eyes, drifting in and out of consciousness as she lay in the truck-pool. She walked her fingers along the bottom of the tarp, running into Kody's hand and walking her fingers away again like a coy crab.

The sun gradually began to warm the water, and her skin with it, but she'd have some time before she'd have to worry about a sun burn. The cab side of the truck sank in, followed by a loud splash. Opening her eyes, she saw Adelais and Lorena in their underwear at the other end.

"Look who it is! Was beginning to wonder if I'd ever see you two out and about. Was starting to think you two wouldn't ever leave your room, you crazy love birds," Alma joked with them.

Lorena and Adelais exchanged looks, Lorena frowning as she looked away. She lifted her leg up, resting it on the side of the truck. She rotated her somewhat swollen, purplish ankle, showing only little pain. "Last thing on my mind is love. 'Sides, what about you?"

"I'm spoken for," Kody said.

Alma patted him on the back, nodding toward Lorena.

"This guy right here? The most loyal stallion you could ever find. Look at his blind devotion to his mistress. Spent—" Alma turned to Kody. "What was it, honey, a week?" She turned back to Lorena. "Spent a week with her, and already acts like he's married. No risk for infidelity here, no ma'am."

Kody turned to Alma, unamused. She offered him a cheery smile of pearly whites, but it seemed to do little. "What, am I wrong? Surely, you'd never do anything to betray dear Crissy's trust. Least of all flirt with your ex—her former bestie, no less." Alma puckered up her lips at Kody, offering him a kiss. He climbed out of the truck, snatching up his clothes and heading back around the building.

"The hell was that about?" Adelais asked.

"Just messing with him. He likes to forget he's kind of a tool. Decent enough in the sack, but I wouldn't trust him with a Klondike bar."

"Alma, ya' were kinda harsh," Lorena commented.

"I guess. But enough about him. Who's up for a threesome?" Alma leaned forward enthusiastically, smiling wide.

They both stared back at her, confused, before uncomfortably looking at each other.

"C'mon…! The last few days have sucked! Can't we have a little fun?"

"Um, Alma, I'm not really—" Lorena spoke slowly, trying to find her words.

"I was kidding about the threesome. It was a joke! I just mean the last few days have been rough. Figure everyone needs to lighten up a bit."

They both continued to stare at her. Alma threw her arms up and climbed out of the truck. She grabbed up her clothes and headed back inside. Still soaked and dripping in her underwear, she offered a wink to the inn manager, who seemed grateful for any kind of attention. After an extended moment of fumbling with the door, she finally got into the room. She walked in on Kody lying nude on the bed during his personal man time.

"Damn, I just say the chick's name and you're already beatin' off. She's not *that* hot."

Kody scrambled to cover himself up, wrapping himself up in a blanket and rolling to face the other direction.

"Don't worry about it, champ. Gonna catch a shower, so you have some time. Go ahead and finish up."

Alma stepped into the bathroom, closing the door behind her. She leaned against it for a moment, keeping her ear pressed on the frame. She ignored her own shallow breaths, continuing to grow louder and louder, and listened for any sign he was continuing. Pressing her body closer into the door, a gradual, filling warmth spread over her as she became wet. Her fingers instinctively wandered toward her hips, grazing over her waistline before she heard Kody shuffling around just outside the door. She quickly shook her head and dropped her underwear, starting the cool shower.

Alma hummed Cobra Starship's club mix of "You Make Me Feel…" to herself as she washed off and cleaned up. She took her time, turning up the heat and enjoying the luxury of a lukewarm shower in spite of the desert heat. Finishing up, she stepped out of the shower and toweled off, realizing she had forgotten to grab a change of clothes. Left with no other option, she wrapped up in the towel and stepped back into the motel room.

Trying to sneak in quietly, she found Kody sitting at the edge of the bed in a dirty pair of pants, avoiding eye contact. She looked around for her bag, trying to find a change of clothes. With it nowhere in sight, she spoke up.

"Where're my clothes?"

"Adelais picked them up. They're doing laundry, I guess."

"So you gave away my only remaining clothes."

"It was that or put those soaking dirt rags back on."

Alma considered his point as she debated between the chair and the bed. Feeling the weight of her karmic debt, she took a seat next to Kody.

"Look, I'm sorry about earlier, okay? I might've been a *little* harsh."

"A little?" He cocked an eyebrow.

"Don't get me started. I know you've been through a lot lately, so me giving you a hard time was probably the last thing you needed."

"You've been riding my ass ever since you got here, Alm. I know I'm a piece of shit for what I did, but I fucked up exactly once. You've been treating me like Zoidberg when I've done nothing but have your back the whole time we were together, before and after."

Kody turned away from her. For the first time in a long time, her heart started racing. Her face flushed, heating up. She grabbed his shoulder, turning him to face her.

"Damnit, Kody! You don't get to do this to me! You don't get to make me feel like shit because of what you did! I fell in love with you!" with light tears now streaming, she lowered her voice. "I fell in love with you. As much as I hated life and everything else, I started believing in having a future—because of you. With you. I started believing in us. I opened myself up to you because you were wonderful to me. Because you loved me. Even now, when they wanted to take Jake, you *did* have my back. But how am I supposed to just forget that you betrayed me? How am I supposed to just accept you back into my life?"

Kody took Alma's hands into his own, holding them in his lap. "I don't have an answer, Alm. But we can't keep fighting each other. Especially out here. Adelais and Lorena are all we've got, and there's no guarantee the shit won't hit the fan and they'll decide we're more useful as bandito bait. At the very least, *we've* got to stick together. I need to know: Can I trust you have my back?"

Alma hesitated as her fingers explored his calloused hands. She licked her chapped lips.

"Only if you swear to watch mine."

She leaned forward, resting her head away from him on his shoulder— her old familiar perch. He released her hands, wrapping his arms around her as his fingers drifted along the base of her neck. She turned her head, bringing her forehead into his collar. She inhaled, her body quivering as it remembered the steps. He continued to hold her close, drawing his fingers further along her back, like old times, allowing them to explore the arch of her spine. She shivered slightly, lifting her head to kiss his neck as the filling warmth returned.

"What was that for?" he asked.

"For having my back."

She lifted her head up, looking into his eyes—the eyes that had once been meant only for her. She leaned forward, bringing her lips to his. Met with no resistance, she pressed on. She wrapped an arm around his head and his back, leaning into him and remembering everything she'd been missing the past few months. She forced his mouth open with her tongue, intermingling the two. His hands still on her back, the towel began to slide off. With it stuck around her waist, she pushed him back onto the bed, climbing on top of him. The touch of his rough hands grasping her breasts caused her to lean into him, feeling the bulge of his pants.

"Hey, didn't you...?"

"I couldn't. Not after you walked in."

Alma climbed off him, keeping the towel wrapped around her waist. He looked up at her, focused on her breasts. She drew her finger from her nipple up to her eyes.

"Heh, you know there won't be any sexy time happening, right?"

He looked at her like a guilty puppy.

"Not for you, anyway. And not because I give a shit about Cris, because I don't. I'm about as worried about her feelings as you are, but that's not the point. The point, which you will keep in your pants, good sir, is no joystick in the glory hole. You lost that privilege."

Alma wagged her finger at him before drawing it above the towel, across her waist.

"However, if you want to start making it up to me, there are several more," she paused, "*recreational* ways you can convince me you deserve a second shot."

Kody couldn't keep his eyes off her, but made no move. She stood before him, sighing. A knock came at the door, getting their attention. Alma pulled the towel up around her chest and answered. Lorena stood at the door with new clothes. She tilted her head, handing the clothes over.

"It's not—just don't, okay?" Alma said curtly. "What do you want?"

"Get dressed." Lorena looked over Alma's shoulder. "Both of ya'. Somethin's come up. Once ya' have some clothes on, come over ta' my room."

Alma closed the door as Lorena walked off, getting dressed and handing Kody a fresh shirt. She set her stuff down and took his hands, pulling him up.

"Look, I don't care what you do, hun. I'm over you, although personally, it's been a while and I could use some good foreplay. But if all you're gonna do is tease me and sit around guilt tripping, then do it on your own time, 'kay? Apparently we have work to do."

Alma waited for no response as she dragged him along, taking him with her as she headed out the door and down the hall to see whatever catastrophe awaited them next.

29. Confederates

"Succeed at any cost—victors can rewrite their history."

– Annals of the Romero Family

Arturo sat uncomfortably in the inn's chair, Kody and Alma on both sides glaring at him in a less-than-friendly manner. Only Lorena seemed to offer any hint of kindness.

"When's Adelais gonna get back?" Alma asked.

"Shouldn't be too long," Lorena replied.

"We don't need Adelais to get started. I'm here because we both have problems that need to be solved."

Arturo blew his dark, mangy locks out of his face, straightening his back and sitting up as best he could in the small chair.

"Not taking help from a bandito. Walk away," Kody commanded.

"Your friend killed my brother. I wouldn't be here if I didn't need to be. Like you said, I'm a bandito, so we can do this the pleasant way, or you can march pigheadedly toward your deaths as you please." Arturo looked over Alma as he spoke.

"Wait, Adelais did *what*?" Lorena asked Arturo as the room door slammed against the wall.

Adelais stormed in, already knowing who was in the chair. Arturo's body lifted from the chair, creating a degree of turbulence as Adelais rushed him against a closet. Throwing a long knee into Adelais's gut, Arturo freed himself, looking up at the man-sized behemoth.

"*You're* Adelais," Arturo said.

"An' yer the bastard's brother."

Adelais swung on Arturo, the latter narrowly dodging a powerful left hook to the temple. Arturo posted Adelais back, creating a gap between them. Before Adelais had an opportunity to renew his assault, Lorena stood between them.

"Back off, Ade. You an' I need ta' have a talk—now."

Adelais pushed through Lorena, who threw a swift knee into Adelais's groin, bringing him down hard. With Adelais reeling on the floor, Arturo took a moment to recompose himself. He took a step forward and offered a hand to Adelais. The hulking vagabond reluctantly accepted Arturo's hand, pulling himself up. Once on his feet, Adelais began his attack anew. Again, Lorena reached out to stop Adelais, but this time was tossed back by his massive hand.

"Adelais!" she cried out.

Kody caught Lorena as Alma lunged toward him, but the barrel of Arturo's .44 caliber Colt Walker resting firmly against his nose finally stopped Adelais. The giant of a man slowly stood down and stepped back. He finally stopped, meeting the gaze of each person in the room. He and Arturo locked eyes, the latter waving his gun toward the door. Adelais moved at once, disappearing beyond the doorframe. Arturo glared at the bystanders gathering outside and put his gun away, calmly closing the door.

"Lorena, there's no way—" Alma started.

"That's enough. Arturo, the plan." Lorena spoke quietly, but firm.

Arturo took a breath, shifting around to stretch and relax his sore muscles. He loosened himself up, alleviating the aches caused by Adelais's outbursts.

"Banditos tried to kill you by burning down your town. I propose we kill them back."

"What? 'Kill them back?' That's your genius move?" Alma questioned him.

"No offense, man, but how is that even possible? There's hundreds of them—they're everywhere. Like ants," Kody added.

"As I told Lorena before, I'm one of the kin leaders. In one fashion or another, we all follow Estaban: some because we believe in him, some because we must. If he were to fall, if they lost the source of their strength, there'd be no one left to hold a grudge against you."

"And the banditos he leads?" Lorena asked.

"They'd war among themselves. Kin leaders would fight for control, but few of them can effectively lead a syndicate like ours, if any of them even managed to succeed Estaban. There'd be chaos, perhaps, but they'd be weakened. At the least, they'd be less of a threat than they are now."

They all stood for a moment, mulling over the options. Alma took a seat on Lorena's bed, staring out the window. After a moment, she turned back to Arturo.

"I only have one pony in this race: do you want Jake?"

"Estaban is the priority."

Alma shrugged and canted her head. "Hey, do whatever you need to, then. I'm out as soon as my brother shows up, so as long you and yours don't mess with us, float your boat. Lorena, you're welcome to come with, by the way."

Lorena shook her head.

"This is my home, and they took my family. I wanna see 'em burn."

Alma nodded and turned to Kody.

"Kody?"

"I dunno." he sighed. "I mean, I respected Siggy, but he's gone. I don't see how me dying helps anything in the long run."

Arturo chuckled to himself, picking up the chair Adelais had tossed over earlier. He straightened out the remaining mess and started making his way toward the door.

"You're leavin'?" Lorena asked.

"It's clear I'm on my own. There's a lot to be done, and time's already too far behind."

Arturo left the room and headed out into the lobby. He apologized to the innkeeper for the trouble caused, and provided generous compensation for the damages. He made his way outside, to the back of the inn where his horse remained tied to a firm post. He undid the lead rope, petting the horse gently.

"Good girl, Viaje. Time to go."

As he prepared to mount the steed, Lorena came around from the far side of the building. He waited as she hobbled up to him.

"Lemme help."

"This is dangerous. If we fail, Estaban will kill us both, slowly, and everyone we've ever known. Even if we succeed, there's still a good chance we'll die."

"Death awaits us all—it's his job. But I don't hold it against him."

Arturo nodded and helped Lorena onto the horse. He climbed on himself, and pulled Lorena's arms around him tightly.

"Shelter those, Lord, who bear me company, from the evils of fire and all calamity," Arturo muttered as Viaje carried the two beyond the limits of the town to begin what he proposed to be their end.

30. Chasing Skirts

"I can't even imagine how simple life would be without women. And how nonexistent."

– Kody's Notebook

"This place is way too wild west-y for me. Ready to find my brother and get the hell outta here?" Alma said as she and Kody sat in their room discussing strategy.

He tried to stop his leg from shaking, but the more he tried to control it, the worse it got. He looked up, met by eager eyes. "Yeah. Let's go."

They headed outside and began walking the streets, devising a plan. Kody recommended bribing people for information, but he couldn't come up with much of a lead on where to start, or where to get the money. Alma suggested bars as a good starting point for both, but changed her mind, considering early afternoon wasn't the best time of day for what she had in mind.

The two continued down the road, discussing where Adelais went, whether Lorena had completely lost it, and if Thomas Dutton would ever make a sequel to *Razia's Shadow*. Walking around, Alma recalled how this was her first real trip to Mexico, briefly visiting Lorena with her mother in the past not counting for much.

"You know, Kodykins, if you think about it, this is the closest any of us ever got to getting that road trip vacation we wanted. Told you we should've come to Mexico."

"Just wish we could've ended up somewhere else. Before I found Lorena, I got stuck in a pretty nice town, a city. It was peaceful, lots to see and do. No one tried to shoot me. You would've liked it."

"Maybe we can stop by on the way back." Alma nudged him.

"Tell me you're not planning another road trip."

He rubbed the back of his head, moseying down the street alongside her. Though he was still dripping with sweat, the desert heat didn't seem as bad.

"Not saying I am, but it is a long drive back. Gonna have to make a few stops anyway… so why not?"

Kody mulled it over as they walked. Months since he'd been home or even back in his home country. The thought of seeing his family again, sleeping in his bed, being safe… he grinned. As they continued down the road, they came upon a small festival in the center of town. Several guitars accompanied an assortment of drums as girls in brightly colored dresses danced around to the music. Alma gasped, and he looked over to see her face light up. She looked to him pleadingly.

"Aren't we supposed to be looking for your brother?" he asked.

"Jake's fine. Or not. Whatever. He'll okay for a little bit. I wanna go dance! And you *owe me* this. I never got to go to the festival you promised me before." She stared into his eyes, eager and waiting. He smiled. She shook her head, singing, "let's go already," doing her best Bender impression.

Kody took Alma by the hand and led her up to the crowd. They watched, catching the scent of grilled chicken as a young man nearby bit into a seasoned empanada. A violin joined the medley of instruments as an older woman began clacking the heels of her shoes against an improvised stage. The woman danced with an older gentleman, taking the stage and putting on a show for the people. Alma grabbed Kody's arm and dragged him through the crowd, joining in.

They moved to the music, enjoying the atmosphere of the festival in the heat of the sweltering sun. Coated in a sheen of sweat, Alma shined as she danced. After a good fifteen minutes of struggling to keep up, Kody snuck his way out of the crowd, taking a breather and grabbing an empanada while watching Alma dance. Having finished his, he went back to grab more empanadas, coming across a small stand selling trinkets.

Among the various things for sale, a brightly colored floral ribbon caught his eye. He picked it up, along with the food, and returned to wait for Alma. He watched her, much like a lead actress so lost in her craft she'd forgotten she was on a stage, until she finally left the crowd some time later, making her way back to him.

"Those for me?" she asked.

"Yeah." He nodded, coming out of his daydream-like haze. "Figured you might be hungry. Gotta be by now."

"Good call."

She took the empanadas, brushing wild split ends out of her face while she ate. As she scarfed the food down, Kody stepped behind her, pulling her hair back and tying it up with the ribbon he'd bought for her.

"Why, Mr. Lehane, if I didn't know better, I'd say you're sweet on me."

"Like you said—I owed you this." He stepped back around.

"Thanks." Alma pressed her greasy, empanada-stained lips against his cheek. "I'm grateful, but don't get the wrong idea. This was about me getting to have my day—that's all. I got no use for a provisional boyfriend."

"Let's go find your brother."

Alma nodded. "Break first though. I'm all kinds of sticky."

Alma chuckled as she wiped the sweat off her forehead. Kody led the way as they returned to the inn. They made their way into their sauna of a room, Kody flinging his shirt aside the minute he passed through the door. He dropped himself onto the bed, Alma following suit closely after, tossing her shirt off and collapsing next to him.

"How have you made it this long with this heat? It's freakin' ridiculous," Alma asked.

"Dunno. Mostly keep myself busy and try not to think about it."

Kody rolled his head to the side, catching sight of Alma. His eyes followed the trail of curves down her sweaty body to the hem of skirt and slowly back up.

"Thinking of ways to take our minds off the heat?" she teased him.

"Don't think that'll help with the heat."

"Don't think the heat is what you're worried about." She slid her hand along his pants until she felt his bulge. "Might need to rethink your privileges. Seems to me I'm the one getting shafted here. Or should be, anyway." She chuckled as she gave a gentle squeeze. The strawberry brunette leaned toward him, her breath hot on his cheek. She drew his face close with her free hand, her tongue inviting itself past his lips. Returning the gesture, he slid his arm along her waistline, well aware of its next destination.

"Good boy," she whispered as she undid his pants.

Their lips apart, he broke free of her for only a moment. He mustered the only thing he could think of as he pulled away. "Uh, maybe you should shower first."

She stared at him, cocking an eyebrow. "Seriously?"

Kody rolled onto his back, resting his hand on hers for a moment before reluctantly plucking Alma's hand from his crotch. She sat up for a moment, looking down at herself, and then to him. She shrugged, and headed to the bathroom. On her way over, she dropped her skirt before disappearing behind the door.

"Damn..." Kody stepped outside the room, slowly pacing back and forth in the hallway. He eventually found himself in the lobby, seated with his head laid on the back of the chair taking deep breaths. "I dunno how much longer I can keep this up," he muttered to himself.

"Hey man, you got a couple a rooms? I'm thinkin' three-ish. Got me, a fine chickarita, and two weird-ass dudes who apparently like burnin' themselves."

Kody lifted his head, convinced he recognized a voice he knew couldn't be there. Turning around, he saw a brownish fella with a boyish man beard.

"G?" he exclaimed.

"Kod-man? Huh, that didn't take long."

Kody stood as Geroge walked around the chair to greet him, the two exchanging a solid bromance hug. Geroge took a step back, waving away Kody's sweaty stench as he took a close look at the boy.

"G, how're you—" Kody noticed G eyeing him suspiciously. "Don't recognize me? It has been a while. Got ju—st a bit of muscle now."

"Uh, no. That ain't it."

Geroge leaned in and brushed off the side of Kody's face, knocking off pieces of greasy empanada lips. Geroge cocked an eyebrow, causing Kody to pull back.

"Dude, I'm not sayin' you're a whore, but uh...I don't really know how to finish that." Geroge cast a glance over his shoulder. "Incoming!"

He pulled Kody close, cleaning off his face and spinning him around in time to see a man walk into the inn sporting a nasty burn on his face. Behind him came Cris, followed by someone who looked remarkably like Glenn. Geroge patted Kody on the back, reminding his boy to breathe.

"Where the hell did he go?" the man he assumed to be Jake asked.

"Over here, man," Geroge responded.

They all turned. Glenn, sporting a similar burn, adjusted his scratched-up glasses while Cris paused, wide-eyed, before running up and snatching Kody away from Geroge. She held him close, squeezing him until air was no longer a commodity of his lungs. Kody hesitantly returned the embrace, inhaling the light scent of cherry that seemed to surround her. He let go as Cris pulled herself away long enough to look him over, refusing to take her eyes off him.

Seeing past Cris's shoulder, Kody couldn't prevent the stupefied expression that must've covered his face as he made eye contact with Glenn. The stoic philosopher said nothing, nodding and shifting his focus to a door opening nearby. Alma came into the lobby, still adjusting her skirt as she walked.

"All right, Kodykins, no more bullshit. I'm all showered off so let's get this thing—" Alma looked up, seeing everyone—Cris—standing in the lobby. She sighed as she rubbed her forehead. "Karma'd," she muttered to herself as she wandered back into her room, slamming the door.

31. The Hacienda Anciana

"I never had much ta' live for. At least now I have somethin' I'm willin' ta' die for."

– Lorena's Prayer Book

The Hacienda Anciana, Mexico

Lorena took Arturo's hand as he helped her down off the horse. They stood before a lithic two-story edifice, older than anything Lorena had ever seen. Along the walls grew varying shades of moss that covered the history of the retreat, affectionately hiding its scars. For a place even nature itself was determined to protect, Lorena found it strange that it served as home to the lord of the banditos. She stayed close behind Arturo as they walked inside.

"Welcome to the Hacienda Anciana, operating base of the northern banditos, and home to our leader, Miguel Estaban."

Lorena continued to examine the stony establishment as they walked inside. Two great arches formed the entrance, leading to a secluded courtyard. Passing through the archway, the air felt instantly cooler due to large trees providing shade for the area. The duo received a few passing glances walking into the courtyard, though all eyes turned away when they seemed to recognize who Lorena was with. On either side of the entrance were walkways, intermixed with plants and pillars, leading to what Lorena assumed were storerooms, or possibly sleeping quarters.

In the center of the courtyard stood a small, ornate chapel. With benches on both sides of the entryway and a fountain between them, the chapel far outshined the small chantry she had maintained back home. Banditos lounged about on top of the chapel, on a balcony, in front of a breezeway that led to private quarters. She assumed it was meant for Estaban.

Realizing that Arturo was staring at her as she stopped to look around, Lorena had to remind herself where she was, and to breathe before she could form coherent thoughts.

"This...this is—" she stammered.

"This is the reason good men choose evil."

Arturo led her through a petrous arcade to a set of stairs heading underground. Though the walkway was well lit, she stopped at the cellar door, refusing to follow.

"What's down there?" she tried to peer down the stairs.

"A substructure. We keep most of our resources underground. They stay cooler, they're protected from the environment, and no prying eyes ever learn of their existence."

"So why do ya' want me down there?" she fidgeted with her fingers.

Arturo met her gaze at eye-level, taking her hand.

"I will not harm you—I promise you. No one else here will make you that offer. Now I need your help, but if you feel more comfortable waiting up here, then you may want to do so by the chapel. I think you'll find it's not unlike your old one."

Arturo turned about and headed into the basement. Holding one calloused hand in the other, Lorena started walking toward the chapel. Her heart began beating violently in her chest as she realized how many banditos had been watching her, more taking notice since her escort left. Small drops of sweat slid down her back, vivid images of her assault still emanating in her mind. Looking at both options, she gritted her teeth and disappeared behind a row of pillars, briskly hobbling to the basement.

The poor lighting throughout the stairwell didn't offer her much in the way of guidance, though it was enough for her to see the stockpiles of weapons, medicine, food, and so many other supplies that awaited at the bottom. Adjusting to the cool, moist air on her skin, she considered why the banditos had been raiding the area for so long. They had a private retreat and enough materials to lay siege to a respectable city. If anyone ever retaliated, they could barricade themselves for months, if they had a will to.

She shivered as she looked for Arturo, unaccustomed to the dank drafts that moved through the cavernous underground hall. Looking back, it was impossible to tell how large the room was, though she thought she could make out the impression of a large door in the far back. As she continued walking along, she tripped over a burlap sack, nearly falling on her face.

"Lorena! Be careful."

Arturo moved out from behind a large crate and a pile of bags to help her up. He returned to his work, and finished laying out some of the bags. Lorena watched as he rearranged them, noticing it had been done throughout most of the basement.

"Arturo, what're ya' doin'?"

"You see the resources we have. There's no one in this part of the country that can challenge us. If Estaban is ever to be stopped, he has to be cut off from his fortress."

"With bags?" Lorena looked back to the sack she tripped over.

"With bombs." Arturo watched her. "Look at the pattern I made over here." He pointed to an arrangement of sacks lain behind the crates. "I need you to do that on the other side of the cellar, and I need you to do it quickly." He shifted his gaze to the stairwell. "There'll be men coming down to check on the supplies soon. They won't question me directly because I'm a kin leader, but if they find us it'll only be a matter of time before Estaban gets involved."

Lorena looked over Arturo's pattern, reluctant to move anywhere near it.

"What if I explode it?" she asked.

"The explosives aren't armed. Don't bang them around too much, but they'll be okay until I prime them. Now hurry!"

Arturo directed Lorena to the other side of the basement, where she began laying out sacks and hiding them just as Arturo had done. Though she moved somewhat slower, she worked hard to keep up with him. Even in spite of dull pain still throbbing in her ankle, she labored and managed to cover most of her side. Exhaustion set in the longer she worked, and unable to tolerate the humidity any longer, she took a seat on one of the crates.

"Ar...Arturo." Lorena panted in between breaths. "I gotta take a break."

"Head up to the chapel. I should be able to finish this."

"Ya' sure?"

"The less time you're down here, the better. Go."

Lorena climbed off the crate, heading back to the stairs. She took her time climbing them, using the opportunity to catch her breath. As she reached the top and placed her fingers on the knob, the door swung open. It hit her nose and abruptly knocked her behind the door into the wall. She grunted, trying to restrain her voice, as a group of banditos headed into the basement. She held still, pressing her body against the cold craggy wall, trying to avoid notice. As she waited, willing even the silence to be quiet, they passed by and continued down to the basement.

She made her way back into the courtyard, taking shallow breaths as she headed to the chapel. She looked back, waiting for a ruckus of some kind, but no noise ever came out of the cellar. Taking count of the area, only a couple of banditos remained about, but most of them maintained a keen interest in her.

She reached the fountain, letting out a small sigh of relief, and cracked the door of the chapel open to peek inside. She observed a wooden altar with several sticks of incense burning before a number of banditos joined in prayer. The intoxicating scents of the incense made her stomach churn, reminding her of home. Regaining her senses, she excused herself back into the courtyard to take a seat on the bench.

She waited. For such a treacherous place, it was surprisingly quiet. She expected a bandito stronghold to be more violent, or chaotic, but it almost seemed... pleasant. She leaned back, trying to relax under the trees in the familiar warmth of the desert, but the tension in her muscles reminded her danger was never far. She listened for some sort of dilemma from the cellar, expecting Arturo to be caught at any time, but nothing came. Instead, a bristly arm forced its way around her waist as an attractive but unwelcome bandito sat next to her, taking hold of her.

"What're ya' doin'? Get offa me!" She pushed him away, but his strong grip on her waist made it difficult to move.

"It's okay, *mami*, I'm not gonna hurt ya'. I think you and me are gonna be real good friends."

"I got friends, thanks." She struggled to get him off.

"Oh yeah, where they at? Don't see 'em." The bandito looked around. "Don't worry, I think you'll like me."

The bandito stood up, half-dragging Lorena with him as they walked toward one of the rooms. Lorena struggled to pull herself away, but the more she tried, the more unwelcome attention it drew from lecherous onlookers. As they neared the room, she began to slide her arm around the bandito's waist.

"Ah, you wanna be friends now?"

Lorena nodded in response to the bandito's question.

"Good, good. I think things go much better for my friends."

She maneuvered her arm under the bandito's, still wrapped around her waist, rubbing her hand along his leg as she worked herself free. They arrived at their apparent destination, the bandito stopping in front of a door to look Lorena over. She opened the door for him, extending her arm forward as she watched his slimy tongue work its way over pristine teeth.

She nudged him through the door, quickly shifting her weight to throw her shoulder into the center of his back. The bandito's foot caught on the edge of the doorway, causing him to fall forward onto his face into the room. Lorena hauled ass toward the entrance, ignoring the pain in her ankle. A thunderous voice boomed out. "Hey!"

She froze in her tracks, craning her head toward the balcony to identify the source of the voice. Looking up, she saw a man who looked very much like Adelais staring back at her. She recoiled, squinting to make sure it was him. She felt a rough squeeze on her hand as the bandito grabbed her wrist and started dragging her back toward the room. She punched him in the arm, but it wasn't enough to detour him. While she was trying to come up with a new way to stop him, the bandito halted his march mid-step.

Lorena looked around him to see Arturo standing before the bandito with a cut on his bruised cheek, still seeping blood. He remained deadlocked with the bandito, expressionless. The bandito forced an audible stream of air through his nose, snorting as he flung Lorena's arm aside. He moved out of the way, around Arturo, and headed back to his room.

Lorena doubled back, running toward the courtyard to get a view of the chapel. She caught sight of the man who looked like Adelais crossing the breezeway above. The man watched her only momentarily, entering into the private dwelling, along with an older gentleman before they disappeared. The men gone, she lost focus as someone approached her from behind.

"Don't be afraid, it's me. We have to go."

Arturo placed his hand on Lorena's shoulder, forcing her to turn, and walking her out of the Hacienda. Lorena stopped him, trying to head back.

"Was that Adelais? What's up there?"

"We don't have time for this. We *need* to go."

"What?" Lorena shouted, flustered.

"You see my face? They thought I was stealing from the reserves. They're been dealt with for now, but even as a kin leader, there's no way to know what Estaban will do once word gets back to him. To you as well as me."

Lorena refused to move, but found herself overwhelmed by Arturo as he respectfully dragged her along. She eventually ceased struggling, accepting Arturo's help to climb onto the horse. She waited as he untied the horse, and helped him up.

"We'll look at your friend's situation once we get some distance and a chance to regroup, but for now we *have* to leave."

"Did ya' at least finish everything ya' needed ta' do?"

Arturo hesitated. "No. And now they'll be looking for me. We'll have to improvise, and do it soon."

Arturo lowered his head as Viaje began to saunter. He led the horse into a full-fledged gallop as they rushed away from the towering Hacienda with no plan and time quickly running out.

32. Bag of Blue Horses

"Only difference between playing an A note on the 5th fret of the 6th string and playing it open on the 5th is whatever suits you best. So pick your method and go with it."

— Jotted in the Tab Book of Geroge Evans

Tapping her feet repeatedly on the floorboard, Cris turned up the air conditioning as she and Kody sat in her car, the quiet reflective melodies of "Lyrical Lies" echoing in the background. She tried to keep her tongue from tasting the dried blood on her lip, having bitten it twice in the last several minutes.

"I missed you," she started.

"Missed you too," he replied.

She looked down at her Sketchers, her feet now shaking back and forth. Her combative shoelaces provided little relief and even less distraction from the angry butterflies fluttering madly in her belly. The dragging silence burned worse than any of the million questions tussling in her head. After a short while, she spoke up.

"Why didn't you call me?"

"I dunno…I think I just needed time to settle things with Alma. So you and I could have a real chance with a clean start, ya' know?"

She offered a blank stare. "No. That sounds kind of crazy. And appreciate that I've been with Geroge and Glenn for the better part of the past few days." She gave Kody the look. "But that's not what matters. After

167

all this nonsense, I finally found you, and you found Alma. So what matters to me is this: what happens now?"

She watched as Kody stared out the window, the two of them listening to Cutie is What We Aim For transition into Damien Rice's wistful "The Blower's Daughter." Cris reached out, placing a hand on his shoulder, but received no response. She retracted her arm, lowering her head. Listening to the slow ballad a moment longer, she turned away, opening her door and stepping out into the heat.

She walked back toward the inn, taking a seat on the steps outside. She laid her head on her knees as a dusty breeze blew by, tossing mahogany locks about. Footsteps approached from behind as Geroge plopped himself down next to her. "Trouble in paradise?" he asked. She nodded, not bothering to lift her head up.

"Ah, finally somethin' I know a thing about! So check it out, back home I got this lawyer I work with. Now he doesn't know much about the law—"

"So you mean he's a regular guy?" Cris asked.

"Huh." Geroge paused for a moment, chuckling. "Yeah, I guess so. Anyway, we got to talkin' about copyrights over a not-love song, and the guy tells me, 'Love is like a bag of blue horses—it can be used for a hundred different things, but no one knows what the hell it's actually for.'"

Cris looked up at him, unable to restrain a self-defeating grin as her eyebrow cocked.

"Yeah, I know right? I still think he's kinda wacked, but he might not be all wrong. If there's a point there, I think it's that ya' do what ya' want with what ya' got. Don't matter what it looks like or how it shapes up." Geroge patted her on the back.

"Ever wonder if your head just takes up space?"

Cris looked up to see Alma standing behind Geroge, knocking on his fuzzy brain carrier. Cris watched as Geroge leaned back, looking up to see Alma and apparently enjoying the view.

"Good to see you too, Alms'ter."

"My charming brother and the cat whisperer are apparently having what passes for a think tank session in there. Figured with all your drugstore philosophy you wouldn't wanna miss out."

Alma tapped him out, waiting for Geroge to excuse himself before taking her place next to Cris. She leaned forward, resting her head on her knees, looking Cris directly in the eyes.

"'Sup bitch?"

Cris rolled her eyes. "Right back at you," she paused before continuing, "What'd you do to *my* boyfriend?"

Alma reeled, falling back onto the steps of the inn trying to control an explosive fit of laughter. Eventually calming down, she took a moment to recompose herself.

"No, no, no, slut action Barbie. The last thing in this glorious dust hole of a world I'm going to do is waste any more time fighting with you over Kody Lehane."

Alma clutched the beaded hemp necklace around her neck, pulling at it until the string gave way. The necklace snapped, loosing some beads onto the ground. Alma gathered them up along with the ones still on the string.

"See this?" Alma showed her the beads. "All yours." She rubbed them in Cris's hair. "I spent so long holding a grudge against you, and you know what it did for me?" Alma pointed to faint circles under her eyes. "This. That's it. You screwed me over, and somehow I got the shit-end of the stick. So I don't really care about all that anymore. It's really not worth it." Alma paused as she got up to leave. Cris watched as she waited for the words Alma seemed to be contemplating. "But there's one thing that is."

Cris looked up, beads falling out of her hair as she tried to conceal her sullen expression.

"Glenn's in there. Kody told me you guys left him for dead, so imagine my surprise when he comes walkin' in with my brother saying you're the reason he's alive. Apparently, karma has Dmetri Martin as one of its writers. Anyway, I'm tired of all this. With everything else, and the fact that you didn't narc on me for taking your car, I'd say we're as close as we're gonna get to being square. So let's call this what it is: you're an evil. prudish bitch, I'm a better not-so-prudish bitch."

A half-smirk crossed Cris's face. "We've been over this: I'm not a prude." Alma frowned, pushing Cris over.

"Please, you're as prissy as they come. I'd take you on right now if I thought you could go half a round with me. But you're all bones these days. Pretty sure one of those wavy car lot balloon guys could take you right now." Alma sighed, rubbing her forehead. "Whatever. Go screw Lehane already. God knows that kid needs to get laid." Alma hesitated before adding, "And I'm sure he misses you."

Alma headed back into the ego-stroking convention taking place in the lobby. Cris stood up, brushing herself off. She started back toward her car, taking several deep breaths. She clenched her fist repeatedly. Getting halfway around the inn, she saw a horse rapidly approaching with two riders. Unfamiliar with rural life, she watched in wonderment as they approached.

As they finally arrived, she observed a rugged-looking cowboy accompanied by a tough young woman. The man tied the horse down as he helped the woman off, and the two made their way into the inn. Hearing them interact with her friends, curiosity got the better of her as she changed course and headed back inside.

"This is Cris. She's the woman Kody's so very much obsessed with," Alma introduced Cris. "These two are Lorena, my cousin, and Arturo, a well-mannered bandito leader who probably gets into more fights than Ryan Atwood."

"Oh my God…is that Mickeyman?" Lorena exclaimed, noticing Cris's mousey tank top.

"What? No." Cris backed up.

"Nah? Never actually seen 'im, figured maybe it was. Well, lemme show ya' around. Arturo?"

"I'll talk to them." He nodded.

Lorena took Cris by the hand and led her back to the room she was staying in. Lorena closed the door behind them, offering Cris a seat on the bed. Cris watched as Lorena sat in a nearby chair, tending to her ankle.

"So you're Kody's girl, huh?"

Cris offered an insincere smile. "We've met before—when you came to visit Alma forever ago. But since it has been that long—it's good to meet you. What happened to your ankle?"

"Bandito crushed it." Lorena seemed lost in thought as she lifted her ankle. "This is one a' the nicer things they've done."

"Why're things so bad out here? How haven't the police stopped them?" Cris asked.

Lorena stared at Cris for a good moment, setting her ankle down and finishing off a glass of water.

"I guess life's different here than where yer from. Even if we had some kinda real police, I don't think most a' 'em would be volunteerin' ta' get shot up ta' make a point."

"Maybe you just haven't gone about it the right way."

Lorena canted her head, her eyes slowly drifting to the side as she considered Cris's words. She lifted her head and continued. "Maybe," she paused, "But we got an idea ta' fix it."

"What?" Cris sat up.

"Arturo and I got a plan. But that's fer tomorrow, and it's nothin' ya need ta' worry about. Reason I asked ya' in here," Lorena lowered her voice as she leaned close, "Was fer you and Kody. I won't be needin' a bed that big any time soon, so I figure someone should get some use outta it." Lorena sat back again, her voice returning to normal volume. "Gonna head back out there. Arturo and I got some more plannin' ta' do before we get everyone on board. If I see Kody, I'll send 'im your way."

Lorena headed back into the lobby. Cris lay back on the bed, clasping her hands in front of her eyes. She lifted them up, dropping them on her face, only to lift them up and repeat the process. She exhaled, continuing this cycle for some time. Taking slower and deeper breaths, her eyelids became heavy, stealing consciousness away from her.

* * *

Geroge opened the driver's side door of the convertible, taking a seat and throwing on Vertical Horizon's "There and Back Again." He looked over to his brother from another mother, watching Kody slumber the sweet sleep of the angels. He tapped on Kody's head, tapping out the chorus to the introspective "Lines upon Your Face."

"Dude, seriously, ya' smell like ass. And I'm not talkin' Burrito Bell ass, I'm talkin' full-on happy hour buffet at Pancho's House of Greasy Delights ass."

He watched as Kody came to, looking around and needing a moment to remember where he was.

"What? Oh, sorry. Still haven't gotten used to the food."

"Yeah huh. Mini K's doin' well, just so ya' know. Her b-day party went off without a hitch. Picked up a stuffed kitty for her, just like ya' asked." Geroge reclined his seat, throwing his boots up onto the dashboard. "But on to other news. Tell me brother man—what's the deal with you and the lady gorgeous? Don't see much lovin' goin' on."

Geroge glanced through the windshield, watching as the sun began its retreat and catching Kody's reflection in the glass. Kody sat rubbing his eyes, equal mix of waking up and being enamored with the same scene. Geroge spoke up.

"Ri—ght. I forgot in the drama land you come from everything's about the latest happenings of your cock. Well, wanna hear a fun fact that ain't about you?" Geroge paused. "Jeany's pregnant." Kody looked over Geroge, saying nothing. "Anyone in half the damn town could be that kid's dad, but I got a feelin'. Don't matter much if it's me or not anyway. Still love the woman, still gonna love the little bastard."

Geroge chuckled, rubbing his matted hair as he watched the horizon devour the sun. Kody offered him a hand, the two shaking on the news.

"G, that's amazing, man! I mean, it's amazing right?" Kody looked over, waiting for Geroge's response. Geroge nodded. "Congrats, man."

"Yeah, thanks. Just found out not too long ago myself, and I didn't wanna tell ya over the phone. It's scary man, it is. It's gonna be hard, and I dunno if we can pull it off. But we're gonna give it our best. The reason I'm tellin' ya this though, other than because I didn't really think it through, is because it got me thinkin' about a lot of things."

Geroge raised his pointer finger and stuck it in Kody's face. "You, my friend, need to stop screwin' around. I don't give a shit if you decide to stick out with the princess or go back to your old fuck-buddy, but I'm tired of watchin' these sweet young ladies gettin' torn apart because of you. Neither one of these fine women deserve the shit you're puttin' 'em through."

"G—"

"That's it brother, said my piece. The rest is on you. So get your shit together so we can go home and Jeany can stop cursin' us both. Got a pregnant girlfriend to look after and you got a godchild to start preppin' for. 'Cause the last thing I want my future son or son-ette to learn is how to pimp from you."

Kody looked over to Geroge, grinning.

"Oh, Jeany's gotta be hatin' me right now."

"You and me both, brother. You and me both. So go, shoo! Fix your shit!"

Geroge waved his hands in Kody's face, pushing him toward the car door. He kept pushing until Kody climbed out of the car and headed indoors. Finally getting a moment to himself, Geroge cranked the radio up and started rocking his head back and forth, practicing his air guitar to Four Star Mary.

33. Sparking the Fire

"I'm pretty much convinced that 'karma' is just another term for 'You're getting the exact opposite of what you expected,'—even if what you expected was the exact opposite of what you should've gotten."

– Alma's Diary

Glenn stepped out of the inn, taking in the sight of the small town at night. He scratched his head, his fingers getting dirty in the oily mess his hair had become in the desert heat. Something brushed against his leg. He looked down, expecting to see his furry companion. He was met not by the regal furr-line, but by brush weeds grazing against his pant leg. A car door slammed not too far off in the distance; he remained in place as he watched Kody approach.

"E-evening," Glenn said.

"Hey," Kody responded.

Kody stopped short of the entrance to the inn, standing a couple of feet behind Glenn. Though he paid no direct attention, Glenn could feel Kody's eyes examining him.

"You know, I d-do speak. You're more than welcome to ask your q-questions."

"Heh, yeah, no…uh…right," Kody stammered. "I dunno. Mind's in other places. This is a little weird for me, man. Last time I saw you, you were pretty much dead. I mean, seriously *at least* one foot in the grave. And then there's that whole you-tried-to-screw-my-girlfriend thing, which I

173

guess I should be mad about, but it's not like I can even really say anything," Kody rambled on.

"L-let's simplify this, s-shall we? We've b-both made trang-gressions that neither of us want to add-dress. Let's just say we're g-good."

Kody paused for a moment and shrugged. "Works for me." Kody's arm fell around Glenn's shoulder, the latter turning toward him trying to figure out what was going on. Kody threw him a reckless grin while he mussed Glenn's hair.

"I know we don't always get along, but it's still good to see ya', buddy."

"L-likewise. Don't you have some 'patching up' to do?" Glenn nodded toward the inn doors.

"Hm... yeah. S'pose I should get back to that, then."

Kody patted Glenn on the back, and moseyed on back into the inn. Glenn exhaled, digging his hands into his pocket. His fingers explored the entirety of his pants multiple times. Frantically, he kept searching until he remembered what had happened to his medication.

"R-right..."

He reached up, scratching his cheek, trying not to pick at the scab forming over the cigarette burn on his face. He slid his fingers over it slowly.

"I c-can do this."

He looked off into the distance, admiring the view of the stars over the mountains. Titans of the land displaying their dominance, breaking free of the loam plane. Was it insurrection? Did the tectonic plates curse their place being buried so far below the realm of the living? Did Tartarus not treat them well? Or did they possess an inert longing to meet their opposition in the empyrean—to see the celestial plane? Perhaps they longed only for equality—to feel the warmth of the sun instead of the heat of the earth. The mother versus the father. Glenn shook his head.

Ignoring the mountains, he rolled up his sleeve to alleviate some of the heat. His hands grazed the larger of his scars on his arm, fingers gliding over them slowly. Not so different from the scar on his cheek, except *that* was a gift from a friend. Could he not give himself gifts, returning to his craft once more? He was an artist, after all. He began digging his nails into his flesh, feeling if he could feel. The discord of faux pain brought a distorted sense of reality to the forefront.

"Stop!" he muttered to himself through gritted teeth.

He remained shaken up, loosening his nails without letting go. He took slow, shallow breaths, calming himself for a minute before sitting down. Finally letting go of his wrist, he leaned forward, resting his head in his palms. He heard the surreal dreaminess of Mitsuda Yasunori's "Radical Dreamers" hummed from behind as a pair of comforting arms gently wrapped themselves around his collar. Soft breasts pressed against his back as Alma's face popped up over his right shoulder.

"Hey, peaches. How's it going?" Alma asked, brimming smile across her face.

"P-peaches? Might be a better n-nickname for you."

"Oh, you're funny now! I like that." She laughed, forcing her bosom against his shoulder blade. "Better?"

Glenn shifted uncomfortably, without moving away. He tried to look her in the eyes, but could see little other than strawberry brunette hair with her being so close. The scent of her sweat mingling with light perfume left him unprepared.

"Aw, don't go all stiff on me. Er—you know what I mean."

"I s-suppose I'm at a loss f-for words."

"Hm…" Alma hesitated. "Was kinda awkward last time we saw each other and all. What'dya say we take this inside and get everything cleared up?"

Without waiting for a response, Alma stood up. She took Glenn's hand into her own, leading him back inside.

* * *

Alma directed Glenn to the bed, sitting him down next to her. She looked him over, taking his wrist into her hands and examining the deepest cut.

"This is the one…the one Cris found, right? The morning after I left?" she asked, thumbing the scar. Glenn nodded.

"I'm so sorry, Glenn. I lost myself and I took it out on you. You didn't deserve that."

Glenn offered no response.

"I'm not asking for forgiveness. I just want you to know I didn't mean to hurt you the way I did. You tried to help me even though you were sick, and I bailed on you. I was in a bad place, and I want you to know that's not gonna happen again." Alma looked over to Glenn, who kept his focus on the wall. "How're you holding up?" She turned his head with her finger to meet his gaze.

"T-trying to avoid reminiscing, m-mostly."

Alma canted her head. Receiving no acknowledgment, she stood up before him, hands on her hips as she looked down to him.

"Are you mad at me? I get the feeling you've been avoiding me ever since you came back, which strikes me as kind of weird since last time I saw you, you tried to fuck me."

"Last time I s-saw you, you threw a lamp at my h-head."

She cast her gaze to the side.

"B-before that, you refused me at the park in T-Texarkana, and b-before that, shot me down in T-tennessee. As I recall, you 'c-can be the spark that b-brightens up my day, but you c-can't be the fire the lights my l-life.' A little n-narcissistic, isn't it? Expecting to be a s-savior for someone you d-don't even c-care about." Glenn paused. "Having b-been one, I'm not a fan of lost c-causes."

Alma stood before him, speechless, as her arms fell to her side. She drew her bottom lip in with her teeth, avoiding eye contact with him as she scanned the floor. She caught sight of a pair of panties she had forgotten to pick up earlier and subtly kicked them under the bed. Glenn rose from the bed, making his way to the door.

"Glenn, wait." She grabbed his arm.

"F-for what?"

"I don't—just don't go, okay? I get that you're bitter about before, but everything was different then. You can't be mad at me for not cheating on my boyfriend." She paused. "That week, anyway." She tried to contain a self-depreciating laugh. "We're different people now. You're the reason I found my brother, and I swore I would help you get better."

She leaned in, thumbing the scar on his cheek. "And I *will* help you get better. The same way you helped me. So let's stick together on this." She slowly brought her face close to his, halted by his index finger against her lips, separating them from his own.

"You want us to 'g-get better'? Then do it p-properly. This isn't a situation that's just g-going to be smoothed over by sex. I t-told you I loved you, Alma. Nothing is going to happen b-between us unless you c-can honestly tell me the same."

Alma brushed her hair behind her ear as she looked at him. She stepped back, turning around to put some space between them. Tapping her foot on the floor, she licked her upper lip, tasting salty sweat and a small piece of empanada from earlier in the day. She turned back around.

"I can't do that."

"I d-didn't ask you to." Glenn replied as he moved to leave.

Alma pushed him back onto the bed. "Stay. I'm not gonna pressure you to get groiny with me—even though I think we could both use it—just stay here, okay? Keep me company."

Glenn exhaled. Alma searched around the room, looking for a relatively clean set of clothes. She asked Glenn to turn around, dropping her pants and taking off her shirt as she lost the bra. She slipped into an old t-shirt then placed her hand on Glenn's shoulder. She began to turn him around, doing a quick once-over to look herself over one last time. After a moment of consideration, she left him as he was, grabbing some lounge shorts off the floor and pulling them over her underwear. Dressed in presentable pajamas, she turned him around.

"See? Sexy free." She looked down to see her sleeping t-shirt was low-cut. "Well, mostly. But I'm not hearing any complaints."

"I s-should go."

"Oh stop. You don't have anywhere *to* go. Pretty low on bed space as it is. Lucky for you, I'm great at sharing."

She dragged Glenn onto the bed, laying him down. With him finally situated and not trying to escape, she lay down next to him, resting her head on his chest as she nudged his shoes off with her feet.

"I let you lay on me last time—it's only fair." She looked up to him. As always, he looked uncertain of himself. She could relate. He finally took his glasses off, laying them on the nightstand nearby. She lay comfortably, pulling his arm around her shoulder, over her, and wrapping it around herself. She rested on his chest, finally able to relax for a little while.

He wasn't the most comfortable thing ever—certainly not her snuggy bear—but she wasn't alone, and neither was he. Reaching for the mp3 player on the nightstand, she put The Killers' last hope for a happy ending, "Dustland Fairytale," on quietly in the background. Before she knew it, the rise and fall of his sleepy breaths nursed her to sleep.

34. Firm Believer

"Where I come from, it's important ta' understand the good side of bad."

– Lorena's Prayer book

"I always wanted a pony," Lorena whispered to Viaje, standing out beneath the stars. She remained low-key behind the motel with Arturo's mare, occasionally keeping a watchful eye on Geroge sleeping in the driver's seat of Cris's car. She drew her fingers through the steed's mane, looking into her deep dark eyes. So similar to those of Perrito. "I bet you're not easy ta' take care of, but I'd treat ya' right. We're not that different, after all. Both strong ladies takin' care of the guys we look after. 'Course, ya'd probably end up getting killed or running off before long, way things have been."

Lorena remained with Viaje, keeping herself alert and listening for any wildlife that might pose a threat to either of them. As she stood with the mare, she found herself lost in the mystery of the waning crescent moon. She'd never had time to think about the moon, or the mysteries of life. Mild pains in her gut, however, kept her from pondering the mysteries too deeply. "Figures," she muttered to herself, forcing a pained grin at her new equine friend.

"What'dya think—ya' figure Ade's a bad man?" she asked Viaje, trying to distract herself.

"He's a man, period. Whether you want to label him good or bad is simply a judgment call," Arturo spoke up, coming around the side of the motel.

Lorena jumped, startled by his presence. "Arturo," she hesitated, "before you said Ade killed your brother. Is that true?"

"Word I received was that a man named Adelais killed Alejandro a couple nights ago. Came from a trusted partner, so I've no reason to doubt him. Do you?"

Lorena recalled Adelais and Siggy leaving the night they had taken her to the makeshift clinic, thinking about how quiet both of them had been when she'd seen them the next morning. She then thought about her conversation with Adelais on whether Alejandro would ever come back to finish what he'd started.

"The first time I met 'im—your brother—he tried ta' choke the life outta me. An' ya' just let him." Lorena turned a sharp eye toward him.

"I'm no more responsible for Alejandro than you are Adelais."

Lorena drew her fingers through Viaje's mane once more before taking a step back, directing her full attention to Arturo. "I don't get you. Ya' pretend ta' be all noble, prayin' at churches and talkin' about bein' forced inta' leadin' banditos, yet you got no problem killin' people and defendin' murders."

Arturo drew his revolver, looking it over. He opened the cylinder, dropping the rounds in his palm as he shook his dark, curly hair out of his face. He tossed the weapon to Lorena, who fumbled as she tried to catch it.

"Look it over," he said. "Would you call that weapon evil? Does it plan nothing but the most foul of crimes? Though it is a gift from the Lord of Banditos himself, it is a piece of metal, like this"—he handed her a round— "and nothing more. I am a man who was told he could change the world. Looking around, I did not like the world I saw, so I accepted that charge. However, a new world cannot be built from, nor upon, nothing. It requires resources, time, devotion, manpower. So there are times when I must kill: to gain what I need to fix the evils of our world, to stop wicked men from causing greater catastrophes. Like letting Alejandro choke you to death, so he'd listen when I implored him to ignore an order to murder a village, or agree to turn against Estaban when we were ready." He took the weapon and loaded a single round, handing it back to her.

"You may call me evil, if you wish, and if you think it better I die now than continue my wicked ways, then take your shot. But I suggest you think about everything that's transpired, and consider what life will be like for you and your loved ones—Adelais—if Estaban is allowed to continue his rule."

Lorena made no hesitation, setting the gun at Arturo's feet. She looked around, checking the ground before taking a seat against the side of the building to relieve the pressure on her ankle. She looked back up to Arturo.

"Good or bad, I ain't a killer," she said.

"Good or bad, sometimes I am," he replied. "That's why I pray." He took a seat next to her, looking at his palms. "My hands are responsible for too much filth to ever be clean, but no man may say if that's true for my spirit. It becomes difficult to see the way forward when the path you've left is littered with the dead. So I seek guidance that I may not become lost, like your friend has."

Lorena leaned her head back, looking up to the sky. She remembered when her mother tried to teach her the constellations: organizing and categorizing the heavens. She'd never paid attention. It didn't matter what their names were—they were shiny and beautiful, and watched over her. That was all she'd ever needed to know.

"Adelais killed your brother." She brushed her hair behind her ear, and began tapping her thumb against her thigh. "And you said he's a bandito. Workin' for Estaban, I guess that's kinda true. I dunno if he was right or wrong, and I don't think I ever will. But he's 'bout the only family I got left, and I need ta' get 'im back. Ever since Siggy…he's lost his path, and if I can't bring 'im home, he'll never find it. He went ta' Estaban to try an' stop all a' this, 'jes like we're doin' now." She looked over to him. "Promise me no matter what, we'll bring 'im home."

Arturo stood up, taking a step closer to his mare. He checked the reins and patted her mane. He nodded to his mare, turning back to Lorena.

"Good men die. You know this already. And yet, you ask me to save the man that murdered my brother." He turned back to Viaje, untying her from the post behind the inn. "If Adelais can help our cause, then he may be worth saving. But I've no sympathy for the devil, or his advocates." Arturo tossed Viaje's reins to Lorena. "She likes you, and like you, she thinks too much. Take her out to clear her head. We'll talk about our plan when you get back." Arturo walked off, not looking back.

Lorena stood up, watching as Arturo approached a man in a leather duster off in the distance. Changing her focus, she looked down, reins in hand. She walked up to the mare, looking her over as she drew her fingers through the horse's hair. "What's on yer mind?" she asked the mare. The steed looked back at her with intrepid eyes.

Lorena checked the mount, gliding her fingers over the rough leather as she adjusted the saddle. She placed her good foot in the iron stirrup, tossing her injured ankle over the side of the saddle. Situated, she took a deep breath as she dug her good heel into Viaje's rib. The steed began to trot, sauntering away from the inn.

Lorena took some time learning how to ride alone, becoming comfortable with Viaje, and remembering her earlier rides with Arturo. She made a few laps around the town, causing Viaje to pick up the pace each time.

"Inwardly cleansed, interiorly enlightened, an' inflamed by the fire of the Holy Spirit, may we ever be able to follow in the divine footprints that guide our way…"

As the two became comfortable with each other, they broke into a full gallop, leaving the town behind and heading off for a quiet ride through the darkly clouded desert sky night.

35. Karma Payment Plan

"When in doubt, go with it; better to regret what you did than what you didn't."

– Kody's Notebook

Kody hesitated a moment longer outside the door before walking away from the room he shared with Alma. He stopped by the night clerk's desk, asking for pencil and paper, and returned to his seat in the lobby.

He sketched sketchy sketches into the sparse plane, burying graphite into the blank universe he tried to create. A ribbon and a bow followed the flow of the circles he spun into madness, resembling either a little girl or a narcissistic pig. Beside his excuse for some sort of sad creation lay his illustrated friends: the duck of combustion, the feline cantankerous, and now a poor puppy with a bad party hat. Though he was no artist, he couldn't call this art.

Turning back to a more familiar craft, he tried spinning words to define an intimate dilemma.

Bitter, burned, buried. The life of a sinful witch, using her gift to help others. Their frail understanding of their own failures must've been her fault. And so her ash was left in a hole to serve as their new albatross. Yet even then, evil happened. Clearly, the dead witch was still at fault

He set the paper down.

He stared at the forgettable ceiling tiles that seemed a poor choice for a poor establishment. His head resting against the back of the chair, he began to drift in and out of consciousness. At some point through his drifting, a swift kick to his ankle brought the world back to his senses. "Damnit, Alm! I'm awake!" He sat up, watching Lorena shake her head as she took a seat across from him.

"I gave up my room fer you, ya' know. On account of I figured you'd be usin' it."

Kody rubbed the sleep from his eyes. "What're you talking about?"

"Cris? Your girlfriend? Gave her my room. For ya' two ta'…ya' know. Figured with all the squabbling between you an' Alma, you must care a lot about Cris. Am I wrong?"

Kody sighed as he rubbed his forehead. "I can't explain how grateful I am for everything you've done, Lorena, but please…stay out of this. I didn't get in between you and Adelais after Siggy…"

Kody trailed off, the pain dwelling in Lorena's eyes more than enough to make him regret ever speaking. He searched for some way to make it right, but he knew right then he was an idiot.

Lorena spoke up. "I get it, okay? After everything, I don't know if Ade and I could ever—especially when he reminds me *so* much of Sig… "She looked away before continuing. "I'll deal with my own problems. But you, Kody, I honestly hope ya' never lose someone ya' love."

Lorena stood up, carefully but firm, and stepped over to him. She leaned forward, pulling him close enough to kiss his forehead. She released him, looking into his eyes. "Because when ya' do, all that's left are the memories, and the time ya wasted on doin' everything but lovin' 'em back."

Kody watched as she solemnly wandered outside. He sat in the chair, thinking about how much time he had already squandered. Time he'd never get back. Matier's speech came to mind, chastising him for wishing he had a little more time, even if only for a moment. Yet here he was, pitying himself over indecision when friends like Siggy had never wasted a moment, and still never had a chance to live.

He balled his fist until his knuckles cracked, slamming it on the arm of the chair. He stood up, ignored by the inn's jaded evening manager, as he headed over to Cris's room. He knocked on her door. After a moment, she appeared from behind the door dressed in little more than the button-up shirt he had left her.

"Kody, hey."

His blood rushed in the wrong direction as his eyes perused her body. He knew how sweet she tasted, and he was nothing short of a sexual tyrannosaurus. But having damned himself on forbidden fruit before, Geroge's advice caused him to pause just once before following his gut, or any other appendages. Kody was becoming adept at regretting his words as he spoke.

"Get dressed. I'll wait out here," he said.

"Everything all right?" she canted her head.

He nodded, and waited for her in the lobby. Before long, she reappeared in the sundress she had worn by the riverside in Texarkana. It still accentuated her features so well—her adorable freckles, her coy smile, the way so many random strands of hair still fell into place in just the right ways. Keeping his eyes all over her, he hardened. Metapod quickly came to mind. He suppressed a laugh while distracting himself enough to focus on the moment. He took her by the hand and led her out onto the porch, the two of them taking a seat on the steps.

"Kody—"

"Let's just take it slow."

He put his arm around her, resting her head on his shoulder—just as they had first done the night of G's concert. Her airy scent— intermingled with a fine tinge of sweat—danced through his nostrils as they watched the glowing lamps of the night sky, listening to nothing other than the sound of each other's breaths. Despite how long they had been apart, they still knew exactly what the other meant. He reached around, pulling the hair from her eyes and tucking it behind her ear. He continued to draw his fingers through her hair.

"Ever my gentleman," Cris muttered as she hugged him tightly, starting to drift off. A light blanket pushed up behind Kody from the other side. He turned back to catch a glimpse of Lorena's half-hearted smile as she turned and walked off. He wrapped it around Cris, who despite the heat, was surely just a bit chilly. She lifted her head enough to give him a light kiss on the cheek, wrapping him up in the blanket with her. He watched from his periphery as her eyelids finally gave way, maintaining watch over his princess as she slept.

* * *

Kody reluctantly opened his eyes as sunlight shone onto his face through the window. Still lying in bed, he pulled the covers over his head until Cris came out of the bathroom, now in jeans and a cozy polo. He rolled over to a knock at the door, watching as Cris answered it. In its frame stood Geroge with his classic aviator sunglasses, waiting.

"Y'all ready?"

"Yes, just give us a minute."

"C'mon, chickarita, grab up your stuff. Everyone's waitin' in the lobby."

Kody climbed out of bed and quickly got dressed as he and Cris grabbed up her belongings, most of his own things having been lost in the fire. They headed out to the otherwise deserted lobby, where a heated debate was underway.

"I ain't doin' it, ya' shit sack, so you can go fuck yerself!"

Jake was about an inch from Arturo's face, the latter looking less than amused with his hand resting on his pistol.

"I didn't make a request. You got Estaban's daughter killed, which makes yours one of the most valuable heads around. Lucky for you, you're more useful to me alive than dead. But if you don't cooperate, I have no problem selling off your corpse and improvising."

Alma jumped in the fray, working with Lorena to try to separate the two as Glenn sat back and observed.

"Hey! No one is killing Jake. That's the end of that very short story. Now, if that means we have to play along with your shenanigans for a bit to get outta here, then maybe we can work something out. Not like I wanna leave Lorena in danger," Alma offered up.

"Then tell your brother to stand down and fall in line," Arturo replied.

"Hey, I don't take orders anymore, asswipe!"

Jake shoved Arturo, causing him to fall back onto the floor. Arturo hopped back up onto his feet, grabbing Jake by the collar and running him into the wall, putting his revolver to Jake's throat. Kody leaned in, moving to help, but Cris held him back. Arturo brought his face close to Jake's, nostrils flaring as they came eye to eye.

"I don't want to kill you. But that's what this very capable pistol is aimed to do if you move against me again," Arturo articulated clearly.

Adjusting his glasses, Glenn stepped up to the two, drawing their attention. Glenn raised his hands, showing they were empty, before slowly lowering Arturo's weapon and separating the two.

"Ar-Arturo, Jake and I will be h-happy to assist you," Glenn said.

"Atty, the hell?"

Glenn turned to Jake, looking at him over his glasses and nodding. Jake snorted and rolled his eyes to the side, taking a seat in a nearby chair next to Alma. Arturo holstered his weapon, inspecting Glenn with a stern expression.

"You're willing to help?"

"You've st-stated your position c-clearly. If your plan is only to use J-jake as bait, then it should pose little d-danger to him, and I imagine you'll p-provide substantial c-compensation, correct?"

Arturo looked Glenn over, chuckling to himself. "You want me to pay him?"

"W-why not? A k-kin leader can surely afford it, and it seems in line with your pr-practices. Given both the d-desperation and necessity of J-jake's assistance, I'd say everyone wins."

Arturo let his head roll back, laughing to himself for a minute before saying anything. He finally held his hand out to Glenn, the two exchanging a handshake. Arturo turned to Jake, who watched nonchalantly.

"You've got clever friends. Stick by them—they just might keep you alive."

"Arturo, give us a minute?" Lorena asked.

Arturo nodded and headed outside. Kody and Cris made their way into the lobby, joining the discussion.

"What's going on?" Cris asked.

"Arturo's gonna blow up the bandito hideout, and he wants to use Jake as bait. And apparently Glenn over here thought it'd be funny to try to sell my brother." Alma leaned against a wall watching both Glenn and Jake unamused.

Lorena stepped up, managing to walk on her ankle well enough, and clarified the situation. "Glenn prolly just saved Jake's life, Alm. Even if Arturo has good ideas, he's still a bandito, an' unlike the rest of ya', I know what banditos'll do ta' get what they want."

"Then why help them?" Alma asked.

"'Cause even though it ain't great, Arturo's way is the closest ta' gettin' peace we got."

"All right, all right...fuck me." Alma sighed, rubbing her head. "If Jake's stuck in this damn thing, then so am I. And so are you, Glenn, for forcing us to go along with this mess. Go ahead and lead us down the rabbit hole, *jefe*."

Glenn nodded. Kody noticed Geroge take off his sunglasses, standing next to himself and Cris. Geroge looked over to Kody, and then Cris, and interrupted the group meeting.

"Hey, this cavalcade of craziness sounds fun and all, but uh…who's driving the bus home?"

The group in the lobby looked at Geroge, and then behind him to Kody and Cris. Geroge shrugged and continued.

"Hey. Don't look me at like I'm runnin' away or somethin'. Ain't been in a real fight since second grade, and I'm thinkin' my grown-up debut against some pissed off dudes with lots of bullets ain't gonna work out too well. Wish y'all the best, but my life's back home, which is where I need ta' be headin'." He turned to Cris. "You drivin', *chica?*"

"Yes. Go load up your bag."

Kody watched as Geroge headed out the door, followed by Cris. The rest of the group turned to Kody. Jake laughed behind him, nudging Alma as Kody turned away and began carrying Cris's bag outside.

"Good luck, Kody, ya' two stay safe," Lorena said, lowering her head.

Alma sprung off the wall, running over to Kody. She ripped the bag from his hand and tossed it on the floor.

"Are you fucking kidding me? *This* is how you have my back? You *can't* bail on me now."

Glenn cocked an eyebrow, which did not escape Kody's notice as Alma confronted him. She grabbed Kody's face and forced him to look at her.

"Kody, when this is thing is over, we're all going home. Together. I don't care what or who you do after that. But right here, right now? We're gonna need every person we can get to make sure that happens."

"What about Cris?" he asked.

"Yes, what about me?"

Cris marched into the center of the lobby, breaking in between the two and knocking Alma back. Alma stood her ground, unwilling to back down.

"Come with us." Alma asked, taking Cris's hands.

"What?" Cris recoiled.

"I meant every word I said. I don't wanna lose anyone. That means *everybody* counts. So come with us. C'mon Crissy, let's bury our issues for now and go home together…please."

Kody shifted back and forth, watching the two. His strawberry brunette and cherry princess. The only women he'd ever loved. The best of friends who grew to hate each other because of him and his lust. But maybe there was a way to change that. His gaze rested on Alma when Cris turned back to him, worry decorating her face. She chewed her lip. Kody spoke up, "I did promise I'd have her back. Besides, didn't you make it your mission to look after Glenn?"

"What? That doesn't even..." Cris trailed off, turning back to Glenn. She looked at him with fondness, and then at Lorena and Alma. "...and G?"

"He can wait in the car, I guess." Kody shrugged.

"So how does this work? What do we do?" Cris asked.

Kody watched as Jake sat in his chair, using a knife to clean his fingernails. Alma turned to Jake, and then Glenn looking for answers.

"There are e-eight of us, so I propose we go in two t-teams. From what I saw, Art-turo rides a horse, and Lorena is g-good with it as well?" Glenn looked to Lorena, who nodded in response. "So Lorena and Art-turo will ride ahead as the advance p-party, and the r-rest of us will squeeze int-to the convertible."

"Where we'll go and sell my happy ass ta' the highest homicidal bidder. Cheers!" Jake offered a toast.

"Yeah, what about that?" Alma asked.

"Once we're s-staged and in p-place, that's where ph-phase two comes in," Glenn responded.

"Phase two?"

Glenn smirked, drawing everyone in as he began laying out his plan.

36. The Apostate's Rebellion

"Hope isn't a method."

– The Annals of the Romero Family

The Hacienda Anciana

Arturo rode toward the towering arches of the Hacienda at sundown with someone bound and sitting behind him. They rapidly approached the steps, meeting guards at the gate. Two banditos trained their weapons on Arturo as he climbed off his horse and unloaded his bounty.

"Arturo Romero, Estaban wants to see you. Now," one bandito said.

"There're rumors you've gone rogue. They're just rumors, right?" the other asked.

Arturo pulled his bounty up, offering him forward to the banditos. "I've been doing what I had to do. Estaban will want to see this man much more than me." Arturo passed through the entryway. The two banditos followed close behind. Arturo made his way to the courtyard, casually glancing toward the basement that was now sealed off and guarded. He looked over to his partner, who chuckled nervously in response. Arturo turned back to the two banditos escorting him.

"What're you two waiting for? You don't recognize Jacob Agramonte? Take him to Estaban now!" Arturo shouted.

"*That's* Jake? *The* Jake? He don't even look like one a' us," one of the banditos sputtered.

Arturo dropped his hand to his holster, glaring at the banditos and offering the hostage to them. The two banditos secured their guest and started marching him upstairs. One of the banditos kept a keen eye on Arturo as they marched.

"What're you looking at? The post you left unmanned? Don't worry about it—I'll find someone who will actually do the job. You'll be lucky if I decide it isn't worth addressing myself and leave for Estaban."

The two banditos, seemingly confused, increased the pace of their march to a set of stairs leading to the second level of the Hacienda. Arturo walked back to the now unmanned gate, scoping out the surrounding area outside of the Hacienda. He found Lorena, Alma, and Glenn crouched near the wall, hiding near his horse as a red car drove off in the distance.

"They on their way?" he asked.

"C-cris and Geroge will get it done," Glenn replied.

"All right, let's go." Arturo nodded to Jake, who stood smoking in the shadows.

The two headed back inside, Jake wearing a large cowboy hat with his duster to conceal his face. With the supply basement cut off, they were forced to reevaluate their plan of attack.

"No way we're gettin' ta' that cellar," Jake said.

"No, we're not. We're gonna have to do this the old-fashioned way."

"Purgatorius Ignis…"

"Grab the oil and start with the rear entrance."

"You and yer fuckin' fire…goddamn pyro."

Arturo walked slowly and upright, garnering as much attention as possible while Jake snuck off into one of the side rooms behind the pillars. Arturo stopped to watch the lighting of the lamps, appreciating the serenity of the Hacienda at night. He shook his head, moving on toward the chapel.

He stepped inside, the few banditos in prayer turning toward him to see who'd entered. They moved to stand upon recognizing him, but with a gesture of his hand, Arturo motioned for them to remain seated. The banditos returned to their prayers as he drew a stick of incense from a small case near the altar and knelt before an effigy of the Holy Mother, lighting the incense.

"Beneath your compassion, we take refuge, O Divine Mother: do not despise our prayers, we your wicked children, in this—our time of pandemonium, but should we fall—deliver us from dangers. O Pure and blessed one, forgive us."

A heavy fist slammed into the chapel door, bursting it open and bringing moonlight into the church. Several banditos piled into the church, calling for Arturo. At the head of the group stood Adelais.

"Tell me ya weren't dumb enough ta' bring her here," he said.

"No dumber than the man walking into the hungry lion's den."

"We got Lehane upstairs. Dunno why ya'd think Estaban couldn't tell the difference between some punk and the man who got his daughter killed."

"Doesn't matter. Estaban won't make a move until he's sure of the situation. Stand aside and I'll deal with him myself."

Adelais refused to move, the remaining banditos circling in around Arturo. He stood his ground, taking a deep breath.

"I saw ya' here earlier with Lorena. Makin' moves on her is already enough of a reason ta' put ya' down. But then I got this list with yer name on it, so… block the doors. No one leaves until this is done."

The banditos fanned out, covering the entrance to the chapel. Adelais stepped up to Arturo, looking down on him to size him up. "Two ways this goes down. Your old friends put bullets in your face, or ya' drop that fancy gun on yer side, and we'll do this decent. Last man standing."

Arturo nodded, unfastening his holster and tossing it to the side. Adelais nodded out of respect, and lunged at Arturo. Adelais planted his fist in Arturo's chest, sending him back into one of the few rows of pews. Arturo regained his footing, and launched himself into Adelais, unable to shake the giant's balance. Arturo dug his feet into the floor, wrapping his arms around Adelais's waist. He shifted around behind Adelais, climbing onto his back and digging his heels into Adelais's thighs in an attempt to put him into a rear naked choke, but was unable to gain the advantage. Adelais dropped onto his back, crushing Arturo as they crashed into the floor.

Leaving Arturo on the ground, Adelais spun back onto his feet. He slammed his boot into the floor, narrowly missing Arturo as the kin leader rolled over and pulled himself up. He threw a long knee into Adelais's gut. Adelais winced, losing his footing, and fell back into the pulpit, splintering it into pieces as Arturo tackled him to the floor. Arturo managed to regain his footing, kicking Adelais repeatedly with his steel greaves. He continued his assault until he felt a sharp pain in his back, hit by a falling piece of the rafters. Climbing out from underneath the wooden debris, he caught the scent of smoke as he pulled himself up, and began looking for an open exit.

Making his way for the door, Adelais tackled him to the floor, pinning him with his knees.

"Helluva fighter, Arturo. Almost a shame ta' put ya' down. Ta' be honest, I've had enough of killin', but peace is more important than you or me." Adelais paused before adding, "An' even though he deserved it, I'm sorry I had ta' kill yer brother."

A deep well of regret surged from within as Arturo thought of his brother rotting in the ground, put there by the vagabond so willing to shed blood. Arturo reached across the floor for his holster, drawing his revolver and firing it off. Adelais recoiled, howling out as he toppled over. Arturo sat up, reaching around to feel his back. His fingers returned wet, coated in a thin layer of red. He regained his focus, watching the chapel burn, engulfed in flames. He looked around to the banditos standing guard, some of them having run off while others remained with weapons drawn.

"Don't die here!" Arturo shouted out. "This man is a fool—you don't have to lose your lives with him. This place is burning away with the old ways—if you want to survive, escape and head to the museum. You'll find refuge." He looked into the eyes of the few men remaining. "You all know me, I've kept you alive, and I intend to keep doing so. Trust me."

Some of the men exchanged glances, while others began moving toward the door. Several banditos fled, leaving only a couple behind. Arturo landed on his back on the floor, his arms refusing to cooperate with the rest of his body as his lungs began to ache. He rolled onto his stomach and started crawling toward the door, trying to escape the heat of the flames. Not far off, Adelais moaned in pain. Arturo reached over for his revolver, picking it up and closing one eye as he aimed for Adelais. He fired off a shot.

The gun slipped from Arturo's grasp as someone pulled him up, bracing him enough to walk. Jake hauled him out of the church.

"You're *saving* me?"

"Sorta. Fresh outta bullets and ya' make a good shield."

Arturo recognized the bastard grin Jake wore as they made it out to the fountain. Turning back, the blaze started dying down as banditos pulled damage control. Re-assessing their situation, Arturo saw banditos on all sides surround them, with Estaban watching from his balcony.

"Shit," Arturo exclaimed.

"Nice *coup d'état*. I see it wasn't a mistake to put you two at the top of my list. Alphabetical order is always such a mistake," Estaban called down. "Arturo, we live in a desert. We're prepared for a little fire. I'm sorry you feel I'm an inadequate leader, but there were probably better ways to let me know. Now you've forced me into a position to prove otherwise. I hate having to prove otherwise." Estaban sighed as he shook his head. "Take comfort in the fact that at least you were a decent man, unlike your piss-stain of a brother." Estaban began looking around. "That reminds me, where's Adelais? Bring him to me." Estaban turned and headed back toward his abode. As he walked away, he shouted out, "Oh, string Arturo up, and bring the other one to me!"

Several banditos pulled Arturo from Jake, separating the two. They dragged Arturo up against the burnt-out—but no longer burning—chapel and left him against the wall as they went inside. He leaned back, recovering as he watched them carry Adelais.

Arturo's arms started trembling, though he was too exhausted to care. He had an idea of what was to come, and he could do nothing to stop it. He exhaled and quietly lowered his head, mumbling a prayer to himself.

"O Divine Mother, I draw nigh to Thee with a contrite and humble heart."

He recited the litany, waiting for the banditos to return. Before long, they came back and stood him up, forcing a needle in his arm. Understanding it as an act of mercy, Arturo offered no resistance as they drugged him. Only marginally maintaining awareness, he felt himself being hoisted. He looked around, but his eyes became lazy and were unable to report much.

Suspended against the building, he lost feeling in his body as he noticed his wrists were being held up by something, tied against the structure. His arms outstretched, his ankles were next to be tied to the building with heavy rope. A noose dropped loosely around his neck, though he did his best to avoid looking at it. The banditos having apparently finished their work, his body dropped slightly, now held up only by the ropes securing his wrists, ankles, and neck.

The rope burned against his neck, but it didn't stop him from breathing. Estaban would want his suffering to last as long as possible. This was the punishment for treason. Arturo shed no tears as his thoughts shifted to his brother, Alejandro, while he hanged against the church, waiting to die.

37. ...A Woman Scorned

"Eye, foot, arm, and half your army for an eye."

– Lorena's Prayer Book

Jake struggled to get free, dragged up the staircase by a small group of banditos. He fought, but to no avail. He remained unable to shake himself free, and was forcefully marched across the breezeway to the private abode he had been to only once before. Thrown onto the petrous floor of the quaint adobe dwelling, he saw Kody sitting just a few feet away, apparently bored.

"The hell? Are you a fuckin' hostage or a guestage?"

Kody shook out his ankle, revealing the chain affixed to the wall. Jake scoffed, kicked aside as banditos made room for Adelais, setting him on a nearby table. Behind the table, Jake noticed something new in the old place: a steel door built into the wall. This revelation was quickly dismissed when Estaban came in behind Adelais, looking a bit worse for wear, but sturdy as ever.

Estaban bypassed Jake on his way to the table, examining Adelais. Jake tried to get a view of him, but received another kick in the ribs as he moved. Grunting at the injury, he attracted the attention of Estaban, who finally took notice.

"Jake. This has been a busy day for me, and I have to admit—I'm not a fan of busy days. My vitality isn't what it used to be. I suspect all this ruckus is due in no small part to you." Estaban walked over to Jake, squatting in front of him. "Big day for you though, I suppose. The brothers that hunted you for so long are dead—you must feel pretty good about yourself. Even if your life is one big, tragic failure."

"I've had worse days." Jake looked up to Estaban, grinning as he shrugged.

"I'm sure that's true. Unfortunately for both of us—mostly me, and a little bit Adelais—that disreputable cur of a lieutenant put a bullet in our friend here. From what I've heard, you know a little about medicine. Do I need to keep going?"

"Ain't any friend a' mine."

Jake crawled off his knees, rising to stand. Estaban met his posture, and walked him over to the table to examine Adelais.

"I imagine not, no. You don't really keep friends. Or hygiene habits. But his family's diversions were the reason you got away in the first place, and they seem like pretty decent folks, so I'd count him among the people you want to stay in this world."

Jake cocked his eye at Estaban as he looked Adelais over, noticing a pool of blood streaming from his shoulder. Jake felt around his body, checking for any other wounds. He felt something in one of Adelais's pockets, and pulled out a small piece of paper. He opened it up, reading the list of names, his and Arturo's being at the top.

"The hell is this?"

"Oh, his list. I guess we can cross one of those off right now, can't we?"

Estaban took the list from Jake, picking up a pen off the table and scratching out Arturo's name. He folded the piece of paper and set it back down on the table.

"An' me?" Jake asked.

"This has been an interesting day. I'll leave that to your friend. It is his list, after all. Though I should tell you, the rest of the names on that list aren't really all that important with the Romeros gone. So, if you're the only thing standing between him and the assured safety of his loved ones…"

"Fuck that."

Jake turned about and headed toward the door, blocked off by several unpleasant-looking banditos.

"Let him die if you want. But if he can't make a decision, I will. And believe me, I've become more than a little absent minded lately. It could take a while before I come up with anything that doesn't involve slow, brutal castration. You took the fruit of my loins, so it only seems right that I aim for the same. You know, for poetry's sake and all."

Jake stared at Estaban, and then at Kody sitting pathetically against the wall. He sighed, pulling out a cigarette and lighting it up as he resumed his examination of Adelais.

"At least let the kid go. He's just a fuck-up we dragged in from outta town."

"Unfortunate for your confederate. Get to work. I have a syndicate that needs attention."

Estaban exited the abode, leaving an ample contingent of banditos to guard it. Jake sucked down the nicotine, embracing the burn and working on patching up Adelais. One of the banditos brought him a first-aid kit and some basic surgical implements, presumably what they kept on hand in case Estaban ever became ill. Jake inspected the sight of injury, and began to extract the bullet.

"Sonuvabitch!"

Adelais's body jumped. Adelais reached for the bullet wound, but couldn't fully extend his arm. Jake held him down, motioning for a few banditos to assist.

"Calm down, big guy. I'm helpin' ya' out, so uh... put in a good word for me, okay?"

Jake inhaled the nicotine once more, snuffing out the cigarette and folding it behind his ear. He wiped his hands off with the first-aid kit's antiseptic and got to work.

* * *

Lorena finally found an opening, waving Glenn and Alma up as they continued creeping around the Hacienda, trying to get to the cellar. They reached the door, unguarded but still boarded up, and took turns pulling security as the other two used assorted debris to remove the planks.

"What'dya think happened?" Lorena asked Alma as they worked on the door.

"My guess? Jake screwed up, and they bailed, which is why we came as backup in the first place. But if the explosives are down here like you said, none of it matters if we can't get to them."

They continued prying the planks off the door one by one, until eventually they were able to get it open. Alma remained up top to keep a lookout while Lorena led Glenn into the cellar, finding most of the explosives still concealed where Arturo had left them. Lorena lit a match, illuminating the dank cavern.

"Thank God…now we just gotta…what was it…plump 'em?" Lorena asked.

"P-prime them," Glenn responded.

"Ya' know how?"

"I can im-improvise."

Lorena watched as Glenn examined Arturo's setup and went through the available resources. He continued moving back and forth, adjusting the layout.

"Hurry up, something's going down up here! I think *el jefe's* making the rounds," Alma called down.

Glenn stopped to readjust his glasses, taking a deep breath. Lorena watched as he reached for a small crate, dousing it in kerosene. He continued messing with the charges while Lorena kept her eyes on the stairs. She jumped as Glenn grabbed her wrist and started heading back upstairs with the crate.

"Wait, what're ya doin'?"

"Most of the blasting caps are m-missing."

"What? What's that mean?"

"We'll have to get c-creative with detonating the explosives."

They made their way back to the top of the stairs, stopping at the door a few feet from Alma, who remained crouched just inside the entryway.

"It's only a matter of time before they notice this door is all not blocked off anymore. Tell me you guys are ready," Alma said.

"Glenn, how much time will I have?" Lorena asked.

"Y-you're not—"

"This is my home. Everything they've done, they've done it to me. I'm returnin' the favor."

Glenn nodded. "Won't be more th-than a handful of s-seconds."

Glenn fell back, receiving a violent blow to the face from a passing bandita. The bandita encroached upon Glenn and Lorena, menacing as she drew close. Lorena balled up her fist, preparing to strike, when Alma launched out of her corner, landing on the bandita's back and dragging her to the ground. She wrapped her arms around the bandita's throat, pulling her into a chokehold until the bandita lost consciousness. Alma smirked as she rolled the bandita off to the side.

"See? Helping you already." Alma took Glenn's hand. "Lorena, you good?"

Lorena nodded. Alma waited for an opportunity, finding her chance and dragging Glenn with her as she ran. Alma looked back only briefly, but was gone within seconds. Lorena did her best to calm her unsteady nerves, setting the box down to stop her hands from shaking. She exhaled.

"They all got out. This is the last time I have to deal with fire, and they all got out."

She made her way back to the stairwell, getting close enough to catch sight of the explosives. Grabbed from behind, she jumped and broke free, falling down the stairs. She managed to grab a rail as she fell, stopping her descent. She looked up to see an eccentric old man in skins approaching.

"I've seen you before. You're that girl Sigurd was infatuated with. What're you doing in my basement? I'm fairly certain I closed it off since my last demolitions expert decided to turn it into an explosive theme park."

Lorena scrambled down the stairs, trying to evade the man. Reaching the bottom, she found herself trapped in a pitch-black basement. She moved slowly, feeling her way around.

"Lorena, right? Adelais talked about you too. Hope he pulls through— he's not doing too well. You can go visit him if you like. Much nicer than down here. No mildew or anything," the old man said.

Lorena clung to the wall, feeling her way to the back of the cavern until she came upon the sealed door. She tapped her foot around, feeling for the crevice that led back across to the stairs.

"I can go see Ade? Right now?" she asked.

"Sure. His schedule's open. You'll need to come with me though."

She listened, and began creeping along the opposite wall as she heard the old man approach. She kicked a rock near the door, following the crevices in the floor as she waited to see what'd happen. She heard footsteps rapidly shuffling toward the door, and quickly made her way back to the stairs, ignoring the pain in her ankle. "This is for you, Sig," she whispered as she lit the book of matches, making out the faint outline of the old man's face in the back of the cavern as she dropped them to the ground, next to a set fuse.

She hobble-sprinted up the stairs, clearing the stairwell and making it back into the petrous arcade. Running until her ankle swelled, the loudest explosion of her life kicked off and shook the very foundations of the Hacienda from below. She continued dashing toward the entrance, the ground behind her beginning to give way. Looking back, she saw a sinkhole beginning to open up, devouring the Hacienda into the earth below.

38. Fools Rush in (Where Angels Fear to Tread)

"If my experience has taught me anything, it's that life doesn't always have a happy end."

– Glenn's Chronicles

Adelais fell off the table, the entire Hacienda rocked by a violent explosion. The bandito guards piled out of the room to check on the situation. Bandaged up, Adelais was able to pull himself up against the wall. Upon getting back on his feet, he was met by Jake, holding at knife pointed at him.

"Ya'd kill me when I can barely move?" Adelais asked.

"You'd do the same, but it would make the time I spent taking care of you kind of a waste. Lemme go."

Unable to do much, Adelais half-shrugged. He watched as Jake peeked out the door, waiting for his moment and taking it. Adelais sat back down on the table, catching his breath. A secondary explosion further shook the foundation, collapsing parts of the roof around the room.

"Adelais, a little help?"

Adelais, woozy and exhausted, looked over to see Kody chained to the wall. He checked his pockets and glanced around the room. No keys lying about anywhere; he checked the drawers of the table until he found a set. He tossed them to Kody and made his way to the door, looking outside.

He looked out over the center of the Hacienda in a dream-like haze. Where the fountain had once been was a giant sinkhole, revealing the entire substructure of the edifice. Worst off, it was growing with all the ruckus of banditos trying to get out with as many belongings as possible.

Adelais felt a hand on his shoulder and turned about, trying to land a blow on his unknown assailant. Kody ducked the unusually slow Adelais and tried to help him along instead. Adelais pushed him off, standing on his own two feet as he resumed leaning against the doorframe.

"Lehane…go find Lorena. Get her outta here."

"Adelais, she's fine. You're the one that—"

"Ain't no one fine with an explosion that big. If any of us deserve ta' make it through, it's her. Go."

Adelais shoved Kody, watching him creep along the breezeway. Looking down over it, the Hacienda was officially a war zone. Banditos who'd held grudges were using the chaos as an excuse to exact revenge. Others were helping each other organize a safe escape, some praying, some holing themselves up with whatever whores they'd managed to find.

Nursing his wounded shoulder, Adelais staggered down the breezeway, making slow but steady progress. A third explosion ignited. Adelais paused, looking around while a strange whistling sound grew louder and louder. A large piece of debris came crashing down in front of him, throwing him back against the door of the private abode and smashing the breezeway to pieces. Adelais lay dazed on his stomach, watching as the debris set the foliage on fire.

Trying to keep his eyes in focus, Adelais spotted something familiar moving among the chaos. For a moment, it looked like Lorena running through the archway. Looking through it, Adelais saw not the young woman he claimed as his sister, but the last thing in the world he'd ever expected to encounter: the Mexican military. "I'm sorry, Sig." Unable to control his stomach's churning, Adelais vomited as he passed out.

* * *

Grabbing Lorena as she made her way through the archway, Glenn quickly pulled her and Alma back behind shrubbery near the entrance as the Mexican military showed up. A platoon of soldiers began establishing a perimeter, apparently surprised the tip they'd received earlier in the day was genuine. Looking past the bread and circus, Glenn saw a red convertible off in the distance, making its way around to the back of the Hacienda to stay out of sight.

"They did it!" Alma shouted.

Glenn covered her mouth, glaring at her over his glasses. She shrunk down, keeping her mouth shut as they watched the operations.

"D-do either of you see anyone e-else?" Glenn whispered.

The women shook their heads. Glenn surveyed the area once more, trying to find familiar faces. With no success, he tapped on the women's shoulders and directed them back inside. Leading the effort, Glenn crept up the stairs back into the Hacienda.

They looked around, staying close to each other in an effort to avoid the rioting. The entire right side of the Hacienda was gone, along with most of the center ground, leaving only the rapidly deteriorating church and arcade. Glenn examined a burnt-out, bloodstained wall across the way, looking up to its balcony. Moving in closer, he saw Kody sneaking across the remainder of the breezeway.

"Kody!" Alma shouted out.

Kody made it to the balcony and looked below, standing up to find a route to reach them. They watched as a bandito ran up from behind and planted its foot squarely into Kody's back, knocking him off the breezeway. He fell several feet, landing in a small garden, on a bed of soft topsoil.

"Kody!" Alma turned back to Glenn. "Find Jake!" She sprinted off around the sinkhole in a mad dash to reach Kody.

Lorena turned back to Glenn, looking up to him. "I gotta find Ade."

"G-go help her. I'll find them."

Lorena hobble-ran after Alma, leaving Glenn to continue exploring the ruins. Glenn stayed close to the main structure of the Hacienda, avoiding the sinkhole as much as possible. He made his way to the edge of the former courtyard, finding a set of collapsed stairs. He took a running start and jumped across, barely managing to cross the gap. He continued heading up, making his way to the balcony.

It appeared most of the banditos were establishing defensive positions, preparing for a final stand as the Mexican military reinforced their control of the perimeter and began moving in. Glenn canvased the area, trying to see through the smoke, though he could barely hear over the gunfire. Between the assorted flames, he was unable to pick out any of his counterparts.

Preparing to move, Glenn felt a sharp pain as a knife entered his thigh. As quickly as it had entered, the blade was gone. Glenn collapsed, finding a bandito fiending with bloodlust standing over him. The bandito pushed him forward, choking Glenn with his own shirt as it caught around his neck. Repeated violent jerks quickly ripped the fabric, allowing air back into his lungs. Stunned from shock, Glenn was unable to move as the bandito clawed at his pants, tearing them off. Regaining some semblance of reality, Glenn tried to crawl away, unable to do so with his pants caught around his knees. Adrenaline jolted fiercely through his body as the bandito tried to mount him from behind. Glenn screamed out, flailing, trying to protect himself.

He jumped forward at the sound of an inhumane screech as his assault suddenly stopped. He turned around enough to see the bandito running off and Jake standing over him. Glenn collapsed onto the ground, sobbing. Jake knelt, taking off his duster and shirt. He tore pieces of his shirt into bandages, making an improvised pressure dressing for Glenn's bleeding thigh.

Sniffling, Glenn rolled himself over and pulled his pants up, although they were too damaged to stay on their own. Jake offered him a piece of bloody, heavy rope lying nearby, which Glenn used to make a belt. Jake put his duster over Glenn's shoulders and helped him up, supporting him. Jake wrapped Glenn's arm around his shoulder, helping him get back to the stairs. Glenn looked down as they headed to the staircase, seeing the remaining flesh of a flaccid, bloody penis.

He and Jake hobbled down the stairs together, nearly walking into a shootout between the banditos and the Mexican military. They doubled back and worked their way over the rubble behind the chapel, heading for a break in the wall near the sinkhole. They took up a position behind the burnt-out chantry, putting a plan into place.

"Atty—see that hole in the wall? It's big enough for us ta' squeeze through."

"There's no way we c-can get over th-there. Too much g-gunfire."

Jake grabbed Glenn's face and pulled him close. "Ya' dumbass, remember what I told ya: dead men got nothin' ta' fear. Now move your ass while I draw their fire."

They made their way to the clearing, looking around to find a path of approach. Jake ran out first, creating a scene while Glenn stumbled after. A minor explosion, whether from the bombs below or a hand grenade Glenn couldn't tell, went off nearby. The concussive blast tossed them back toward the chapel, ringing Glenn's eardrum as his body slammed against a wall.

* * *

Glenn slowly regained his senses, unaware of how much time had passed. As far as he could tell, he was still caught in the war zone. He looked over to Jake, who was heaving and bloody with his back against the wall, returning fire. "Jake, j-just go," Glenn spurted out. Jake slapped him upside the head, wrapping Glenn's arm around his shoulder. "C'mon, Atty, quit bein' a bitch. You know better than anyone: ya don't leave a fallen comrade."

Glenn tried to walk, but was unable to continue with the knife wound in his thigh. Jake hoisted Glenn up around his shoulders, fireman carrying him across the little remaining ground covered in debris. Sticking to the wall and keeping a low profile, the two made it the hole in the wall.

Jake knelt, lighting a cigarette as he peered through the hole. Looking through it, he appeared to be checking if it was safe enough to crawl through. Several bullets hit the wall next to Glenn, drawing Jake's attention to the group of banditos pointing Mexican military assault rifles in their direction. Glenn crawled out in front of Jake, providing cover. Severe pain erupted in his thigh as Jake threw his fist into it, dropping Glenn onto his knee. Jake looked to him, smiling, with a cigarette dangling out of his mouth, shoving Glenn through the hole.

"Heh, take care a' my sister, Atty. She deserves a real man, not some pussy boy like Lehane. Fuck 'er good."

Glenn turned back only once, watching Jake drop to the ground as a volley of rounds transformed his silhouette into something unrecognizable. Turning his head forward, Glenn scrawled violently through the crevasse in the wall. He struggled, getting caught in the narrow cement passage. Forcing himself with everything he had left, he barely made it out to the other side. He gave his utmost effort, but was unable to push himself any further. He tried to call out with a raspy voice but produced little more than dry air.

Unable to lift his head, Glenn had nothing left. His body collapsed. He began to suffocate as his head fell into a puddle of mud. Reflexive coughing burned his throat, wet sediment jerking up and down his trachea. It hurt, but it could've been worse. It wouldn't be too much longer until he could finally rest…

* * *

Something yanked at Glenn's wrist, a rough grip on the scar he was so very fond of. His eyelids rose enough to see a dark hand with a cotton wristband pulling him up. His body landed on something soft. Glenn looked up, trying to discern the visage when the voice made his savior all too clear. Geroge climbed back into the driver's seat, next to Cris who held and was stroking the hair of a busted-up Kody. His senses slowly coming around, Glenn realized he was lying on Alma's lap. She kept her eyes on the ground, silent.

39. Black Autumn Snow

"People can talk for hours and not say a word."

– Geroge's Tab Book

Los Tios, Mexico

Geroge scrubbed the front seat, trying to get as much ash and dried blood out of the car's interior as possible. Kody's plunge off the top of the small chapel didn't kill him, but it didn't do any kindness to the convertible's upholstery either. Geroge waged a strong campaign, but eventually settled for throwing a blanket over the seat. He looked up into the afternoon sky, watching remnant ash and cinder from the Hacienda fall like black autumn snow. He carried the bucket and rags back inside the inn.

Geroge made his way to Lorena's room, knocking before entering. He left the bucket and rags near the bathroom, putting them out of sight. He took a seat, watching Lorena stare vacantly out the window while Glenn held a tearful Alma in his arms.

"Hey. I, uh…I don't mean to interrupt, but I'm headin' out."

Alma looked up, pushing Glenn's arm from her shoulder. She solemnly stood up and walked over to Geroge, giving him a hug. "Be careful, G. Take it slow and make sure you take a lot of breaks. Say hi to Jency for me."

"I will." Geroge nodded, returning the embrace. He got up and headed for the door, stopping short of the doorframe. "Lorena, you sure you don't want a ride? The old place ain't too far from here."

"I'll make my own way," she replied, never turning back.

"All right. Good luck with rebuilding your bar. Lemme know if it ever gets off the ground. The Bards could come down and do a show or something."

Lorena didn't respond. Geroge lingered for a moment before leaving the room. He walked back into the hallway, heading over to the other room. He peeked inside, seeing Cris passed out in a chair next to the bed. He stepped inside, tapping her on the shoulder.

"Hey, chickarita, thanks for lending me your car—I'm gonna head on home. You guys really gonna stay?"

"We have to, for now." Cris looked over to Kody, badly bruised and resting in bed. "Besides, I'm not fond of this place, but after what I saw last night…Lorena could use the help. Once she gets back on her feet, Kody and I will come home. Let Tabby and my sister know we're okay?"

"Always do. But you gotta promise to phone Jeany and let her know what happened to me after Emma's done beatin' me to death. Don't think you remember how much of a temper your sister has."

"Heh…try texting her." Cris shrugged.

Geroge leaned in, kissing Cris's forehead. She reached up and hugged him, holding him tight. He sighed, letting her go. He walked over to Kody, kissing his forehead.

"No hetero, brother. Get better, all right? You got a godchild to meet."

Cris looked up, but Geroge said nothing as he headed out of the room. He stopped outside the door, staring into the lobby, before moving on. He headed out in the unusually humid autumn afternoon, Glenn leaning unevenly on the side of the porch.

"You guys party way too hard, man. Make sure you take care of the Alm'ster, G. I know I give her a lot of crap, but she's a good woman," Geroge said.

"I t-told you b-before: you're G, not I."

"Yeah yeah… tell me somethin'."

Glenn turned his head toward Geroge.

"You think the banditos are gone for good?"

"History shows that di-dissentious elements never d-disappear. I think the d-destruction of the Hacienda will set them b-back, and hopefully quiet things d-down for a while, but…" Glenn trailed off.

"But what?" Geroge asked.

"What happened after J-julius Caesar was killed?"

"They had a funeral?"

Glenn looked at Geroge over his glasses, adjusting them as he turned away. Geroge waited, but Glenn appeared to lose interest, watching something going on down the road. Geroge turned his head to see Lorena untying a horse. He watched as she climbed up onto the mare and rode off toward the ruins of her old bar.

"D-don't worry about her. Things should be c-calm for a while." Glenn paused. "And she w-wanted some time alone."

Geroge moved up to Glenn, offering him his hand. Glenn took it, and Geroge threw him into a bro hug. Shortly after the two parted, Geroge headed back to the car. He put up the hood of the convertible, keeping the falling ash out as a dust storm started to kick up. Looking over to the passenger seat, he went through his bag, making sure he had the beads he'd scavenged after Cris tossed out Kody's old necklace. Making sure everything was set, he hit the gas and threw the radio on to Coldplay's song of self-discovery, "Don't Panic" as a dust storm started rolling in.

I guess it'd be all fine and dandy if things ended there. Ya know, on a high-ish note. But I'm guessin' you want a little more. And why shouldn't you? Loose ends and all. Think I can swing a little encore. I'll fill you in on a bit I caught through the rumor mill's grapevine.

40. The King of the Dark and Forgot

"Order and chaos work hand in hand. In accordance with the laws of nature, the rise of one evokes the rise of the other."

– The Autobiography of Miguel Estaban

The *Profunda Gruta*, Mexico

The wily old man in animal skins tried to re-open the sealed doors of the cavern, but was met with little success. The debris of the Hacienda's foundation held the blast doors firmly shut. He turned back, walking along the dimly lit path of the cool grotto. He walked for several minutes along the crude limestone trail, making his way back to the central hub.

As he returned to the underground stronghold, he was greeted by several banditos, who escorted him to a small, hobbled-together treatment table on one of the higher ledges. Winded, Estaban took a seat along the craggy wall, the few scant pieces of furniture available already in use.

"Estaban, do you require assistance?" one of the banditos asked.

"I'm old, not dead. Though the way things are going lately, either is fine."

The old man took a moment to catch his breath before standing. He quietly looked over his protégé. The man on the makeshift table was still breathing, though not in any kind of respectable shape. Estaban turned to the slightly less old, homely doctor working on his patient.

"What's the prognosis? Is he going to be able to get back in the game? I know he had his heart set on playing this season," Estaban asked.

"I'm not inclined to help this bastard in the least. He's the one person around here worse than you. But uh…" The doctor looked back, noting the banditos holding him at gunpoint. "Since you asked so politely, he'll live. Can't say much for his arm, though."

Estaban came around the side of the table, looking down to the injured bandito. He uncapped a bottle of water, offering the wounded a small drink. The bandito on the table took slow sips, laying his head back down.

"Now, now. Take your time. Need you to rest up and get better. If this nonsense has taught me anything, it's that it's getting to be that time. I need to find a nice quiet place to live out the rest of my hopefully boring days. I can think of no one more capable—other than myself—to take my place."

The injured bandito tried to sit up, assisted by Estaban and the doctor as he did. He looked over to Estaban, still somewhat groggy due to the pain medications.

"Lorena okay?" he slurred.

"Heh, you picked a hell of a woman. She blew the whole damned place up, trying to kill you, me, Scruffy, and everyone in between. And you're still worried about her. She's fine, and she'll remain that way so long as you keep playing for the home team. But then again, why wouldn't you?"

Adelais lay back down, exhausted, and fell back asleep. Estaban felt his forehead, checking to see if the fever had started to subside.

"Not that I care, but why would you want a man who's done nothing but kill your people off to take over for you?" the doctor asked.

"He and his brother have served me faithfully, and far better than most. Besides, what we need now is ambition and motivation. Both qualities this young man possesses in abundance."

"But again the part where he's tried to kill pretty much everyone, including you."

"I failed to protect his brother from my psychotic former successor. Seems fair. But it's that exact rage that I'm counting on to end all of this."

Estaban lifted his hand, feeling Adelais's fever finally starting to subside. He nodded to a bandito in the corner, who began moving toward the doctor.

"Send some men out to the museum to see what the commotion is all about. Seems some of our old friends are rallying over there, and I really do believe we've seen enough surprises. The nonsense in this place has gone on long enough—it's time to bring order to this madness."

Estaban spoke to his men as the bandito in the corner dropped a sack over the doctor's head, tied a heavy rope around the neck, and dragged him off.

Gotta say, even remembering now, it's still a bit crazy to think about all the nonsense these dudes and dudettes got themselves into. Especially Sig. From what I heard about that kid—such a damn shame. But uh, what's the old saying? When one door closes, ya get a nice glass of lemonade? I dunno, something like that. Pretty sure lemonade was a thing. But the kid was smart. I'm sure he wouldn't let his dream go down like that.

So I'm bettin' at this point you've got all sorts of burning questions on your mind like, "What about the Bards? This story hasn't been Bard-tastic at all!" And you're absolutely right. It has been a little light on our usual rock star action, for what I think by now are obvious reasons. I don't wanna say we're on hiatus, so let's say the band is taking a life pause. We'll be back rockin' before long.

Anyway, got a Jeany-situation to take care of, so I'm gonna see to it. But don't worry, got plenty of juicy details and fan service to fill ya in on soon enough.

Until then.